mS

"I know you are trying to provoke me, sir—"

"Indeed? I thought the reverse was true for once!" Guy exclaimed.

"Very well!" Sarah met his eyes. "I'll admit that I said something that I deeply regret! Pray accept my apologies, my lord!"

The dance had ended, but Guy was still holding her hand. They were standing on the edge of the dance floor, surrounded by couples milling about, yet it seemed to Sarah that they were entirely alone. When Sarah looked up into Guy's eyes she saw an expression of desire overlaid by wicked mischief. So strong was the conviction that he was about to kiss her that Sarah took an instinctive step backward.

"Do not worry." Guy spoke so only she could hear. "I will not do it—at least, not here! But the temptation, Miss Sheridan, is acute."

Color flamed into Sarah's face as she realized he had read her thoughts. "Believe me," she said with as much composure as she could muster, "so is the temptation to slap your face!"

Praise for Nicola Cornick's recent titles

The Virtuous Cyprian

"...this delightful tale of a masquerade gone awry will delight ardent Regency readers."

—Romantic Times

The Larkswood Legacy

"...a suspenseful yet tenderhearted tale of love..."

—Romantic Times

Lady Polly

"...a solid, cozy read with many delightful characters..."

—Romantic Times

DON'T MISS THESE OTHER TITLES AVAILABLE NOW:

#627 CHRISTMAS GOLD

Cheryl St.John/Elizabeth Lane/Mary Burton

#628 BADLANDS LEGEND

Ruth Langan

#629 MY LADY'S HONOR

Julia Justiss

The Blanchland Secret

Nicola Cornick

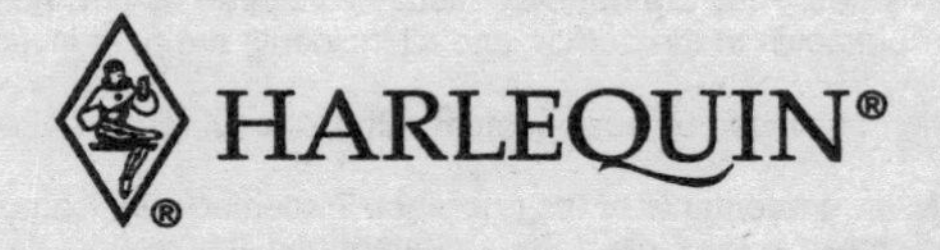

TORONTO • NEW YORK • LONDON
AMSTERDAM • PARIS • SYDNEY • HAMBURG
STOCKHOLM • ATHENS • TOKYO • MILAN • MADRID
PRAGUE • WARSAW • BUDAPEST • AUCKLAND

ISBN 0-373-29230-9

THE BLANCHLAND SECRET

First North American Publication 2002

This edition published by arrangement with Harlequin Books S.A.

Visit us at www.eHarlequin.com

Printed in U.S.A.

Available from Harlequin Historicals and NICOLA CORNICK

Lady Polly #574
The Love Match #599
"The Rake's Bride"
Miss Verey's Proposal #604
The Blanchland Secret #630

Please address questions and book requests to:
Harlequin Reader Service
U.S.: 3010 Walden Ave., P.O. Box 1325, Buffalo, NY 14269
Canadian: P.O. Box 609, Fort Erie, Ont. L2A 5X3

Chapter One

Mr Julius Churchward, representative of the famously discreet London lawyers of the same name, had a variety of facial expressions he could draw upon, depending on the nature of the news he was imparting to his aristocratic clients. There was sympathetic but grave, used when breaking the news that an inheritance was substantially smaller than expected; there was sympathetic but rueful, for unsatisfactory offspring and breach of promise; finally, there was an all-purpose dolefulness, for when the precise nature of the problem was in doubt. It was this third alternative that he adopted now, as he stood on the doorstep of Lady Amelia Fenton's trim house in Bath, for if the truth were told, he knew nothing of the contents of the letter he was about to deliver.

Mr Churchward had travelled from London the previous day, stopped overnight at the Star and Garter in Newbury and resumed his journey at first light. To undertake such a journey in winter, with Christmas pressing close upon them, argued some urgency. The morning sun was warming the creamy Bath stone of Brock Street but the winter air was chill. Mr Churchward shivered inside his overcoat and hoped that Miss Sarah Sheridan, Lady Amelia's companion, was not still at breakfast.

A neat maid showed him into a parlour that he remembered from a visit three years before, a visit during which he had conveyed to Miss Sheridan the disappointing news that her brother Frank had left no estate to speak of. At the back of his mind was an occasion some two years before that, when he had had to proffer the even more depressing intelligence that Lord Sheridan had left only a small competence to keep his daughter from penury. Miss Sheridan had borne the news with fortitude, explained that she had very few material needs and gained Mr Churchward's admiration in the process.

He still felt the inequity of her situation keenly. A lady of Miss Sheridan's breeding should not, he felt, be reduced to acting as companion, even to so benevolent a relative as her cousin, Lady Amelia. He was sure that Lady Amelia was too generous ever to make Miss Sheridan feel a poor relation, but it was simply not fitting. For several years Mr Churchward's chivalrous heart had hoped that Miss Sheridan would make a suitable match, for she was young and looked well to a pass, but three years had gone by and she was now firmly on the shelf.

Mr Churchward shook his head sadly as he waited in Lady Amelia's airy drawing-room. He tried hard not to have favourites; it would have been quite inappropriate when he had so many esteemed clients, but he made an exception in the case of Miss Sarah Sheridan.

The door opened and Sarah came towards him, hand outstretched as though he was a great friend rather than the bearer of doubtful news.

'Dear Mr Churchward! How do you do, sir? This is an unexpected pleasure!'

Mr Churchward was not so sure. The letter he carried seemed to weigh down his document case. But such misgivings seemed foolish in the light of day. The parlour was bright with winter sunlight; it shone full on Miss Sheridan, but she was a lady whose face and figure could withstand the harshest of morning light. Indeed, her cream and rose complexion seemed dazzlingly fresh and fair and her slender figure was set off to advantage by a simple dress of jonquil muslin.

'How do you do, Miss Sheridan? I hope I find you well?'

Mr Churchward took the proffered seat and cleared his throat. He was astonished to find that he was nervous, too nervous to indulge in talk of the weather or the journey. He bent to unbuckle his case and extracted a letter in a plain white envelope.

'Madam, forgive my abruptness, but I have been asked to deliver this letter to you. The manner in which the request came about is quite extraordinary, but perhaps you would wish to read the letter first, before I explain…' Mr Churchward was unhappily aware that he was rambling. Sarah's wide and beautiful hazel eyes were fixed on his face with an expression of vague puzzlement. She took the letter and gave a slight gasp.

'But this is—'

'From your late brother. Yes, ma'am.' Mr Churchward groped for his all-purpose solemn expression, but was sure he was only achieving the anxious look of a man who was not in complete control of the situation. 'Perhaps if you were to read what Lord Sheridan has written…'

Miss Sheridan made no immediate attempt to open

the letter. Her head was bent as she examined the familiar black writing and the sunlight picked out strands of gold and amber in the hair that escaped her cap.

'Are you aware of the contents of the letter, Mr Churchward?'

'No, madam, I am not.' The lawyer sounded slightly reproachful, as though Francis Sheridan had committed a decided *faux pas* by leaving him in ignorance.

Miss Sheridan scanned his face for a moment, then walked slowly over to the walnut desk. Mr Churchward heard the sound of the letter-opener slicing through paper and felt relief wash over him. Soon they would know the worst…

There was silence in the little room. Mr Churchward could hear the chink of china from the kitchens, the sound of voices raised in question and answer. He looked around at the neat bookshelves laden with works he remembered from Blanchland; books that Sir Ralph Covell had dismissively thrown out of the house he had inherited from his second cousin, Lord Sheridan; books that Sarah had gladly retrieved for her new home.

Miss Sheridan did not speak at all. Eventually she crossed to the wing chair that mirrored Mr Churchward's on the other side of the fireplace and sat down. The letter fell to her lap; she looked him straight in the eye.

'Mr Churchward, I think I should read you the contents of Frank's letter.'

'Very well, madam.' Mr Churchward looked apprehensive.

'Dear Sal,' Miss Sheridan read, in a dry tone, 'if you get this letter I shall be dead and in need of a favour. Sorry to have to ask this of you, old girl—fact is, I'd rather trust you than anyone else. So here goes. I have a daughter. I know that will surprise you and I'm sorry I never told you before, but to tell the truth, I hoped you'd never need to know. Father knew, of course—made all the usual arrangements, all right and tight. But if he is gone and I'm gone, then the child needs someone to turn to for help, and that's where you come in. Churchward will tell you the rest. All I can say is thank you and God bless you.

'Your loving brother, Frank.'

Miss Sheridan sighed. Mr Churchward sighed. Both were thinking in their different ways of the insouciant Frank Sheridan who would have fathered a child so lightly, made cheerful provision for her future perhaps, but not really given the matter the thought it deserved. Mr Churchward could imagine him dashing off such a letter before he went off to join the East India Company on yet another mad attempt to make his fortune...

Sarah's voice broke into Mr Churchward's thoughts. 'Well, Mr Churchward, can you, as Frank suggests, throw any more light on this mystery?'

Mr Churchward sighed for a second time. 'I confess, madam, that I did know of Miss Meredith's existence. Your late father...' He hesitated. 'Lord Sheridan came to me seventeen years ago to ask me to make arrangements for a certain child. I thought...'

'You thought that the child was his own?' Sarah said calmly. For a moment, Mr Churchward could have sworn that there was a twinkle in Miss Sheridan's eye, a look that was surely inappropriate for a young lady when confronted with the evidence of some improper connection of her family.

'Well, I assumed—' Mr Churchward broke off unhappily, aware that it was dangerous for lawyers to make assumptions.

'It was a natural supposition,' Sarah said kindly, 'especially since Frank could have been little more than eighteen himself at the time.'

'Young men…wild oats…' Mr Churchward made a vague gesture. He suddenly realised the impropriety of discussing such a matter with a young, unmarried lady, cleared his throat purposefully and pushed his glasses up his nose. He deplored the necessity of giving Miss Sheridan this information, but there was nothing for it. Best to be as businesslike as possible.

'The child was placed with a family in a village near Blanchland, I believe, madam. The late Lord Sheridan paid an annuity to a Dr John Meredith each year during his lifetime and…' he hesitated '…left a sum to him in his will. Dr Meredith died last year, at which time his widow and daughter were still resident near Blanchland.'

'I remember Dr Meredith,' Sarah said thoughtfully. 'He was a kindly man. He attended me when I had the measles. And I do believe he had a daughter—a pretty little girl some seven or eight years younger than I. She went away to school. I remember everyone saying that the doctor must have some private income—' She broke off, a rueful smile on her lips as she realised that the mystery of the doctor's finances was now solved.

The arrival of some refreshments—a pot of coffee for Mr Churchward and a strong cup of tea for Miss Sheridan—created a natural break in the conversation and gave the lawyer the opportunity to move smoothly forward.

'I do apologise for springing such a surprise on you, Miss Sheridan—'

'Pray do not, Mr Churchward.' Sarah smiled warmly. 'This is none of your doing. But I understand from

Frank's letter that you were to contact me if Miss Meredith was in need of help. In what way may I assist her?'

Mr Churchward looked unhappy. He reached for his bag again and extracted a second letter. It was smaller than the first, the paper of inferior quality, the hand round and childish. 'I received this three days ago, Miss Sheridan. Please...'

Once again, Sarah read aloud.

Dear Sir,

I am writing to you because I am in desperate need of help and do not know where to turn. I understand from my mother that the late Lord Sheridan gave her your direction, instructing her to contact you should either of us ever be in dire need. Please come to me at Blanchland, so that I may acquaint you with our difficulties and seek your advice.

I am, Sir, your most obedient servant,
Miss Olivia Meredith.

There was a silence. Mr Churchward was aware that he should have felt more at ease, for provision for illegitimate children and difficulties raised by said children was very much a part of Churchward and Churchward's business. Never before, however, had he been confronted by the situation in which an errant brother had asked his younger sister to offer help to his byblow. Frank Sheridan had been a likeable man, but thoughtless and devil-may-care. He had indubitably put his sister in a very awkward situation.

'Miss Meredith makes no mention of the precise nature of her difficulties,' Sarah said thoughtfully. 'And when Frank wrote his letter he would have had no notion of the sort of help she would need—'

'Very difficult for him, I am sure, madam.' Mr Churchward still looked disapproving. 'He wished to do the right thing by the child without knowing what that would be.'

Sarah wrinkled up her nose. 'I fear I am becoming confused, Mr Churchward. May we go over this once again? I shall call for more coffee and tea.'

The pot was replenished, Sarah's cup refilled, then the maid withdrew once again.

'Now,' Sarah said, in her most businesslike voice, 'let us recapitulate. My late brother left a letter with you to be despatched to me in the event of a plea for help from his natural daughter, Miss Meredith. Frank was, I suppose, trying to guard against my niece being left friendless in the event of his death.'

'I assume that to be correct, madam.'

'And there has never been any request for help until three days ago, when you received this letter from Miss Meredith?'

Mr Churchward inclined his head. 'All contact with Dr Meredith and his family ceased on your father's death, ma'am. I believe that Lord Sheridan left them a sum of money—' Mr Churchward's lips primmed as he remembered that it was a not-inconsiderable sum of money '—in order that the child should want for nothing in the future. Why she has seen fit to contact us now…'

'The help Miss Meredith needs may not be of a financial nature,' Sarah observed quietly, 'and she is still my niece, Mr Churchward, despite the circumstances of her birth.'

'Very true, madam.' Mr Churchward sighed, feeling

reproved. 'This is all most irregular and I am not at all happy about it. For you to have to return to Blanchland is the most unfortunate thing imaginable!'

Once again, the lawyer thought that he detected a twinkle in Miss Sheridan's eye. 'Certainly, Frank asks a great deal, Mr Churchward.'

'He does indeed, ma'am,' Mr Churchward said fervently. He shuddered, thinking of Sir Ralph Covell, the late Lord Sheridan's cousin, who had inherited Blanchland Court upon Frank's death. In the following three years Covell had turned the place into a notorious den of iniquity. Gambling, drunken revels, licentious orgies... The tales had been wilder each year. It seemed impossible to believe that Miss Sarah Sheridan, respectable spinster and pillar of Bath society, would ever set foot in the place.

'Your cousin, Sir Ralph Covell, is still in residence at Blanchland, Miss Sheridan?' Mr Churchward asked, fearing that he already knew the answer.

'I believe so.' The warmth had gone from Sarah's voice. 'It grieves me to hear the tales of depravity at Blanchland, Mr Churchward. It is such a gracious house to be despoiled by such evil.'

Churchward cleared his throat. 'For that reason, Miss Sheridan, it would be most inappropriate for you to return there. If your brother had known what Covell would do to your home, he would never have suggested it. Besides...' Churchward brightened '...he has not actually asked you to go to see Miss Meredith yourself! You may advise her through an agent, perhaps—'

Churchward broke off as Sarah rose to her feet and crossed to the window. She gazed into the distance. The bare trees that lined the Circus were casting shifting shadows onto the pavements. A carriage rattled past.

'Perhaps someone could represent your interests at Blanchland,' Churchward repeated, when Sarah did not speak. He was desperately hoping that she would not ask him to be that person. His wife would never stand for it. But Sarah was shaking her head.

'No, Mr Churchward. I fear that Frank has laid this charge on me alone and I must honour it. I shall, of course, gratefully accept your advice when I have ascertained the nature of Miss Meredith's problem. I imagine that it should be easy enough to find the girl and see how I may help her.'

Mr Churchward was ashamed at the relief that flooded through him. There was an air of decision about Miss Sheridan that made it difficult to argue with her, despite her relative youth, but he still felt absurdly guilty. He made a business of shuffling his papers together and as he did so he remembered the piece of news that he had still to impart. His face fell still further.

'I should tell you, ma'am, that I took the liberty of sending a message to Miss Meredith to reassure her that I had received her letter. By chance I passed my messenger on the road as I made my way here. He had been to Blanchland and was on his way back to London.'

There was a pause. Sarah raised her eyebrows. 'And?'

Mr Churchward looked unhappy. 'I fear that he was unable to find Miss Meredith, ma'am. The young lady was last seen approaching the front door of Blanchland Court two days ago. She has not been seen since. Miss Meredith has disappeared.'

Later, as he was driving back to London, Mr Churchward remembered that he had forgotten to tell Miss Sheridan about the third letter, the one that Francis

Sheridan had requested be despatched to the Earl of Woodallan. His spirits, which had been depressingly low since leaving Bath, revived a little. Woodallan was Sarah's godfather and a man of sound sense into the bargain. It was a pity that Mr Sheridan had ever thought to involve his sister in such an undignified situation, but at least he appeared to have had the sense to apply to a man of Woodallan's stature to support her. Mr Churchward sat forward for a moment, debating whether to ask the driver to turn back to Bath, then he caught sight of a signpost for Maidenhead and sat back against the cushions with a sigh. He was tired and nearing home, and, after all, Miss Sheridan would learn of Lord Woodallan's involvement soon enough.

Lady Amelia had already left for her morning engagements by the time Mr Churchward departed for London, so Sarah had no chance to confide in her cousin. She thought that this was probably a good thing, for her natural inclination had been to rush and tell Amelia all, when perhaps it would be better to think a little. Frank had not laid any strictures of secrecy on her, but Amelia was the least discreet of people and no doubt the tale of Sarah's niece would be all over Bath in a morning were Amelia to be made party to the story.

Sarah sat on the edge of her bed and thought of Frank and of her father, paying for his granddaughter's upkeep, and of neither of them breathing a word to her. She suspected that neither of them had ever intended that she should know. But perhaps Frank had had some premonition of his own end when he was about to set sail for India that last time. At least it would have been some comfort to him to think, as he lay racked by fever so far from home, that he had made some provision, hasty and thoughtless as it was, for Olivia's future…

Sarah stirred herself. She could sit here thinking of it all day, but she had errands of her own to attend to—some ribbons to match at the haberdasher's and bouquets to collect from the florist for the ball Amelia was holding the following night. Sarah replaced her lace cap with a plain bonnet, donned a sensible dark pelisse, and hurried down the stairs.

Mrs Anderson, Lady Amelia's housekeeper, was lurking in the stairwell, a look of slightly anxious eagerness on her homely face. She started forward as Sarah reached the bottom step.

'Was there…did the gentleman bring any good news, Miss Sarah?'

Sarah, adjusting her bonnet slightly before the pier glass, smiled slightly. News travelled quickly and a visit from the family lawyer was bound to cause speculation.

'No one has left me a fortune I fear, Annie!' she said cheerfully. 'Mr Churchward came only to tell me of a request my brother Frank made a few years ago. Nothing exciting, I am sorry to say!'

Mrs Anderson's face fell. In common with all the other servants in the house, she thought it a crying shame that Miss Sheridan should be the poor relation, and her a real lady, so pretty-behaved and well bred. Not that Lady Amelia ever treated her cousin as though she was a charity case, but it was Miss Sarah herself who insisted on running errands and doing work that was beneath her. She was doing it now.

'Would you like me to collect the vegetables whilst I am out?' Sarah was saying. 'It is only a step from the florists to the greengrocer's—'

'No, ma'am,' Mrs Anderson said firmly. It was one

thing for Miss Sheridan to carry home a bouquet of hot-house roses and quite another for her to be weighed down with cauliflower and lettuce. She moved to open the door for Sarah and espied the portly figure of a gentleman just passing the gate. 'Why, ma'am, 'tis Mr Tilbury! If you are quick to catch him up, he may escort you to the shops!'

'Thank you for warning me, Annie,' Sarah said serenely. 'If I walk very slowly, I am persuaded he will lose himself ahead of me! I just pray that he does not turn around!'

Mrs Anderson shook her head as she watched Sarah's trim figure descend the steps and set off slowly up Brock Street towards the Circus. There was no accounting for taste, but to her mind a marriage to a rich gentleman like Mr Tilbury was far preferable to being a poor spinster. Unfortunately, Miss Sheridan seemed too particular to settle for a marriage of convenience. Mr Tilbury was older, a widower with grown-up children, and if he were a little dull and set in his ways, well…

Mrs Anderson closed the door, noticing in the process that the housemaid had left a smear on the polished step. She walked slowly back towards the kitchens, still thinking of Miss Sheridan's suitors. Bath was a staid place and could not offer much in the way of excitement, but there had been several retired army officers who would have been only too happy to offer for Miss Sheridan if she had given them the least encouragement. And then there was Sir Edmund Place—an invalid, with a weak chest, but a rich one! And there had been young Lord Grantley—very young, Mrs Anderson admitted to herself, barely off the leading reins, in fact, but infatuated with Miss Sheridan and no mistake! Old Lady Grantley had soon whisked her lamb out of harm's way, declaring to all and sundry that Miss Sheridan was a designing female! Mrs Anderson bridled. Miss Sarah was more of a lady than Augusta Grantley would ever be!

Still, there was always hope. Cook's sister, who was Lady Allerton's housekeeper, had overheard her ladyship mention that a number of new visitors had been listed in the *Bath Register*, chief amongst whom was Viscount Renshaw, son of the Earl of Woodallan. Not just that, but his lordship was rumoured to be staying with his good friend Greville Baynham, one of Lady Amelia's beaux... Still plotting, Mrs Anderson called for the housemaid and made some pungent remarks about the slovenliness of her cleaning.

The subject of these musings, completely unaware that her cousin's matchmaking staff had plans for her, had purchased two very pretty pink ribbons for the bodice of Amelia's ballgown and was just leaving the florist with her arms full of specially cultivated roses. No matter how she tried to avoid it, the events of the past hour kept flooding back into Sarah's mind. A niece of seventeen! And she was only four and twenty herself! Frank, her senior by eleven years, had begun his womanising young. He had always been one with an eye for the prettiest maids. And who had been Olivia's mother? Sarah paused on the street corner. Surely it had not been the doctor's prim little wife? Mrs Meredith had been so very proper...

Aware that she was speculating in a most ill-bred manner, Sarah smiled a little. She was certain that Churchward had been shocked by her lack of sensibility when acquainted with the news! Engrossed in her thoughts, she stepped off the pavement and someone bumped into her, knocking all the breath out of her body. The roses went flying across the cobblestones. Sarah lost her balance and would have fallen were it not for an arm that went hard around her waist, steadying her.

'I beg your pardon, ma'am!' a masculine voice exclaimed. 'Devilish clumsy of me!'

The gentleman set Sarah gently on her feet and removed his arm from about her with what she considered to be unnecessary slowness. He turned to gather up the scattered flowers, but he was too late. A carriage, bowling along at a smart pace, neatly severed the heads of half of them.

'Oh, no!' Sarah went down on her knees again to try to rescue those that were left, but even they were bruised, their petals drooping. Amelia would be furious. The red roses were the centrepiece of her decoration the following night and the florist had grown them especially for the event. With all her heart Sarah wished she had left the roses to be brought round later on the cart with the other flowers, but she had been looking forward to walking through the winter streets with such a splash of colour. She sat back on her heels, holding the sad bouquet in her hand.

'Pray have some sense, madam! You are likely to be squashed flat if you remain in the road!'

The gentleman took Sarah firmly by the elbow and hauled her to her feet again. There was considerably less courtesy in his voice this time.

Sarah stepped back and glared at him furiously. 'I thank you for your concern, sir! A pity you did not think of the danger before you consigned my roses to precisely that fate!'

The gentleman did not answer at once, merely raising

one dark eyebrow in a somewhat quizzical fashion. His thoughtful gaze, very dark and direct, considered Sarah from her skewed bonnet to her sensible shoes, pausing on her flushed face and lingering on the curves of her figure beneath the practical pelisse. Sarah raised her chin angrily. Her experience of gentlemen was indisputably small, but she had no trouble in recognising this one as a rake—nor in reading the expression in his eyes.

His was a tall and athletic figure, set off to perfection by an elegance of tailoring seldom found in conservative Bath society. London polish, Sarah thought immediately, remembering Amelia's description of her years in the capital and the intimidatingly handsome gentlemen who had flocked to her balls and soirées. This gentleman had thick fair hair ruffled by the winter breeze, its lightness a striking contrast to the dark brown eyes that were appraising her so thoroughly. A slight smile was starting to curl his firm mouth as he took in the angry sparkle in Sarah's eyes, the outraged blush rising to her cheeks.

'I can only apologise again, madam,' the gentleman said smoothly. 'I was so taken in admiring the beauties of this city—' the amusement in his eyes deepened '—that I was utterly engrossed!'

Sarah felt an answering smile starting and repressed it ruthlessly. There was something here that was surprisingly hard to resist; some indefinable charm, perhaps, or, more dangerously, an affinity that was as disturbing as it was unexpected. The gentleman exuded a careless confidence and a vitality that seemed to set him apart. Bath was full of invalids, Sarah realised, and it was almost shocking to meet someone who seemed so very alive.

The strangest thing of all was that he seemed vaguely

familiar. The combination of fair hair and dark eyes was very unusual and definitely stirred her memory. She paused, unaware that she was staring and that the quizzical twinkle in the gentleman's eyes had changed to thoughtful speculation.

'I beg your pardon, but have we met before, sir?' Sarah frowned slightly. 'There is something familiar—'

Too late, she realised just how he might misinterpret her question. She had been thinking aloud and bit her lip, vexed with herself.

The gentleman's dark eyebrows rose fractionally and there was a certain cynicism in his drawl as he said, 'You flatter me, ma'am! I should say that we could be very good friends if you so choose.'

The colour flooded into Sarah's cheeks. She stopped dead, regardless of curious glances from the other shoppers in Milsom Street.

'That was hardly my intention, sir! I would scarcely attempt to scrape an acquaintance in so ramshackle a manner, particularly with a gentleman who is an undoubted rake! Your assumptions do you no credit! Good day to you, sir!'

He was already before her as she turned on her heel to leave him standing there.

'Wait!' He put out a hand to detain her. 'Forgive me, ma'am! It was not my intention to offend you!'

Sarah looked pointedly down at his hand on her arm, and he removed it at once. 'I should have thought that that was precisely what you intended, sir!'

'No, indeed!' He would have seemed genuinely contrite were it not for the glint of amused admiration she could see lurking in his eyes. 'I intended quite otherwise—' He broke off at the furious light in Sarah's eyes. 'You must allow me to apologise for my deplorable manners, ma'am! And for the roses…' He gave a wry smile to see the drooping posy in Sarah's hand. 'I hope it is a simple matter to procure some more?'

It was said in the tones of someone who had never had any difficulty in finding—or paying for—two dozen red roses for his latest *inamorata*. Sarah, who was finding it extraordinarily difficult to remain angry with him, managed a severity she was proud of.

'I fear that these were the last roses to be had, sir,' she said frostily. 'They were grown especially. And even if they were not, I can scarce afford to go around Bath buying up flowers in an abandoned fashion! Now, you will excuse me, I am sure!'

The gentleman appeared not to have heard his dismissal, although Sarah suspected that he had, in fact, chosen to ignore it. He fell into step beside her as though by mutual consent.

'I trust that you were not injured at all in the accident, ma'am?' The undertone of amusement was still in his voice. 'It was remiss of me not to enquire before. Perhaps I should escort you home to reassure myself that you are quite well?'

Sarah raised her eyebrows at such flagrant presumption. She wondered just how blunt she was going to have to be to dismiss him. It was difficult when a part of her was drawn to him in such a contrary fashion, but she was not accustomed to striking up a conversation with strange gentlemen in the street. Besides, no matter what her errant senses were telling her, such behaviour was dangerous. This man was definitely a rake and had already shown that he would take advantage.

'It is quite unnecessary for you to accompany me, sir. I am indeed well and will be home directly!'

'But it is not at all the done thing for a lady to wander

around unattended, you know,' the gentleman said conversationally. 'I am sure that Bath cannot be so fast as London; even so, the worthy matrons would not approve of such behaviour!'

Once again, Sarah was almost betrayed into a smile. He was outrageous, but surprisingly difficult to resist.

'I am sure that *you* are aware, sir, that it causes less speculation to walk around unchaperoned than to be seen in company with a complete stranger! That being the case, I shall continue alone and wish you a pleasant stay in our city!'

So saying, she gave him a cool nod and walked away, every line of her body defying him to follow her.

Guy, Viscount Renshaw, watched the slender figure walk purposefully away from him. A faint, rueful smile curved his lips. He saw the lady reach the corner of the street, saw her pause to exchange greetings with a gentleman coming the other way and noted with quickened interest that the gentleman was his good friend, Greville Baynham. Reflecting that it was fortunate that Bath society was proving to be so close-knit, Guy strolled across the street just as Greville took his leave of the lady.

'Sorry I was so long, old fellow!' Greville gave his friend an amiable grin. 'Saw a pair of Purdeys that took my fancy. I hope that you found enough to amuse you in my absence!'

'Oh, I was well entertained,' Guy said lazily, watching Sarah disappear out of sight. She had a very trim figure, he thought, good enough to challenge any of the accredited London beauties. Those hazel eyes, set in the wide, pure oval of her face, were magnificent... He realised that Greville had addressed another remark to him and was waiting patiently for his response.

'I merely asked whether you would care to take the spa waters?' his friend said with a quizzical look. 'Though perhaps you have found other attractions more to your liking? Bath is a slow place these days, especially out of season, but—'

'But not as slow as all that!' Guy turned a thoughtful look on his friend. 'Tell me, Grev, who is the lady to whom you were speaking just now?'

Greville frowned, pushing a hand through his ruffled brown hair. 'The lady?' His brow cleared. 'Oh, you mean Miss Sheridan? Save yourself the trouble if you thought to strike up a flirtation there, Guy! She don't give rakes the time of day!'

Guy laughed. 'I believe you, although she did claim an acquaintance with me! Thought I had mistaken her quality until she gave me the coolest set-down I've ever experienced!' Guy frowned a little. 'Sheridan, did you say? The name *is* familiar... Why, yes, I remember her! Well, I'll be damned!'

Greville burst out laughing. 'Doing it too brown, Guy! I don't believe you've ever met the lady before!'

'No, I assure you!' Guy looked triumphant. 'Miss Sheridan is the sister of the late Lord Sheridan, is she not? She is also my father's goddaughter and, though I have not seen her for an age, it must be the same girl! We were practically childhood friends!'

Greville's shoulders slumped. 'Devil take it, Guy! Of all the cursed luck!'

Guy gave his friend a pained look. 'Surely you mean it is a charming coincidence! And, as you evidently know the lady, you will be able to furnish me with her direction—'

Greville groaned. 'Don't do it, Guy! Miss Sheridan is Lady Amelia Fenton's cousin and Amelia will string me up if you try to get up a flirtation with Sarah!'

Guy smiled. He had heard quite a lot about Greville's hopeless passion for Lady Amelia only the previous night, when his friend had been in his cups and musing on the cruelty of womankind. Guy had imagined that Bath would prove very shabby genteel now that it had passed its heyday as a fashionable spa, yet the staid society was promising several intriguing possibilities. Greville had made no secret of the fact that he intended to press his suit with the lovely Lady Amelia and now there was Miss Sheridan…

Remembering the flash in those beautiful hazel eyes as Sarah had administered her set-down, Guy was forced into a reluctant grin. He had noticed her as soon as she had come out of the florist with those wretched roses in her arms. Beneath the prim bonnet, her hair had been the colour of autumn leaves; not brown or gold or amber, but a mixture of all three. She had held herself with an unconscious grace, slender and straight; despite her demure appearance, she was far from priggish. There had been a hint of laughter in her eyes and a smile on those pretty lips, and he had known that, for all her propriety, she had been attracted to him.

It was a shame that his father was also Sarah Sheridan's godfather. Guy acknowledged that that would preclude the sort of relationship that had sprung to mind on first seeing her. Nevertheless, it gave him the perfect excuse to pursue the acquaintance and that was a thought that held definite appeal. He drove his hands into his coat pockets.

'Has Miss Sheridan never wished to marry?' he asked, still following a train of thought of his own.

'No money,' Greville said succinctly, watching his friend with deep misgiving. 'Here in Bath everyone is looking to marry a fortune. Sarah goes about with Lady Amelia, writes her letters and so on—' He broke off at the look of distaste on Guy's face.

'Miss Sheridan a lady's companion? Surely not!'

'It is hardly like that,' Greville said, leaping to Amelia's defence. 'Lady Amelia is most sincerely attached to her cousin—they are friends rather than employer and employee! Why, Amelia is the sweetest-natured creature—'

Guy held up a hand in mock surrender. 'No need for such heat, old fellow! You'll be calling me out next! I had no intention of casting doubt on Lady Amelia's generosity, but it seems…' he hesitated '…incongruous to think of Miss Sheridan in such a situation. I wonder if my father knows? At the very least he would offer her a dowry…'

Greville's mouth twisted wryly. 'Thought it was something else you had in mind to offer Miss Sheridan, Guy!'

'I won't deny it crossed my mind,' the Viscount murmured, ' but m'father wouldn't like it! Tell me, Grev, if all the roses in Bath had been sold, where would you go to buy a posy for a lady?'

Greville stared at him as though he had taken leave of his senses. 'Don't know what the devil you're talking about, old chap! Roses in winter?'

'It is very late for them, I suppose. Would I be able to send someone to purchase red roses in Bristol, perhaps?'

'You can buy anything with your sort of money,' Greville said, without rancour. 'Though why you would wish to go to the trouble—'

'A favour for a lady,' Guy explained.

'I collect you mean to win a lady's favour!' Greville said glumly. 'Well, I can't stop you! But be warned, Guy—Miss Sheridan is no fool! She will see through your schemes! And as for Lady Amelia, well, I would not like to be in your shoes if she takes you in dislike!' His gaze fell on the one red rose that Guy had rescued from the street and which he still held in one hand.

'Must you walk round carrying that thing?' he besought. 'Devil take it, Guy, you look like a cursed dandy!'

Chapter Two

'Sarah! You cannot return to Blanchland! I absolutely forbid it! Why, your reputation would be in shreds as soon as you crossed the threshold!'

Lady Amelia Fenton, her kittenish face creased into lines of deep distress, threw herself down onto the sofa beside her cousin. 'Besides,' she added plaintively, 'you know that you detest what Ralph Covell has done to the house, and have never wanted to set foot there again!'

Sarah sighed, reflecting that the only positive thing about the current situation was that it had successfully deflected Amelia from bewailing the loss of the red roses. She had been beside herself to discover that her artistic centrepiece was ruined—until Sarah had casually mentioned her plan to travel to Blanchland on the day following the ball.

Amelia got to her feet again and paced energetically up and down before the fireplace. She looked quite ridiculous, for she was far too small to flounce about. All Amelia's features were small but perfectly proportioned, in contrast to her fortune which was big enough to make her one of Bath's most sought-after matrimonial prizes.

Realising from Sarah's expression that she looked absurd, Amelia sat down again, frowning. 'I know you think I am making a cake of myself, Sarah, but I am truly concerned for your welfare!' She sounded small and hurt. 'Whatever you say, it will be the ruin of you to go there!'

Sarah sighed again. 'Forgive me, Milly! I must go. It is at Frank's request—'

'Your brother has been dead these three years!' Lady Amelia said incontrovertibly. 'It seems to me that it is asking a great deal to expect you to grant his requests from beyond the grave!'

Sarah, reflecting that her cousin had no notion quite how much Frank was indeed asking of her, tried to console her.

'It will not be for long, I promise, and it is no great matter. I am sure Sir Ralph cannot really be so bad—'

'Ralph has made Blanchland a byword for licentiousness and depravity!' Amelia said strongly. 'You may pretend that you are happy to accept this commission, but you *know* it will ruin you! What can be so important to force you back there? Oh, I could murder Frank were it not that he is dead already!'

Sarah burst out laughing. 'Oh Milly, I truly wish that I could confide in you, but I have been sworn to secrecy! It is a most delicate matter—'

'Fiddle!' Lady Amelia said crossly. She looked at her cousin and her anger melted into rueful irritation. She could never be cross with Sarah for long.

'Oh, I am sorry, my love! I know you were most sincerely attached to your brother and that you believe you are doing the right thing, but...' Her voice trailed away unhappily.

'I know.' Sarah patted her hand. At four and twenty she was Amelia's junior by five years, yet often felt the elder of the two. It was Amelia who rushed impetuously at life, Amelia whose reckless impulses could so often lead to trouble if not tempered by the wise counsel of her younger cousin. Amelia, widowed for five years, still seemed as heedless as a young debutante. Yet now it was she who was counselling caution and Sarah who was set on a foolhardy course.

'And to travel now!' Amelia said fretfully. 'Why, it is but two weeks to Christmas and I am sure we are in for some snow!'

'I am sorry, Milly, it is just something I feel I must do—'

'Excuse me, madam.' Sarah broke off as Chisholm, Amelia's butler, stepped softly into the room. 'There are two gentlemen here to see you—'

'I am not at home!' Amelia cried vexedly. 'Really, Chisholm, you know that I am not receiving!'

'Yes, ma'am, but you did give orders that Sir Greville—'

'Greville!' Amelia cried. 'Why did you not say so, Chisholm? What are you waiting for? Show him in at once!'

Not a muscle moved in the butler's impassive face. 'Very well, madam.'

Sarah, repressing a smile, wondered whether Amelia appreciated the long-suffering patience of her servants. They were all most sincerely attached to her, despite her grasshopper mind.

'Sir Greville! How do you do, sir? I had no notion you were returned from London!'

Amelia, her ill temper forgotten, smiled sunnily as her visitors were shown into the room. Indeed, Sarah felt that a less good-natured man than Sir Greville Baynham might have read far more into the warmth of his welcome than was intended. Greville had been Amelia's most constant admirer for the last few years and though she showed every evidence of enjoying his company, she had never accepted any of his proposals of marriage. Sarah privately thought that, should Sir Greville's attentions be permanently withdrawn, Amelia would miss him rather more than she anticipated. Unfortunately her cousin showed no sign of recognising that fact.

'Lady Amelia,' Greville was saying formally, 'please allow me to present Viscount Renshaw. Guy is staying with me at Chelwood for a few days. Guy, this is Lady Amelia Fenton and...' he turned to smile at Sarah '...her cousin, the Honourable Miss Sarah Sheridan, whom I believe you have already met.'

Sarah's heart had skipped a beat as she recognised the tall figure following Greville Baynham into Amelia's elegant drawing-room. Guy Renshaw. What dreadful bad luck that he should appear again just when she had succeeded in banishing from her mind that wicked smile and those disturbing dark eyes. And worse, it seemed she had been correct all along in recognising him, though there was little resemblance between the gangling youth who had once teased her mercilessly and this very personable man.

Guy Renshaw sketched an elegant bow. 'Lady Amelia, how do you do? I have heard much about you!' His voice was low-pitched and very agreeable, as melodious as Sarah remembered from that morning. She found that her heart was beating fast and had to take a deep breath to steady herself.

Amelia blushed and smiled as she gave the Viscount her hand. Sarah tried not to laugh. Judging by the rueful look on his face, Greville might be regretting introducing his friend to the lady he ardently wished to marry! Amelia was quite the most dreadful flirt and did not deserve his devotion whilst Guy Renshaw, as Sarah now knew, could scarcely be trusted.

'And, Miss Sheridan…' Lord Renshaw turned to her. There was a smile playing around the corners his mouth. He really was quite shockingly attractive and Sarah was sure that he knew it. The thought served to calm her. She would not provide the confirmation!

'Not only have you and I have met before, ma'am,' the Viscount was saying, 'but I would go so far as to say that we were childhood friends!'

'Were you indeed, Sarah?' Amelia's eyes were bright with curiosity as they moved from one to the other. 'How intriguing!'

Sarah looked at Guy Renshaw very deliberately and saw his smile deepen into challenge as he awaited her response.

'Lord Renshaw mistakes,' she said slowly. 'We were never childhood friends.'

It gave her a certain satisfaction to see the swift flash of surprise in his eyes. Guy Renshaw, Sarah thought, was all too sure of himself and his power to attract.

'How could we be,' she added sweetly, 'when Lord Renshaw spent the whole time tormenting me with spiders and toads? I do believe I thought him an odious boy!'

Amelia gave a peal of laughter. 'Dear me, Lord Renshaw, it seems my cousin has a long memory for childhood slights! You will have to try hard to win her good opinion!'

'I shall endeavour to do so, ma'am, if Miss Sheridan will give me a second chance!' There was speculation as well as amusement in the look Guy cast Sarah. She felt a shiver of awareness, as though he had just issued a challenge she was unsure she could meet. She looked away deliberately.

Amelia was patting the sofa beside her. 'How long do you plan to spend in Bath, Lord Renshaw? No doubt you will find our society sadly flat after London!'

'I doubt it, ma'am,' Guy murmured, casting another glance at Sarah. He took a seat beside his hostess. 'I fear, however, that I am only here for a few days. I am but recently returned from the Peninsula and am anxious to see my family again. I shall be returning to Woodallan the day after tomorrow.'

'Then you must come to my ball tomorrow night!' Amelia gave him a ravishing smile. 'It will be most apt for a returned hero, for I am celebrating the allied successes!'

They fell to discussing the Peninsular War and Sir Greville came across to Sarah and sat down next to her. She let herself be distracted by small talk. At least the arrival of the two men had had the effect of diverting Amelia's attention from her proposed visit to Blanchland, but Sarah suspected that it was only a temporary respite. Amelia was known for her tenacity and if Sarah was really unlucky the topic of the roses might be raised as well. Sarah had managed to skate adroitly over the cause of her accident but she would not put it past Guy Renshaw to mention the whole story just to put her out of countenance.

A footman and maid arrived with refreshments and

somehow, Sarah was not quite sure how, Sir Greville and Lord Renshaw exchanged places. It was done in the neatest and most unobtrusive manner, but Sarah did not miss the look of gratitude Sir Greville flashed his friend as he took his place by Amelia, and her opinion of Guy went up a little. She only hoped that the Viscount's motives towards herself were as irreproachable.

'May I join you?' Guy was smiling at her, the smile that made her heart do a little flip despite herself. 'I can assure you that it is quite safe—my preoccupation with arachnids and amphibians is a thing of the past!' He leaned forward to help Sarah to a Bath biscuit. 'I am most sincerely sorry for the spider on your chair—'

'It was a toad on my chair,' Sarah said severely, 'and a spider in the schoolroom! I beg you not to regard it, Lord Renshaw. I do not believe that I sustained any lasting hurt!'

'I am relieved to hear it,' Guy murmured, 'as I wish above all things to make a good impression upon you, Miss Sheridan!'

'A little late for that, my lord, when you were so destructive to my roses!' Sarah observed sweetly.

He lowered his voice. 'Was your cousin very displeased? If only you had vouchsafed your name and direction, Miss Sheridan, I could have escorted you back here and apologised to her!'

Sarah knew he was trying provoke her by reminding her of the set-down she had given him. A smile tugged at the corners of her mouth, but she repressed it ruthlessly.

'You know that that would scarcely have been appropriate, my lord! As for Amelia, she was a little dismayed. She is the dearest creature, but even she cannot concoct a red, white and blue flower arrangement without the red!'

'Ah, I see. The patriotic theme?'

'Precisely so!' Despite herself, Sarah found that they were smiling together. Guy was sitting forward, his entire attention focused on her in a most flattering manner. It was very disconcerting.

'I am so very sorry that I did not recognise you when we met earlier, Miss Sheridan,' he said softly, 'but how was I to know that the gawky schoolgirl I used to know had grown into such a beautiful woman? Such a transformation is enough to throw a fellow completely!'

Sarah felt a blush rising at the teasing note in his voice. There was admiration in the look he gave her; admiration and a more disturbing emotion. It seemed astonishing that she could be sitting here in Amelia's drawing-room with a gentleman she had just met again for the first time in thirteen years, and be feeling this intoxicating and entirely improper stirring of the senses.

'You are outrageous, sir!' she said, to cover her confusion. 'I believe you have not altered one whit!'

'Oh, you must allow me a little improvement!' Guy looked at her with mock-reproof. 'At the very least, I am taller than when you last saw me!'

'That was not at all what I meant! It seems to me that you were always given to the most excessive flattery! Why, I distinctly remember you practising your charms on my grandmother! She professed herself scandalised that one so young should be so adept at flirtation!'

'Well, I'll concede that I was ever inclined to practise on susceptible ladies!' Guy said lazily. 'You may find, however, that my scandalous behaviour has developed in other directions since then!'

Sarah was sure that he was correct and it seemed likely that the type of outrageous behaviour indulged in by a man of nine and twenty was infinitely more dangerous to her than that of a youth primarily obsessed with practical jokes.

'I do not doubt it, sir! Pray do not furnish me with the details, it would not be at all proper!'

'But then I am not at all proper,' Guy said ruefully. 'Though, to my regret, I believe you to be a very pattern-card of correctness, Miss Sheridan!'

'So I should hope! Pray do not pursue this line of conversation, sir!'

'Must I not?' There was a look of limpid innocence on Guy's face. 'I was presuming that our previous acquaintance would allow a certain informality—'

'Informality!' Sarah realised that she had raised her voice when she caught Amelia's look of curiosity. She hastily dropped her tone again. 'You presume too much, my lord!'

Guy shrugged, gracefully conceding defeat. Sarah had the distinct impression that it would only be a temporary reversal. She cast around for a safe change of subject. Genteel Bath society had scarcely prepared her for dealing with so flagrant a flirtation. She plumped for something she hoped would be innocuous.

'I understand that you had been abroad for some years, sir. Your family must be eager to see you after all this time.'

Guy took her lead courteously, though there was a flash of amusement in his eyes that told her he knew she was trying to deflect him.

'Yes, indeed,' he said agreeably. 'I was serving with Wellesley in the Peninsula for four years and only returned because my father's health has deteriorated and he needs my help at Woodallan.'

'I am sorry to hear of the Earl's ill health,' Sarah said, concerned. 'I hope that it is not too serious?'

For once the humour dropped away from Guy's expression and he looked sombre. 'I hope so, too, Miss Sheridan, but I fear the worst. It is very unlike him to admit that he needs my help, but he has intimated that he wishes me to take on more of the running of Woodallan and the other estates...' He made an effort to try for a lighter note. 'No doubt my mother will be glad to see me back—she has been cursing Bonaparte these four years past for prolonging the war!'

'It is several years since I saw your parents, although your mother and I still write,' Sarah said, with a smile. 'She told me in her last letter that she had high hopes of your swift return. She is kind—she sent me a very sympathetic letter when my father died.'

She looked up, to see Guy watching her. For all his levity, those dark eyes were disconcertingly perceptive. 'It must have been a difficult time for you,' he said gently. 'You must have been very young, no more than nineteen, I imagine? And then to lose your brother and your home in such quick succession...'

Sarah's mind immediately flew to Blanchland again. It seemed strange that she had so completely forgotten about Frank's letter during the past few minutes. She had lost a brother, but it appeared that she had gained a niece. What sort of a girl would Miss Olivia Meredith prove to be? Her letter had been very neat and proper, the writing of a young lady educated at one of Oxford's more select seminaries. But how to find her? She had to concoct a plan...

Sarah realised that Guy was still watching her, his

searching gaze intent on her face. It made her feel oddly breathless.

'I beg your pardon. I was thinking of home…' She tried to gather her thoughts and steer away from further confidences. 'Yes, I thank you… It was a difficult time.'

'And now you reside with Lady Amelia?' Guy smiled, looking across at where Amelia and Greville were engrossed in conversation, her chestnut curls brushing his shoulder as she bent forward confidingly. 'I imagine that must be quite amusing!'

Sarah laughed. 'Oh, I have been most fortunate! Amelia's society is always stimulating and she has been as generous as a sister to me!'

Guy lowered his voice. 'Do you think she will ever put Grev out of his misery and accept his suit, Miss Sheridan?'

It was a surprisingly personal question. Sarah raised her eyebrows a little haughtily and saw him grin in response.

'I beg your pardon, Miss Sheridan, if you think me impertinent. I am only concerned for my friend's future happiness, for I know he holds Lady Amelia in high esteem. But perhaps you think me presumptuous—again?'

Sarah unbent a little. 'There is nothing I would like more than to see them make a match of it, my lord. I have been promoting the alliance these two years past! Alas, Amelia is not susceptible to my arguments!'

'Nor to Greville's, it would seem,' Guy said, shifting a little in his chair. 'And you, Miss Sheridan? No doubt you have many suitors! I should be glad to have happy news of your own situation to take back to Woodallan with me!'

If the previous question had been bold, this one took

Sarah's breath away. Once again there was a teasing light in his eyes, daring her to give him the snub he deserved.

'I shall be happy for you to tell your family that I am in good health and spirits,' she said, with a very straight face, 'and to give them all my very best wishes!'

Guy did not seem discomposed. His smile broadened with appreciation. 'I shall take that as encouragement for my own hopes then, ma'am!'

'You should not do so, my lord,' Sarah said crushingly. 'I had not the least intention of encouraging you!'

'I was thinking that the gentlemen of Bath must all be slow-tops,' Guy said, apparently undaunted by her coldness, 'but now I perceive that you are very high in the instep, Miss Sheridan! Your good opinion is not easily gained!'

'Certainly not by an acknowledged rake who carelessly destroys my roses!' Sarah said coolly. 'Pray do not repine, however, my lord! There are any number of young ladies in Bath who would be delighted to flirt with you!'

'Minx!' his lordship said, with feeling. 'I have to tell you that I have no interest in them, Miss Sheridan!'

'Indeed?' Sarah hesitated over administering yet another set-down to him in a single day. She had the feeling that it would be inviting trouble.

'Naturally I do not include you in their company, ma'am! Will you dance with me at your cousin's ball tomorrow night?'

Sarah raised her eyebrows again. There was no doubt that Viscount Renshaw possessed a most persistent and provocative disposition, and that he was deliberately trying to incite a reaction.

'It is not certain that I shall attend, sir,' she said, still cool. 'I have other plans—'

His eyes danced with a secret amusement. 'Oh, surely you would not disappoint your cousin, ma'am? Shall I appeal to her to persuade you?' He glanced across at Amelia and Greville, still deep in conversation.

'Pray do not disturb them,' Sarah said hastily, aware that her colour had risen again. It was an understood thing that she would be present at Amelia's ball, for it would be the highlight of Bath's winter season. She suspected that Guy had guessed as much. His amused gaze rested on her face, moving over each feature with slow deliberation. Sarah felt inordinately uncomfortable under that observant scrutiny.

The clock chimed.

'Oh!' Amelia got hastily to her feet. 'I do beg your pardon, gentlemen! I am promised to Mrs Chartley's card party! Pray excuse me or I shall be very late!'

Greville and Guy stood up, Greville offering his escort to Amelia, who accepted prettily.

Guy took Sarah's hand and pressed a kiss on it. 'I am sure we shall see you this evening, Miss Sheridan. Do you go to the dance at the Pump Room?'

'Oh, yes, we shall be there!' Amelia said cheerfully, seeming blissfully unaware that her cousin was about to deny it. She gave Guy Renshaw a melting smile. 'It is the last public dance of the year, you know! But how charming to be able to see you again so soon, Lord Renshaw!'

Guy bowed. 'The pleasure will be all mine, Lady Amelia! Your servant, Miss Sheridan!'

They all went out together. Sarah watched from the window as the Viscount parted from Greville and Amelia with a casual word and a smile. She was aware of a certain conflict inside her and a faint disappointment. Guy Renshaw was a charming man and he had made his admiration for her very plain, but he was also a dangerous flirt who probably did not mean a word of it. It would be very foolish to read anything into his behaviour and even more imprudent to allow an unexpected physical attraction to disturb her.

Besides, he would be leaving Bath in a couple of days and so would she. Abruptly, Sarah remembered her commitment to visit Blanchland, and felt depression settle on her. She did not want to see what Ralph Covell had done to her beloved family home, nor to become embroiled in the problems of Frank's natural daughter, nor to ruin her own reputation in the process. Amelia was quite right—she must be mad. And Churchward had even offered her a way out by suggesting that an agent could represent her interests, yet for some reason she had chosen not to take it…

Sarah felt the beginnings of a headache stir. Since she had resolved on this rash course of action, she must at least plan how to accomplish it with a minimum of fuss. Blanchland was less than a day's journey from Bath, and if she were fortunate she would be able to find Miss Meredith quickly, discover the girl's difficulties and instruct Churchward on the best way to resolve them. The whole matter could be decided in a week—ten days at the outside. And no one need ever know.

The presence of Viscount Renshaw and Sir Greville Baynham caused quite a stir at the Pump Room that night. Sir Greville, whose family home was a few miles north of the city, had always been a universal favourite, with several young ladies expressing themselves willing to console him if Lady Amelia refused his suit. The

Viscount caused an even greater commotion, being fortunate enough to be rich, handsome and heir to an Earl into the bargain.

It was a clear, starry night, and Sarah and Amelia had walked the short distance from Brock Street to the Pump Room, enjoying the fresh chill of the night air that brought the colour to their cheeks and made their eyes sparkle. As they handed over their cloaks and Amelia cast a thoughtful look over her cousin, Sarah saw her smile of approval.

'How pretty you look, Sarah! I would not have dreamed of saying anything before, but I am so glad you have cast off that hideous half-mourning!'

She saw Sarah's expression and added hastily, 'I know you were a most devoted sister to Frank, my love, but surely you are too young to wear black forever?'

Sarah could feel her lips twitching as she tried to suppress a smile. Milly could be amazingly tactless at times.

'I know the black was ageing,' she agreed mildly, 'but surely the lavender became me a little?'

Amelia looked contrite. 'Oh, sweetly pretty, my love, but for a whole year? And even then you habitually chose drab colours that are nothing to this delicious rose tint you are wearing now!' She cast her cousin a sideways look. 'I did wonder whether the advent of Viscount Renshaw was the reason for your sudden—'

'Oh, look, Milly, it is Mr Tilbury and his sister!' Sarah was aware that she had never shown much inclination for the Tilburys' company before now, but felt she had to distract her cousin. Amelia, however, was far too determined for that.

'Yes, I fear we will be in for much the same company as ever tonight, especially with it being the end of the season! As I was saying, it is fortunate that Greville has brought that charming man, Guy Renshaw, with him! I declare, Bath society seldom offers the opportunity to meet so prodigiously attractive a gentleman!'

Sarah knew that she was blushing and prayed that it could be put down to the heat of the room after the cold outside. She would never have admitted to Amelia that she had spent twice as long as usual at her toilette and agonised between the rose pink and the aquamarine silk. Sarah had been aware of a growing sense of anticipation all afternoon, and found that she was feeling quite nervous as she and Amelia entered the ballroom. She experienced an altogether unfamiliar sensation of breathlessness, her heart suddenly racing and butterflies fluttering frantically in her stomach. Her slender fingers tightened on her fan. This was ridiculous! Good gracious, she was very nearly in a fit of panic, and all because of Guy Renshaw, who had once put a toad on her dining-chair!

She could see Guy across the ballroom, deep in conversation with Greville and attracting considerable attention from the female guests. The reason was not hard to seek: the classical good looks of the Woodallan family, combined with the immaculate black and white of the evening dress, made him look extremely handsome and ever-so-slightly dangerous.

'Half my female acquaintance have already heard that the Viscount called on us earlier and have begged an introduction,' Amelia was saying, with a giggle. 'I declare, we have not seen so much excitement in an age!' She linked her arm through Sarah's and the cousins walked slowly down the edge of the ballroom.

'Greville looks very handsome tonight,' Sarah observed, giving Amelia a meaningful look. 'Not even Lord Renshaw can put him in the shade!'

'Oh, Grev looks very well,' Amelia said, so carelessly that Sarah wanted to shake her, 'and I am very fond of him, of course, but in a brotherly sort of way!'

'A favourite brother, perhaps,' Sarah said tartly.

Amelia cast her a look from under her lashes. 'Oh Sarah, do I treat him so badly? I do not mean to!'

'You know you do not value him as you ought! Greville would never lose all his money at cards, or drink himself into oblivion the way your late husband did—'

'No...' Amelia sighed soulfully '...Alan was such exciting company!'

Sarah sighed. In her opinion, Alan Fenton had been a wastrel with nothing to commend him, and she could never understand why Amelia appeared to value his dashing looks over Greville's integrity. They were almost upon Sir Greville now and she saw the glad light that sprang into his blue eyes as he looked at Amelia. It was too bad.

'Miss Sheridan.' Guy Renshaw took her hand, his touch evoking much the same shiver of awareness as it had done earlier in the day, and Sarah was instantly distracted. 'You look delightful. I would ask you to dance, but I fear that the excitement of the minuet might be too much for me!'

Sarah looked reproving. 'I know you find our entertainments dull, my lord, but there are country dances after eight, if that is your preference!'

'What, no waltzes?'

'Oh, the waltz is much too fast for Bath!'

'A pity! Perhaps I shall have to settle for a country dance after all, if you will so honour me. In the meantime, do you care for a little supper?'

'Thank you.' Sarah let him take her arm and steer her away from the others and into the refreshment room. He helped her to a seat in a secluded alcove, then crossed to the buffet table, where several young ladies immediately gravitated towards him and one of them artfully drew him into conversation over the merits of the strawberries.

Behind a pillar to Sarah's right, the young ladies' mamas were watching with gimlet eyes. Sarah tried not to listen, but at least half of her wanted to eavesdrop on their conversation. She was no cynic, but she knew that despite the pungent denunciation they would inevitably make of Guy's character, either would marry him off to their daughter with triumphant haste.

'A shocking reputation, Mrs Bunton, quite shocking!'

'Really, Mrs Clarke? Just how shocking would you say it is?'

'Oh, quite dreadful! Of course, that was before he went to the War—perhaps the rigors of campaign have instilled some respectability...but I doubt it!'

'Once a rake—' Mrs Bunton said meaningfully.

'Though marriage to a good woman may redeem him, of course!'

Both ladies paused, evidently dwelling on the benefits of a match with their particular daughter.

'They say that Lady Melville was his mistress for a whole year—'

'Oh, yes, I had heard that, too! A most impassioned liaison, by all accounts!'

'And then there was the business of Lady Paget—'

'Dreadful! They say her husband never recovered! But the family is rich, of course,' Mrs Clarke said, as if in mitigation, 'and rumour has it that Woodallan wishes him to settle down.'

'Emma could do worse…'

'Much worse… Or your own dear Agatha, though they say Lord Renshaw prefers blondes…'

It was perhaps fortunate that Guy chose that moment to extract himself from the bevy of debutantes and return to Sarah, whose ears were becoming quite pink from what she had been obliged to hear. His observant dark gaze did not miss her high colour; as he put the loaded plate before her, he gave her a wicked grin.

'Dear me, Miss Sheridan, whatever can have caused you such discomfort? You look positively overset!'

'I am very well,' Sarah snapped, trying to keep her voice discreetly low, 'just embarrassed at having been obliged to overhear a rehearsal of your amours, sir! It is well that you will be leaving Bath soon, you have caused such a flutter in the dovecotes!'

'Good gracious, I had no idea you could be so frank, Miss Sheridan!' Guy said admiringly, eyeing her outraged face with amusement. 'To bring yourself to mention such matters! I was fair and far out in thinking you a prim Bath miss!'

'I am prim! That is why I am so agitated!' Sarah took a steadying draught of champagne. 'I do not think it wise for you to distinguish me with your attentions, my lord!'

'Why not?' Guy looked genuinely hurt. 'Because you are so respectable and I am not? But you see, Miss Sheridan—' he lowered his voice '—I am very grateful for the condescension you are showing me! Your respectability cannot but help improve my shocking reputation, you see! If the good ladies of Bath see that you are prepared to bear me company, perhaps they will not think me so bad after all!'

'Nonsense! You speak a deal of nonsense, sir!'

Their eyes met and Guy smiled, the lightness of his tone belied by the intensity of his gaze.

'Very well, if you don't like my nonsense, perhaps the truth will serve instead! I have the oddest feeling, Miss Sheridan...' his fingers brushed the back of Sarah's wrist lightly but with a touch that seemed to burn her '...that we are kindred spirits, despite our differences...or perhaps because of them...'

Very deliberately Sarah freed herself and took a mouthful of food, glad that the hand that held the fork was so steady. Her heart was racing at his touch, so light, but so confusing. He was still watching her with that disconcerting mix of speculation and challenge.

'Tell me, Miss Sheridan, have you never wished for any excitement?'

Damn the man, would he never change the subject? Sarah felt acutely vulnerable. Just how far was he going to press this particular topic?

'My life is quite exciting enough, I thank you, my lord.' Her voice was quite calm. 'I have my books and my letters and my friends. There are concerts here at the Pump Room and if the weather is fine I may promenade in the park!'

'It sounds a positive orgy of entertainment,' Guy murmured, his eyes mocking her above the rim of his glass. 'Have you never been to London?'

'No, I have not.'

'You had no come-out, like other debutantes? No...' he looked at her thoughtfully '...I suppose your father died before you were old enough, and then your brother was too wrapped up in his travelling...'

'I liked living in the country,' Sarah said truthfully, 'and Bath is very pleasant.'

'That's certainly true. All joking aside, it seems a

delightful place. But have you no wish to recapture your youth?'

'I was not aware that I had yet lost my youth, sir,' Sarah said tartly. 'I am scarce in my dotage!'

'How refreshing to meet a young lady who does not think she is at her last prayers! So you consider that you still have plenty of time to throw your bonnet over the windmill!'

'What an extraordinary idea!' Sarah could not help smiling in return. 'I assure you I have no intention of doing so, my lord!'

'Ah, well, who can say?' Guy raised his dark eyebrows. 'Look at you this evening, Miss Sheridan, giving countenance to a rake!'

'I scarcely think that I am giving you countenance, my lord!'

'Maybe not, but I notice that you do not dispute the other half of my statement!' There was a teasing note in Guy's voice.

'As to that, I cannot say.' Sarah spoke with equanimity. 'Nor,' she added quickly, seeing the spark of devilment in his eyes, 'do I have any ambition to find out!'

'What a sensible lady you are, Miss Sheridan,' Guy murmured. 'So measured, so composed! Lady Amelia must find you a positive paragon of a companion!'

Remembering the concern she was currently causing her cousin, who had wasted another twenty minutes earlier that afternoon trying to persuade her against her trip to Blanchland, Sarah could not agree with him. She was almost glad to see the ponderous figure of Mr Tilbury approaching to request a dance. Guy did not demur when she excused herself and Sarah was annoyed that this should be so, then was even more irritated with herself for so out-of-character contrariness. She watched

Guy performing a succession of country dances with Bath's most eligible debutantes and told herself that she did not care in the least.

Guy presented himself a little late for his promised dance with her for he appeared to have had difficulty in tearing himself away from his previous partner, the extremely young and pretty Miss Bunton. Sarah discovered that this engendered in her a feeling of acute vexation akin to indigestion, the like of which she had never experienced before. She had to fight a hard battle with herself in order to greet him civilly, and was mortified to see the sardonic light in his eye that suggested he had seen and noted her reaction. Sarah was obliged to remind herself yet again that she had only met the man that very day and could have neither interest in nor opinion on his behaviour. Nevertheless, she kept her gaze averted from his, for she had the lowering suspicion that he could read her mind.

'You are very quiet, Miss Sheridan,' Guy observed softly, when the movement of the dance brought them together. 'I know it cannot be that you need to concentrate on your steps, for you dance too well for that. Have I then done something to displease you?'

Sarah saw the flash of mockery in his eyes and, in spite of all her good intentions, she felt her temper rise. He really did have the most regrettable effect on her composure!

'How could that be so, my lord?' she asked sweetly. 'I scarcely know you well enough to claim the privilege of being annoyed by your behaviour!'

She saw the look of amused speculation on Guy's face before the dance obliged him to move briefly away. Sarah tried to get a grip on her bad temper. She had no wish to betray the fact that he had the power to affect her, nor to be drawn into a conversation that could be dangerous, and she was afraid that she had already said too much. She received confirmation of this a moment later.

'I collect that you mean that one must care sufficiently for someone before their behaviour can influence one's feelings?' Guy said lazily, when they came back together again. 'In that case, I shall hope that time will see you quite exasperated with me!'

Sarah reflected ruefully that she had probably deserved that and would think twice before crossing swords with him again.

Guy seemed disinclined to let the matter drop, however, for when she did not reply he raised an eyebrow and said, 'What do you say, ma'am? Do you think you could find it in your heart to dislike me a little?'

Sarah smiled a little shamefacedly. 'I know you are trying to provoke me, sir—'

'Indeed? I thought the reverse was true for once!'

'Very well!' Sarah met his eyes squarely. 'I'll admit that I said something that I now deeply regret! Pray accept my apologies, my lord!'

The dance had ended, but Guy was still holding her hand. They were standing on the edge of the dance floor, surrounded by couples milling about as they either retired for refreshments or joined the set that was forming, yet it seemed to Sarah that they were entirely alone. Guy smiled and when Sarah looked up into his eyes she saw an expression there that was compounded of desire overlaid by wicked mischief. So strong was the conviction that he was about to kiss her that Sarah took an instinctive step backwards.

'Do not worry,' Guy spoke so softly that only she

could hear, 'I will not do it—at least, not here! But the temptation, Miss Sheridan, is acute.'

The colour flamed into Sarah's face as she realised that he had read her thoughts. 'Believe me, my lord,' she said, with as much composure as she could muster, 'so is the temptation to slap your face!'

Guy burst out laughing. 'So the honours are even, Miss Sheridan!' He pressed a kiss on her hand. 'Until our next meeting!' And he sauntered away to the card-room, leaving Sarah feeling breathless and outraged in equal measure.

Chapter Three

Sarah slept well that night, but awoke early with thoughts of Blanchland pressing on her mind once again. She was aware that she had as yet made no plans for her journey to her former home, other than a vague decision that she should set off the following day. This was all very fine, but she needed to be better prepared. She could not predict how Sir Ralph Covell would greet the unexpected arrival of his late cousin's daughter, nor had she decided whether she should take him into her confidence or not. If Churchward's information had been correct and Olivia had last been seen approaching Blanchland Court, this might prove a very bad idea indeed.

Sarah shivered and burrowed deeper under her blankets for both warmth and comfort. Not for the first time she reflected that she was involving herself in a situation that appeared to have Gothic overtones, but she was a most practical girl and could only believe that there was a perfectly simple explanation for Olivia's disappearance. No doubt the girl had gone to stay with a relative and forgotten to tell anyone. And the desperate matter on which she required advice would probably prove to be a romance, or, at worst, the need to go out into the world and earn a living as a governess. There was no need for worry.

Sarah threw back the bedcovers and crossed to the window. There had been a hard frost and the winter sun was rising in a pale blue sky. The house was astir with the peculiar excitement that characterised the day of a ball. Sarah had promised to help Amelia with her preparations, but she knew that her cousin would not be rising early and she needed some fresh air.

Amelia kept a small stable in the mews behind the buildings. There were her carriage horses, a gentle white mare that she occasionally rode in the park, and a decidedly more spirited one that Sarah enjoyed putting through its paces. The morning, with its crisp, fresh air, was perfect for a ride.

It seemed that Astra thought so, too, for her ears pricked up as soon as they left the quiet streets behind and reached the springy turf of Lansdown. Sarah enjoyed a fine gallop, leaving the toiling groom far behind, and only as she skirted Greville Baynham's land did she slow down and allow herself to think about the previous night.

There was no doubt that some kind of peculiar affinity existed between herself and Guy Renshaw, and she knew that if she had any sense she would leave it well alone. Sarah sighed, allowing the horse to pick its own way along the steep path. She could not deny that in some senses Guy was a very eligible *parti*, so eligible, in fact, that he would look to marry far higher than a penniless companion, no matter how well-connected. In other respects he was utterly ineligible, for his reputation and evident disinclination for settling down rendered him not just unsuitable but positively dangerous.

Sarah sighed again. She had had plenty of opportunities to marry in the previous six years, but somehow none of her suitors had quite matched her expectations and she had been too fastidious to marry just for the sake of it. She wondered now whether that had been a mistake. Living with Amelia was enjoyable, but how long would it continue? Besides, she had had the running of Blanchland and missed having her own establishment. Yet it seemed typical that when her inclination had finally settled on a gentleman who more than met her expectations, her choice should be totally inappropriate…

'Good morning, Miss Sheridan! It is a beautiful morning, is it not?'

Sarah came out of her reverie in time to see the subject of her thoughts let himself through the gate that separated the downs from Chelwood Park. He brought his horse alongside Sarah's and gave her a smile, his gaze openly appreciating her pink cheeks and bright eyes.

'That's a very spirited creature you have there, Miss Sheridan! It would be difficult to tell which of you looks as though they have enjoyed the gallop more!'

He sat his own chestnut hunter with a skill that Sarah did not find at all surprising and the casual elegance of his attire would be enough, she thought, to have all last night's impressionable debutantes swooning again. This morning, with the breeze ruffling his thick, fair hair and the sun lighting those expressive dark eyes, Lord Renshaw looked utterly devastating.

'Your cousin does not ride with you?' he asked, looking down the hill to where the groom was exhorting his labouring horse up the slope. 'I see that you are alone, to all intents and purposes.'

'I think not.' Sarah could not help wondering what intent or purpose he might have in seeking her out alone. She would have to be careful. 'Amelia does not care for riding, but I brought the groom.' She gestured down the hill, where Tom was still making heavy weather of getting the old cob to catch up. Guy laughed.

'So I see—and promptly left him behind again! I did not imagine you to be so keen a rider, Miss Sheridan! You did not mention it as one of your ruling passions last night!'

Sarah cast him a look under her lashes. 'I grew up in the country, so it can be no great surprise that I ride!'

'No, but you ride very well indeed, which is rare. I'll allow that it is commonplace enough to meet ladies who can prance about in the park and think that they look most accomplished!'

'You are very severe this morning, my lord!' Sarah could not help laughing. 'I am glad that my own small skill gains your approval rather than your censure!'

Guy smiled lazily. 'Oh, I am renowned as a hard critic, but I cannot find fault with you, Miss Sheridan!'

Sarah felt herself blushing under his scrutiny. For some perverse reason all she could think of was his threat—or was it a promise?—to kiss her on some future occasion. Would such a manoeuvre be possible on horseback? It was an intriguing thought. It would certainly require considerable skill, but— Sarah suddenly realised that Guy was still watching her, one dark eyebrow raised in teasing enquiry. Afraid that he would read her thoughts again, as he had the previous night, Sarah turned her horse's head abruptly away and was relieved to see the groom struggling up the last incline to join them on the level summit.

'There is an exceptional view from up here,' Guy

observed, looking out across the city to the Somerset hills beyond, 'and a keen breeze. It leaves me sharp set! Will you join us at Chelwood for breakfast, Miss Sheridan?'

Tom the groom, who had been encouraging his exhausted horse, cast Sarah a scandalised glance. She smiled.

'Thank you, my lord, but I do not think that would be very proper! I fear I must return to Brock Street for my breakfast!'

'My sensible Miss Sheridan! A bachelor household, even one so unimpeachable as Chelwood, is not an appropriate destination for a single lady!' Guy's dark eyes were full of mockery. 'A pity if you were to starve on your way home as a result!'

'I must be going, at any rate,' Sarah said, trying to crush her foolish excitement at his use of the phrase 'my sensible Miss Sheridan'. She turned Astra's head towards home. 'Amelia will need help with all the preparations for her ball tonight. Good day, my lord.'

'A moment, Miss Sheridan.' Guy put his hand over hers on the reins. 'Does Lady Amelia intend to be so fast as to have the waltz this evening?'

Sarah paused. 'I believe so, my lord.'

Guy let her go and raised his whip in a salute. 'Then save me a dance, Miss Sheridan!'

Amelia was in great good spirits. Silk drapes in red and blue swathed the walls and pillars of the ballroom, white candles filled the sconces and huge vases overflowing with red roses formed the centrepiece of her decorations.

The roses had arrived in the late afternoon and had caused much excited giggling and shrieking amongst the maids as they had tried to find sufficient receptacles in which to place them all. Several old, chipped vases had been pressed into service for the less prominent of arrangements and a chamber pot had even been proffered, though Sarah had seen Chisholm hastily hide it behind the umbrella stand before Amelia had noticed. There had been no card, which had led to much gossip and speculation, but when the pack of maids had gone and Amelia had swept off to see to the menus, Chisholm had stepped forward with a tiny, delicate posy of pale pink rosebuds with a card tucked inside. There were only two words, written in a strong black hand that Sarah had never seen before, yet instantly recognised: 'Penance? Renshaw.'

And now Sarah was wearing one of the rosebuds pinned to the bodice of her aquamarine gown and was full of a most heady excitement at the thought of seeing Guy again.

'Your decorations look very fine and patriotic,' Sarah said, catching her cousin at a quiet moment between the arrival of two parties of guests. 'I know you would not give away the secret before, but how have you managed the red, white and blue theme for the menus, Milly?'

'Oh,' Amelia laughed, 'the trout with garlic and tomatoes is red and there is woodcock in a white wine sauce—'

'And the blue?'

'Ice cream with bilberries! We call it *glace du Napoleon*! Cook has been swearing that this is his finest hour!' Amelia smiled as her gaze rested on the roses. 'They are magnificent, aren't they? Are you sure you have no idea of their provenance, Sarah?'

'Good evening, Lady Amelia. And Miss Sheridan! I am so glad that you decided to attend after all, ma'am!'

Sarah swung round to see Viscount Renshaw bowing punctiliously. She was not sure whether she was glad to see him or not. On the one hand, his arrival was timely in diverting Amelia from her question. On the other, there was a decidedly wicked twinkle in his eye.

Amelia opened her eyes wide. 'Lord Renshaw! Good evening, sir! But whatever can you mean? Why should Sarah not attend my ball? Sarah, you know you have been promised for tonight this month past!'

Sarah gave Guy Renshaw a fulminating look. 'I have no notion what his lordship can mean, Milly!'

'I beg your pardon.' Guy gave her a look of limpid innocence. 'I must have misunderstood you, ma'am. Lady Amelia, do I have your permission to take your cousin off and dance with her?'

Amelia looked speculatively from one to the other. 'You have my blessing, Lord Renshaw, but whether Sarah will agree is another matter!'

Guy took Sarah's arm. 'It is a waltz and you did promise me...'

He appeared to take her acquiescence for granted, steering her towards the dance floor and taking her in his arms in a manner that might be entirely appropriate for the waltz, but nevertheless deprived Sarah momentarily of speech. Their bodies touched for a brief second before he held her a little away from him with impeccable propriety.

Sarah was an accomplished dancer, but she found that waltzing in Guy's arms was a very different experience from attempting the boulanger with Mr Tilbury. Dancing with Guy was unnerving; the touch of his hands through the silk of her dress felt like a caress. His head was bent close to hers, and when their eyes met she could see the admiration in their depths, the flash of desire that he did not trouble to hide. It disturbed her and stirred something strange and sensual within her. Sarah closed her eyes momentarily, startled by her own feelings.

'You dance beautifully,' Guy said, after they had circled the floor a couple of times in silence. 'I remember that you were musical even as a child. You used to sing and play most prettily.'

'I do not recall that you were so eager to dance with me in our youth,' Sarah said, with a slight smile, glad of an innocuous topic of conversation when her thoughts had been anything but innocent. 'There was one children's ball at which you spurned me quite ruthlessly, my lord!'

Guy's arms tightened momentarily. Looking up, she saw a look of brilliant amusement in his eyes and her heart did a little somersault.

'I had no discernment in my youth,' he said regretfully, 'and our parents were forever trying to throw us together. I believe they wished us to make a match of it and naturally enough, I tried to rebel! What boy of sixteen wishes to contemplate matrimony—least of all with a young lady of eleven!'

'Perhaps they were a little misguided—'

'Just premature, I believe, Miss Sheridan!'

Sarah was vexed with herself for giving him the chance to flirt with her. Just when she had thought they could talk on uncontroversial subjects, he had turned the topic around! He richly deserved a set-down.

'More of your nonsense, sir!' she said crossly. 'I am no green girl to be taken in by your flattery!'

'No, indeed,' Guy agreed amiably, his smile teasing her. 'I forgot that you had so many years in your dish,

Miss Sheridan! My reputation is quite safe with you, is it not?'

Sarah was rendered momentarily speechless by his impudence. Before she could marshal her thoughts to deliver the cutting remark he deserved, the music whirled to a close.

Guy bowed. 'Perhaps you will spare me another dance later, Miss Sheridan?'

'I do not think that would be at all respectable, sir!' Sarah said pertly, unable to resist. 'As you have just pointed out, you must have a care for your reputation, and two dances could be considered fast!'

She saw him smile and knew he would have replied in kind had Amelia not arrived at that moment, bringing with her a very young man who had a hopeful look in his eye.

'Lord Renshaw, pray forgive my interruption,' Amelia began, 'but Mr Elliston believes that you may have been serving with his elder brother in Portugal, and is most anxious for any news...'

Guy bowed. 'Of course. You must be Richard Elliston's brother? I remember him well.' He gestured to the refreshment room. 'We could talk over a glass of wine if you wish...'

Young Mr Elliston looked quite overwhelmed at such condescension. Amelia smiled, taking Sarah's arm and drawing her away.

'He is very kind. Poor Jack Elliston has been quite worried—the family has had no news for nigh on six months!' She looked closely at Sarah. 'Are you quite well, my love? Your colour is very high! I do hope you have not taken a chill!'

'I do not believe so.' Sarah was astonished how calm she sounded when inside she felt quite shaken. For all that she had acquitted herself well enough, flirting with Guy Renshaw was an occupation requiring sterner nerves than hers. No doubt the society ladies who indulged in a little intrigue to relieve the boredom of their marriages were well versed in playing such sophisticated games. She was not, having little or no experience of the art of dalliance.

'Lord Renshaw seems to have been most charming to you,' Amelia was saying, her voice casual but her gaze alert as she took in Sarah's becomingly pink cheeks and sparkling eyes. 'I do believe he is trying to get up a flirtation with you, Sarah!'

Sarah took a glass of wine gratefully from a passing servant and drank half of it straight away before answering. Amelia's intent look deepened.

'Sarah! Whatever ails you? Are you sure you are quite well?'

Sarah laughed and pressed her cousin's hand. 'I am feeling very well, I thank you. I believe you must put my uncharacteristic behaviour down to Lord Renshaw's bad influence!'

Amelia's eyes widened to their furthest extent. 'Gracious, Sarah, how diverting! Surely you have not been encouraging him?'

'Not precisely, but…' Sarah hesitated '…I wonder if I have discouraged him sufficiently? He is, as you say, so very charming that it is difficult to resist…'

Amelia began to laugh. 'I should not worry, Sarah! You are scarcely a hardened flirt and Lord Renshaw is experienced enough to know the difference between a lady of easy virtue and a respectable spinster! I am more concerned that your own heart should remain whole!'

Sarah wrinkled up her nose and reached for her wineglass again. 'Really, Amelia! Respectable spinster! You make me sound at least sixty and as dull as ditchwater into the bargain!'

'Better to be respectable than give in to Guy Renshaw's blandishments,' Amelia said drily. 'He has a truly terrible reputation, Sarah! Why, Mrs Bunton tells me—'

'Thank you,' Sarah said hastily. 'I have already heard her on the subject! I am in no real danger, I assure you, either from his lordship or from my own feelings! I know he can have no serious intentions and will not allow him to progress with any dishonourable ones!'

A little frown still marred Amelia's forehead. 'That is all very well, but it would not do to like him too much!'

'I know.' Sarah felt a little lurch of the heart as she spoke. Amelia had hit upon the very problem, for she was beginning to like Guy Renshaw very much indeed, and against her better judgement.

She let Mr Tilbury carry her off for the cotillion, noting that Amelia still looked concerned. She knew that her cousin had her own best interests at heart. Guy Renshaw could not be seen in the light of a suitable connection for a penniless companion. Her ineligibility could only mean that he could have no serious intentions, and designs of a less respectable nature would have to be ruthlessly crushed.

For a moment, Sarah felt an extraordinary disappointment. Guy's charm was very potent and Sarah knew that her own inexperience made it difficult for her to treat his admiration lightly. Then there was the peculiar physical attraction he held for her, the like of which she had never even dreamed of, let alone experienced before. For a moment, Sarah let herself imagine being in Guy Renshaw's embrace, recalling the hard strength of the arms that had held her in the waltz, the ripple of muscles beneath the smooth material of his jacket, the curl of that sensuous mouth…

Suddenly heated, Sarah felt her body diffuse with warmth and the colour flood into her face. It was fortunate that Mr Tilbury was rather unobservant, for it would have been impossible for him to believe that his own conversation could cause his companion to blush so vividly.

Sarah tried to concentrate on his observations on the price of coal, furiously castigating herself for allowing her thoughts to wander in so improper a direction. And this was hardly the first time!

The dance progressed in pedestrian fashion, with none of the zest of the previous waltz.

Guy was nowhere in sight, perhaps still talking with Mr Elliston, but Sarah noted a knot of people set a little back from the dance floor, with Mrs Bunton at its core. Several of the most influential hostesses in Bath had their heads bent close, their hairpieces waggling, their mouths forming shocked and horrified circles. One of them glanced in Sarah's direction and looked away again hastily. Sarah frowned. Surely her behaviour with Viscount Renshaw had not caused such scandalised debate? One waltz, even with a notorious rake, hardly constituted a social solecism. Besides, Mrs Bunton had been pushing her own daughter in Guy's direction only the night before.

Mr Tilbury addressed another of his remarks to her and Sarah temporarily forgot the group of gossiping matrons. However, she was reminded again swiftly as the dance drew to an end. As Mr Tilbury escorted her from the floor, Mrs Clarke drew her skirts aside and turned her back in the most pointed of snubs. Sarah stopped in surprise and Mr Tilbury's face flushed with outrage.

He was about to speak when Mrs Clarke said loudly, 'What can one expect with such low family connections? There's bad blood in the Covell family, which no doubt accounts for his cousin throwing her lot in with him! I wonder at Lady Amelia giving countenance to a woman who is clearly lost to all sense of decency!'

Shock rendered Sarah temporarily speechless. All around her she could see the looks of speculation and hear the chatter of rumour and gossip. She looked about desperately for Amelia, but her cousin was across the room, talking to Greville Baynham. There was no help closer at hand. Mr Tilbury was opening and closing his mouth like a stranded fish, his own expression one of painful embarrassment. Everyone else merely watched to see what would happen next.

Murmuring an incoherent apology to Mr Tilbury, Sarah hurried from the ballroom, almost ran up the stairs and instinctively sought shelter in her own room. Once there, she closed the door softly and leant back against it with her eyes closed. Mrs Clarke's sharply cruel words echoed in her mind: 'Lost to all sense of decency...'

There could be no mistake. Somehow, word of her intention to visit Blanchland had leaked out, been seized upon by eager gossips, and passed around the ballroom. Sarah felt outraged and humiliated. How dared they speak of her like that, make her the butt of their slander, rip her reputation to shreds in her very presence? She had seen them all, some condemning her already, others merely excited by scandal, but all watching her reactions for their own entertainment. Sarah had heard of times when the collective disapproval of Bath society had ruined someone's reputation, or left them a social outcast. It was just that she had never been on the receiving end before.

And why should she hide away here as though she had something to be ashamed of? Eyes flashing, Sarah flung open the door, ready to do battle in the ballroom. She would show Mrs Clarke and Mrs Bunton and all the other quizzes that she did not give a rush for their disapproval! She would not let them judge her and run away from them…

Sarah closed the door behind her and walked towards the stairs, still burning with outraged anger. She did not see the figure on the shadowed landing until it moved, and then she spun round with a gasp of alarm.

'Lord Renshaw! Good gracious, you gave me fright! Whatever are you doing up here, sir?'

'I wanted to speak to you, Miss Sheridan,' Guy said, coming forward into the circle of light cast by the single candelabra. 'I heard you come running up here and thought it best, perhaps, that we did not have an audience for our conversation.'

Sarah looked at him in puzzlement. There was something curious in his tone, some element that she could not define but that made her uncomfortable. It was impossible to decipher his expression in the flickering candlelight.

'I do not understand you, sir,' she said uncertainly. 'Surely it would be better to return to the ballroom—'

'Very well, if you are determined to face the extraordinary rumours that are circulating there,' Guy said coolly. 'Perhaps we could invite the whole of Bath society to join the conversation since they are taking such a close interest in your affairs!'

Sarah let out her breath in a long sigh. 'Oh, so you have heard—'

'I have! I could scarce believe it! Either you are seriously lacking in judgement, Miss Sheridan, or you are not the woman I thought you!'

Sarah stared at him, her temper soaring dangerously. She had been expecting him to sympathise with her in the face of the small-minded and malicious scandalmongers, and to find herself condemned unheard was adding insult to injury.

'Oh really, my lord!' she burst out. 'It is the outside of enough to have to put up with the ill-informed gossip of spiteful matrons without such as yourself picking pieces in my good character as well!'

'Indeed?' Guy stepped closer to her, his physical presence completely overwhelming her. Now that he was so near, Sarah could sense the slow burn of his anger, though she still did not understand its cause. 'At the least you do not pretend ignorance! Are you telling me that the rumours are untrue, Miss Sheridan?'

Sarah hesitated for a fatal second, trapped by her own honesty. 'Yes! No! At least…I do intend to visit Blanchland, but it is not as you imagine…'

Guy brought his hand down on the banisters with a force that seemed to make the delicate ironwork shiver. 'Surely it can be no surprise that your apparent desire to spend the winter in a house of ill repute should set the town by the ears, Miss Sheridan! Good God, Blanchland is a place where no woman of respectability should dream of setting foot! You will not have a shred of reputation left to you!'

Sarah glared at him. 'I can scarce believe that you are giving credence to chance-heard rumours, my lord!

I should have thought better of you! You have not even paused to request an explanation!'

Guy had turned away, his face tight and angry, but now he swung back towards her.

'There can be no reasonable explanation! At least,' he corrected himself punctiliously, 'the best construction I can put on your conduct is that you lack any sense of proper behaviour and the worst—' his dark eyes narrowed murderously '—is that you are accustomed to the sort of society and pursuits that Blanchland has to offer! Neither is an adequate excuse!'

Sarah seldom lost her temper. The even tenor of life in Amelia's household was hardly ever ruffled by upset or disturbance, but now she found herself furiously angry. Guy's stubborn refusal to see anything but the worst in her was as distressing as it was infuriating. The situation was further exacerbated by the fact that she could not understand why he was so angry. Worst of all was a shaming desire to cry, as she realised that, despite the brevity of their acquaintance, his good opinion was something that she valued deeply. She swallowed hard and made a conscious effort to whip up her anger as a defence against the hurt she was feeling.

'That is enough, sir! I do not wish to hear you slander my reputation! And as for your playing of the moral arbiter, it is rich beyond belief! You are the greatest hypocrite I have ever come across!'

Sarah made to walk past Guy and seek the sanctuary of her room again, all thoughts of returning to the ballroom forgotten. She was shaking with anger and mortification. She had no clear idea of how such a confrontation could have occurred, nor did she wish to prolong it. For Guy to take her to task in such a way was not the conduct of a gentleman, but deeper than that, more hurtful, was his evident contempt and unjust condemnation.

Guy shifted slightly, but he did not move to let her past. There was something wholly unyielding about his stance, as though he had no intention of letting her go easily. For a long moment their eyes met in angry conflict, then Guy stepped forward and trapped Sarah between his body and the balcony rail.

He bent his head and brought his mouth down on hers in a kiss that was searching and utterly ruthless. Disbelief and fury welled up in Sarah. She pummelled his chest hard with her clenched fists, but he only tightened his grip on her, rendering her protests useless.

'I am living up to my reputation now, Miss Sheridan,' he said, raising his lips an inch from hers. 'I suggest that you start to do the same!'

His mouth returned to hers with a fierce demand. A shocking excitement swept through Sarah, setting her trembling in his arms. She could smell the faint, crisp scent of his lemon cologne, taste the sweetness of wine as his lips parted and moved over her own, lightly one moment, deepening again the next, but always in inexorable control. The merciless hands holding her hard against him did not relent for a moment.

Sarah gave up the struggle. She had no strength left to resist him, no will to do so. Despite the calculated nature of his embrace, to be kissed by him was such exquisite pleasure that she never wanted it to end. Her fingers uncurled against his chest and she slid her arms up about his neck. One of Guy's hands slipped down her back and over her hip, drawing her against the hardness of his body. He slid his other hand under the hair at the nape of her neck, his caress on the tender skin there causing Sarah to shiver. She made a small, inarticulate sound of surrender, pressing closer, completely abandoned to the kiss.

Something had changed, although Sarah was too adrift to realise what it was. Guy's cruel grip had eased and the touch of his lips, his hands, became gentle, exploring mutual pleasure rather than administering punishment. The aquamarine dress was slipping off Sarah's shoulders and the lace fichu tumbled to the floor. She felt the featherlight touch of Guy's fingers graze her collarbone before his lips left hers to trace a downward path from the line of her throat over the exposed curve of her breast. His breathing was as ragged as her own now. Sarah arched against him, weak with desire, stunned by her reaction to him.

His mouth returned to hers roughly, plundering its softness. He held her face still with one hand, upturned and open to his, his fingers tangled in her hair. His other hand gently brushed aside the silk of the dress and bared Sarah's heated skin to his touch. The deep, sweet invasion of her mouth went on and on. The pins tumbled from Sarah's hair and fell with a soft tinkle on to the marble floor of the hall below. She did not notice; did not notice as her hair fell from its carefully arranged curls to swirl about her bare shoulders, did not notice as her bodice slipped to her waist, leaving her half-naked in Guy's arms, did not notice as a door below opened abruptly and people spilled out into the hall.

'Oh!' There was a squeal from one of the women. 'I almost stepped on a pin!'

Sarah heard the voices, but could make no sense of them through the desire that clouded her mind. It seemed, however, that Guy retained just enough presence of mind to drag her back from the balcony and into the shadows before the assembled company turned as one to gaze up into the darkness of the upper hall.

'I say! Whatever is going on? Is there anybody up there?'

There was a giggle from one of the women, a guffaw, hastily repressed, from one of the men, and some murmured words and laughter before they all drifted off into the cardroom. Then there was silence.

Reality hit Sarah like a tidal wave. How could she be standing here in the candlelight, her clothing all awry, having allowed this man the most appalling liberties imaginable? Only seconds before he had questioned her virtue, and now she had comprehensively proved his point! She was trembling, her whole body shaking not with passion but with the enormity of what she had done. Where would it have ended? With her naked on the landing in full view of Amelia's guests? Her cheeks burned as she realised that she had been so lost in desire that she had not even thought of whom might see her. How could this have happened? She had always found Guy Renshaw attractive, but their verbal sparring had given her no clue to the shocking physical awareness that would flare between them. Why, when she had made to leave him on the landing she had not even liked him any more! And yet...

Sarah pulled her dress up over her shoulders and bent to pick up the discarded scrap of white lace. The point of a fichu, she remembered her mama telling her years before, was to preserve a lady's modesty. Well, she had no need of that! Her own behaviour had proved as much! And worse, memory stirred to remind her just how much she had enjoyed it, how she had ached for Guy's kisses, the touch of his hands on her body... How was it possible to dislike someone and want them at the same time? The thought made her despair.

More distressing still was the look of stony contempt on Guy's face. Whatever emotions had shaken her, they had evidently left him singularly unmoved. He still had hold of her wrist, but Sarah wrenched it from his grasp and walked past him to the door of her bedroom, her head held high and the effect ruined by the knowledge that his gaze had taken in the decadent effect of her plunging neckline. Her heart sank as Guy followed her into the room. All she wanted to do now was recover from her humiliation in private.

'You will oblige me by leaving me alone now, sir.' Sarah knew she had not achieved the icy tone she sought and could hardly bear to raise her eyes to his.

'A moment.' Guy's searing gaze swept over the dishevelled curls about Sarah's shoulders and lingered on the shadowy cleft between her breasts. 'You're good, I'll say that for you! Just enough untutored innocence mixed with passion!' He gave a cynical laugh. 'Good enough to leave me in some doubt! Anyway, I came to make you an offer—one that you may look kindly upon after your performance just now. I wish to spare you the trouble of looking for a protector at Blanchland. I am rich enough for any taste and I'm sure I can satisfy you! What do you say?'

The colour drained from Sarah's face. This was the final insult. She had refuted his accusations only to fall into his arms and apparently prove herself experienced. Was *carte blanche* the logical outcome? She supposed that might be so. Could she blame him for thinking of her as he did? Perhaps not, and yet she had hoped he would know her better than that. She had cherished secret dreams that had been far removed from this tawdry reality. She could scarcely believe that everything good and pure and sweet between them had been ground into the dust.

'Get out of my room!' It felt to Sarah that she must have shouted, but her words came out as a whisper. Guy's expression was blank for a moment, then he turned on his heel and the slam of the door echoed through the entire house.

'Sarah?' Amelia's tap on the door was almost silent and her cousin barely heard her whisper. 'Sarah, are you there?'

As Sarah struggled to sit up, Amelia turned the knob and stepped into the darkened bedroom. The lamp was turned down low, but there was enough light to see Sarah's stricken face and Amelia hurried forward in obvious alarm.

'Sarah! Whatever has happened?'

Sarah raised a face so blotchy and tear-stained that it was almost unrecognisable. A few minutes before she would have sworn she had no more tears left, but now she burst into tears all over again.

'Oh, Milly!'

Amelia sensibly did not press for an explanation, but gathered her cousin into her arms without a word. Eventually Sarah's sobs subsided a little again and she looked up.

'Has he gone?'

'He? Who?'

'Lord...Lord Renshaw...'

Several things became clear to Amelia at the same time. 'Yes, he left about an hour ago. I did not see him, but Grev said that he had gone. Was he with you before that, Sarah?'

A nod of the head was her only reply. Amelia's thoughtful gaze took in her cousin's tumbled hair and the blue dress that was lacking a piece of material it had certainly started off with. She raised her eyebrows. 'Here? He was with you here?'

Sarah nodded again.

Amelia glanced from her cousin to the bed. Try as she might, she could not keep the horror out of her voice. 'Oh, Sarah, surely he did not make love to you—?'

Sarah made a noise that was halfway between a sob and a laugh. 'No, it is not as bad as that!' She pushed the damp hair back from her face. 'Not quite, but nearly...' Slowly the story of the encounter came out, with Amelia sitting quite still and quiet as she listened.

'I felt so dreadful,' Sarah ended bitterly. 'I had told him that he had misjudged me, and then I behaved like the veriest trollop! Is it any wonder that he treated me like one? When he said—' She broke off on a sob, swallowed and started again, 'He made it all sound so sordid, Amelia, and that is exactly how it was!'

'You must not blame yourself,' Amelia said carefully, after a moment. 'I knew that you were more than a little in love with him, whatever you said before! Lord Renshaw had no right to speak to you as he did and, despite his reputation, I had not really thought that he would—' She broke off. 'Truly, the man is unforgivable!' She passed her cousin another handkerchief and patted her hand encouragingly.

Sarah blew her nose hard. 'Oh, dear, this is a terrible! To offer me *carte blanche*—'

'A poor reflection on Lord Renshaw rather than on yourself, my love!' Amelia said stringently. 'Pray put him from your mind. I doubt we shall see him again!'

Sarah thought that this was probably true. The idea gave her so much pain that she had to bite her lip to prevent herself from crying again. Yet if it was distressing to think of never seeing Guy again, it upset Sarah even more to think of the opinion of her that he would carry away.

'Will you still go to Blanchland, Sarah?' Amelia was asking carefully. 'Unfortunately, it is true that everyone is talking about it. I swear I told no one, but I wonder if the servants overheard—'

'Probably,' Sarah said tiredly. She got up and moved to turn up the lamp. 'Let people talk! I still intend to go tomorrow!'

'Sarah!' Amelia seemed uncertain whether to be glad or sorry that her cousin's familiar determination was reappearing. 'You cannot! Oh, surely you must see that it is impossible now! If you stay here and we put it about that it was all nothing but malicious gossip, the outcry will soon die down—'

'You mistake, Amelia.' Sarah was already pulling a couple of canvas bags from the cupboards, her actions showing a feverish energy. 'I intend to go, now more than ever! I will not have the likes of Guy Renshaw standing in judgement on me!'

Sarah rose early after a night with almost no sleep at all. Amelia had left her with a kiss after spending a fruitless half hour trying to persuade her cousin to change her mind. The more Sarah thought about it, the more her conviction grew. The misery she had felt at Guy Renshaw's stark contempt was hardening into anger now, humiliation turning into a burning fury. She was angry with herself for falling into his arms and confirming his opinion of her, but she was even more angry that he should ever have doubted her virtue. In the dark shadows of the night she had painfully admitted to herself just how much she had liked him. So much had been built upon so little: the roses, a couple of conversations, one waltz. And now she would have to learn to forget him.

With a heavy heart, Sarah dragged her bags to the bedroom door. If she was lucky, she could avoid Amelia, who always got up late on the morning after a ball. She could not bear another scene. She would take a hack down to the Angel and get the coach to the Old Down Inn and from there…

Sarah went out onto the landing, intending to tiptoe downstairs and find herself some breakfast before she left. She averted her gaze from the spot at the top of the stairs where she and Guy had had their encounter the previous night.

Far from being quiet, the house seemed very noisy. The shutters were flung back and servants were scurrying about in a frenzy. As she descended the stairs Sarah could see two large trunks, neatly bound with red rope, standing by the front door. Chisholm, looking as harassed as Sarah had ever seen him, was taking down what seemed like an endless list of instructions from his employer. Sarah stared in disbelief.

'…and cancel my attendance at Mrs Chartley's breakfast, if you please, and the card party at Colonel Waring's and any other invitations I have forgotten!'

'Yes, my lady.'

'And make sure that any invitations from Mrs Bunton and Mrs Clarke are returned unopened—'

'Yes, my lady.'

Amelia, looking fresh and radiant in a coffee-brown travelling dress and matching hat, turned to see her cousin watching her in amazement from the top of the stairs.

'There you are, Sarah! At last! Hurry and take some breakfast! Oh, and Chisholm—' her voice hardened '—if Sir Greville Baynham calls, pray tell him that I have left town and that his friends are not welcome in my house again—'

'Oh, Milly, you cannot do that! It is not Greville's fault!' Sarah recovered the use of her voice and hurried down to her cousin's side.

'No matter!' Amelia's chin was set defiantly. 'Sir Greville is to blame for having such poor taste in his friends! Now, are you almost ready, my love?'

Sarah watched bemusedly as two footmen threw open the main door and staggered out to the carriage under the huge weight of Amelia's baggages.

'Yes, but…what…?'

'I knew that I could not persuade you to change your mind,' Amelia said, seizing her arm and steering her towards the breakfast parlour, 'so I have changed mine! Dearest Sarah! I am coming with you!'

Chapter Four

'Seems to me you've made a dashed mess of things, Guy,' Greville Baynham said frankly, helping himself to a large plate of devilled kidneys. 'Didn't even give the poor girl a chance to explain!'

Guy stared gloomily out of the breakfast-room window. He had spent the best part of the night playing high and drinking deep, and this morning was left with a vicious headache and a feeling of sick disgust. At the back of his mind was the thought that Greville was very probably correct.

In his salad days he had tumbled into love several times with females who were either unsuitable or ineligible or both. It had not mattered then; his suffering was usually of short duration and there were plenty of ladies willing to help him recover and move on to the next conquest. As he had grown older he had seen that love rarely had much to do with these transactions and was quite content for this to be the case. The fact that his father wished him to settle down and provide an heir for Woodallan he viewed as a completely separate issue. Or, he *had* viewed it as such until he had met Miss Sarah Sheridan.

Guy shifted in his chair. He had told Greville about the rumours that were circulating about Sarah and a little of the scene between them, though, naturally enough, he had not imparted the whole tale. Greville had been frankly incredulous.

'Sounds all a hum to me,' he said judiciously. 'The Bath tabbies usually prefer fiction to fact! They find it so much more scandalous. Ten to one the whole thing is nothing more than a Banbury tale!'

Guy pulled a face. 'I would like to agree with you, Grev, but Miss Sheridan practically confirmed it! When I asked her if it was true she was visiting Blanchland, she did not give a convincing denial! What was I to think?'

Greville waved his fork about descriptively. 'That she was visiting her old nurse? That Ralph Covell wanted to hand over some of her father's paintings? I don't know—anything except what you clearly *did* think, old chap!'

Guy did not deny it. Now he said, 'I suppose…I may have been a little hasty—'

'Seems to me you should think about why you reacted as you did,' Greville said drily, demonstrating his disconcerting habit of hitting the nail on the head. 'I believe you must owe Miss Sheridan an apology, Guy. Do you care to accompany me to Brock Street this morning? I was intending to call on Lady Amelia anyway.'

Guy hesitated. He sincerely doubted that Sarah would either offer an explanation or give him the chance to apologise. It seemed most likely, in fact, that she would never speak to him again. He thought again of the previous night, of how Sarah's initial resistance to him had melted into response and how he had taken ruthless advantage of it. Much as he would have preferred to deny it, her willingness had raised an echo of genuine passion in him that had transcended the blind fury that had first prompted him to punish her. He had been as shaken as she was—or as she had appeared to be.

Guy paused. Supposing—just supposing—Sarah had been the innocent he had always thought her to be? How must she have felt to have her inexperienced reactions construed as calculated passion? How would she be feeling that morning, confronted with the discovery of her own desires and the memory of his contempt? There were no excuses. He had taken disgraceful advantage of her.

Guy gave a groan and buried his head in his hands. Looking at matters in the cold light of day, he was both stunned and disconcerted by his violent reaction to the gossip he had heard. As Greville had said, he needed to analyse why he had responded so furiously and the answer was not far to seek. Although he had not previously acknowledged it, his feelings for Sarah Sheridan ran very deep indeed. The knowledge was a shock on one level, but on another he was obliged to admit that he had known it from the first. The fact that he had known her such a short time was irrelevant to his feelings. And now he had made the most godforsaken mess of the whole business… He groaned again.

Greville was eyeing him with concern. 'I'll ring for an ice bag,' he said, getting up. 'And, Guy, have a shave before you go out. It won't help your cause to arrive in Brock Street looking half cut!'

The house in Brock Street was shuttered and it seemed to take an inordinate amount of time before Chisholm answered the bell. Nor was his demeanour particularly encouraging when he did so, for there was a look in his eye that seemed to imply that they should be using the tradesmen's entrance.

'Good day, Lord Renshaw. Good day, Sir Greville. May I be of service?'

Guy and Greville waited to be allowed over the threshold, but Chisholm remained obdurately in the way. Greville raised his eyebrows.

'Good day, Chisholm. Is Lady Amelia receiving visitors? Pray tell her that we have called!'

Chisholm folded his lips into a thin line. His stance seemed to suggest that such good humour was sorely misplaced.

'I regret to inform you, sir, that Lady Amelia has left town.'

There was a pause. Guy stepped forward. 'And Miss Sheridan? Is she at home?'

Chisholm's gaze seemed to turn even more glacial. 'I fear not, my lord. However, her ladyship asked me to give Sir Greville the following message.' He cleared his throat and avoided looking directly at either of them. 'Her ladyship wishes it to be known that she has gone to the country with her cousin. Further, whilst you are still welcome to visit here, Sir Greville, the same invitation does not extend to your friends. Good day, sir.'

Chisholm bowed neatly, stepped back and closed the door firmly.

Both Guy and Greville stared at the wooden panels in stupefaction, then Greville took a hasty step forward and reached for the bell again. Guy laid a hand on his arm.

'Grev! Wait!'

Guy did not think he had ever seen his friend so angry. Greville's grey eyes were burning with fury.

'How dare he say such things! The confounded impertinence of the man! Why, I'll—'

'He is only doing as he was instructed,' Guy pointed out quietly. 'Come away, Grev. There are people watching.'

It was true. Several curious passers-by, including the ubiquitous Mrs Clarke, were occupying the pavement at the bottom of the steps.

'Oh, Sir Greville!' that lady trilled, stepping forward to block their way. 'Lord Renshaw! Have you heard the news? Lady Amelia has gone to Blanchland with her cousin! I can scarce believe it, but it must be true for Mrs Bunton heard it from Lady Trippeny, who—'

Greville set his shoulders. He gave the gossip a look of comprehensive dislike. 'It is perfectly true, Mrs Clarke, but of no great import! Miss Sheridan has been called to Blanchland on an urgent family matter and her cousin has gone with her as chaperon! That is all! And I do beg you to remember that, before you indulge in idle speculation about the lady who is shortly to become my wife! Why, I shall be joining her at Blanchland shortly myself!'

Mrs Clarke's mouth rounded in astonishment. 'Oh, Sir Greville! And, Lord Renshaw—' she swung round on Guy accusingly '—were you aware of this?'

Guy tried not to laugh. 'Which part, Mrs Clarke? The bit about Lady Amelia chaperoning her cousin to Blanchland, or the part about Sir Greville being betrothed to Lady Amelia and joining her at Blanchland tomorrow? Or even…' his smile broadened '…the fact that I am shortly to announce my own engagement to Miss Sheridan? Yes, I am aware of all of it!'

Mrs Clarke backed away from them, almost tripping over the kerb in her haste to escape and acquaint Mrs

Bunton with her news. The two men nodded amiably to the rest of the crowd and strolled off down Brock Street with every appearance of nonchalance.

'I cannot believe we just did that,' Guy said under his breath, as they turned into The Circus and paused for a moment. 'The story will be all over Bath in less than a half hour! Did you mean what you said?'

'Of course!' Greville looked grim. 'You know I've been meaning to marry Amelia this past age! This ridiculous jaunt to Blanchland has simply precipitated matters!'

'Hope she sees it in the same light as you, old fellow,' Guy said feelingly. 'Do you mean to go there to offer her your protection?'

'Well, I hadn't thought of it until five minutes ago,' Greville admitted, 'but now I see I need to talk some sense into the foolish woman!'

Guy repressed a grin. 'Well, in that case you'd better travel with me! I'm for Woodallan, and you can break your journey there before travelling to Blanchland on the morrow.'

'Thank you!' Greville seemed to be recovering his good humour. The tense lines on his face eased a little. 'And what of your own plans, Guy? Thought you were touched in the attic when you said that about marrying Miss Sheridan!'

Guy shifted a little. 'Couldn't leave Miss Sheridan as the only one with a stain on her reputation, could I, Grev? That odious woman would rip her to shreds!'

'But will you keep your word?' Greville pressed. 'If not, Miss Sheridan will be thrown to the wolves anyway!'

'I suppose I'm honour bound to try to persuade her…' Guy gave his friend a lopsided grin. 'You may count this as your fault, for telling me to examine my feelings! Truth is, I'd offer for Sarah like a shot if I thought she'd have me, but I doubt she'll even consider it. Too much to forgive, I suppose! Devil take it, how have I managed to make such a confounded mess of things in such a short space of time?'

Greville laughed. 'Cupid's arrow, old chap! Strikes when and where, at will! And it seems to me that, of the two of us, you have the harder task!'

'Amelia, you know this will not serve! Instead of saving my reputation, you are only ruining your own! Why, both of us will be tarred with the same brush!'

Sarah and her cousin had been arguing all the way from Brock Street to Combe Hay. The beauty of the winter countryside had been ignored and the discomfort of the twisting road scarcely noticed as Sarah desperately tried to persuade Amelia to change her mind. The irony of the situation was not lost on her. Amelia had spent considerable time and effort in trying to persuade her to abandon the trip to Blanchland, yet here she was sitting in Amelia's carriage with Amelia's servants in attendance and Amelia herself beside her. And her cousin was adamant.

'I am a respectable widow whose good reputation can only help to protect you, dearest Sarah. Since it seems you are determined to go through with this mad plan, I feel it my duty to accompany you and save you from yourself!'

'You are very noble,' Sarah said, uncertain whether to laugh or cry, 'but pray do not make this sacrifice on my account! You have told me yourself that Blanchland is the most licentious house in the kingdom—you must know that even *your* good name will not be able to withstand the scandal! Oh, Amelia, pray do not go through with this!'

Amelia turned her dark gaze on her cousin. 'You have not told me why this visit is so important to you, Sarah, but I have to believe that it is of great consequence. If it matters so much to you that you are prepared to risk your reputation on it, I am prepared to do the same to help you. There! We shall have no more arguments!' She turned her shoulder and looked out of the window.

Sarah gave a sigh of exasperation. She could not deny that it was pleasant to have company on the journey and it was infinitely more comfortable to travel privately than on the public stage. But those were small benefits in comparison to the damage that this escapade would cause. No doubt the whole of Bath society would already have heard what had happened, and how could either of them ever show their faces there again? It was melancholy to think of Amelia being ostracised for an act of misplaced kindness.

Sarah looked at Amelia's determined profile. She felt a strong sense of guilt that she had not confided her quest in her cousin, but something made her hesitate. Time enough for that when Miss Meredith had been found and the mystery solved. At least arguing with Amelia had distracted her from melancholy thoughts about Guy.

They stopped for luncheon and to change the horses at the inn at Clandown, and Amelia confidently predicted that they would reach Blanchland by late afternoon, for the roads were good for the time of year. Sarah started to feel very nervous. How would she find her home after all these years? And how would Ralph react to their unexpected arrival? She barely knew her father's cousin; though she bore him no ill will for inheriting her home after Frank's death, she could hardly bear to think what he had done to it.

The journey progressed uneventfully until they neared the Old Down crossroads, where a sudden downpour took them by surprise and set the road awash. Within moments the horses had lost their footing and the carriage lurched off the road and into the ditch.

'No harm done, ma'am,' the coachman reported cheerfully as he helped Amelia and Sarah down on to the road, 'but it might be better if you took shelter in the inn whilst we haul it out. A nice dish of tea should help you over the shock!'

The Old Down Inn was accustomed to passing trade and soon put a private parlour at the disposal of its unexpected guests. Amelia regarded her dripping figure with deep displeasure, whilst outside the rain splattered against the window and emphasised the sudden decline in the good weather.

'Oh, I look hideous,' Amelia declared, wringing water from her cloak into a bucket helpfully provided by the landlady. 'This bonnet is quite ruined, and I have only worn it twice! A fine pair of figures we will cut, arriving at Blanchland in such a state!'

She glanced critically over Sarah, whose hair was drying in corkscrew curls about her face. 'Humph! Well, at least you look the part, Sarah, with your wild hair and soaking dress! Oh, this is too bad!'

'Thank you,' Sarah said drily. 'It is comforting to know that I already look like a demi-rep and I have not even set foot in the house yet! Do you care for tea and cakes, Milly? It might improve your temper!'

Amelia looked rueful. 'I'm sorry, Sarah, I know I am like a bear with a sore head! Truth to tell, I was feeling nervous before, but now I just feel downright unpresentable! Oh, to arrive in so undignified a state when we do not even know what we will find…' She took a cup of tea and moved over to the window. 'I had better not sit down or I shall cause a puddle! I wonder when this storm will cease—' She broke off with an exclamation and Sarah looked up from the fire, which she had been trying to coax into reluctant life with the poker.

'Whatever is the matter, Milly? You look as though you have seen a ghost!'

'It is Greville!' Amelia whispered, looking as though she was about to rush from the room. 'Greville and Lord Renshaw! Sarah, they are here!'

Sarah felt her heart leap into her throat. 'Oh, no, it cannot be! You must be mistaken, Milly!'

'I tell you, they were right outside the window—'

Amelia broke off at the sound of voices in the passageway outside. The parlour door opened.

'Good afternoon!' Greville Baynham said affably, as though he were meeting them in Milsom Street. 'An inclement day! I am glad to see that you appear to have suffered no injury when your coach left the road!'

Neither Sarah nor her cousin were up to answering him in kind. Sarah met Guy Renshaw's quizzical gaze, blushed crimson and looked hastily away. As he came towards her, she backed away from the fire, still holding the poker, and took refuge behind the parlour table. Amelia, obviously viewing attack as the best form of defence, burst into speech.

'You!' she said, in tones of ringing outrage. 'Whatever are you doing here, Sir Greville?'

'Came to find you,' Greville said imperturbably. He crossed to the fire and kicked it into a blaze, warming his hands. 'Heard you'd gone off on some mad start and thought that you might need some help—'

Amelia drew herself up to her full—tiny—height. 'Well, we do not, sir! Not from you, at any rate! We can manage perfectly well on our own!'

'I doubt that,' Greville said coolly. 'You have only been on the road for a few hours and already you are in a scrape! And as for your destination—well, that proves you have not the least notion of how to carry on! Good God, two gently bred ladies visiting a house of ill fame! Fit for Bedlam, both of you!'

Amelia's stormy gaze swept from Greville to Guy Renshaw and rested there for a moment. 'Do not preach to me, sir, when you keep such poor company!'

Sarah winced. Amelia seldom lost her temper properly, but when she did so the results could be spectacular. This promised to be one of those occasions. She caught Guy Renshaw's eye and saw that he was looking rather amused. A slow smile was curling the corners of his mouth and Sarah felt an answering gleam and stifled it at once. The last thing she wanted at that moment was to experience any kind of kindred feeling for Guy. He had humiliated her and insulted her, she reminded herself severely, and his charm was of the most superficial kind.

'It ill becomes you to speak of bad company when you are planning so rash an escapade, madam!' Greville said to Amelia, more coldly than Sarah had ever heard him. 'Do you forget that this will ruin your reputation forever? And yet you disparage those who seek to offer you their aid—'

'Offer their aid!' Two spots of colour were burning on Amelia's cheeks now. 'Forgive me, sir, but it seems to me that you came to censure rather than to support!

My cousin and I can do very well without such dubious assistance!'

'You may claim so, but you have as much idea of how to go on as a pair of schoolgirls! Less! At least a schoolroom miss knows her manners!'

Sarah caught her breath sharply as Amelia made a noise like an enraged kitten. The combatants faced each other fiercely across the table, Amelia with her fists clenched and Greville with a singularly unyielding look on his face.

Sarah could feel Guy watching her across the room and she found herself looking around for a means of escape. Guy was between her and the door, the window was too small and she could scarcely scramble up the chimney. A strange panic took hold of her as he came towards her.

As Amelia drew breath for another salvo, Guy reached Sarah's side and took her arm.

'I believe that we may safely leave these two to settle their differences, Miss Sheridan. May I beg a word in private?'

'Certainly not!' Amelia snapped, before Sarah could speak. She flashed Guy a look of contempt. 'Stand aside from my cousin, Lord Renshaw! You have done her enough harm!'

Guy looked from Amelia to Greville. 'My dear Lady Amelia, pray confine your quarrel to Sir Greville and leave Miss Sheridan to deal with me!' He removed the poker from Sarah's hand. 'I should feel safer if you were without this!'

Sarah had forgotten that she had been stirring the fire when they had arrived. She relinquished her weapon and edged away from Guy towards the door.

'A moment, Miss Sheridan.' Guy had turned back to

her with exquisite courtesy. 'Pray do not leave just yet! It is still raining and your carriage is not fit for use! Will you grant my request of a private interview?'

Sarah shook her head. 'My cousin is in the right of it, sir. I do not care to have my business discussed in a wayside inn!'

Guy inclined his head. 'Then come back with us to Woodallan and discuss it there!'

'Impossible!' Amelia retorted, her colour still high. 'We must reach Blanchland before nightfall—'

'Must you?' Guy strolled into the middle of the room and turned back to smile at Sarah. 'Had you thought what might happen if you arrive at dinner time?' he asked conversationally, looking from her to Amelia. 'Why, Sir Ralph may well be indulging in one of his famous orgies and you would walk right into the middle of it! Time enough for that once you have been there a little while! But if you leave it to the morning, you will find them all still abed. Not ideal, of course, but less…active, perhaps, than the night before!'

'Outrageous!' Amelia declared.

'But true,' Greville said coolly.

'I fear Lord Renshaw may be right, Milly,' Sarah said after a moment. 'Perhaps we should bespeak rooms here for the night—'

'Out of the question,' Guy said briskly. 'You could not so offend my parents' hospitality, Miss Sheridan, as to take rooms within two miles of their house!'

Sarah flushed. 'If you were not to tell them we were here—'

'Alas, I would find it quite impossible to keep the truth from them! Their own goddaughter preferring the dubious comforts of an alehouse to Woodallan! I am sure my mother would be quite distraught!'

Sarah reached for her cloak. Somehow they had been outmanoeuvred. 'Very well, my lord. Since I do not trust you to spare your mother's feelings, we will come with you. However—' she glared at him '—do not think to dissuade us from our errand, nor to enlist the support of your parents in such an enterprise!'

Guy's dark gaze mocked her. 'Miss Sheridan! I could not possibly tell my parents that you intended to visit Blanchland! The shock might kill them!'

He held the door open for her. 'You look very pretty, Miss Sheridan,' he added, in tones low enough that only Sarah could hear. 'To see you with your hair like that gives me ideas—'

'I thank you,' Sarah snapped. 'I heard enough of your ideas last night, sir! I wonder that you dare to speak to me of them again!'

Guy detained her with a hand on her arm. 'In point of fact, Miss Sheridan, that is what I wished to discuss with you. I wished to apologise, but I will save it until we have gained the privacy of Woodallan!'

Sarah's lips tightened angrily. 'It may be that I do not wish to hear any of your excuses, Lord Renshaw!'

'You will hear me out, however,' Guy said, with what seemed to Sarah to be breathtaking arrogance. He offered her his arm, and laughed when she swept past him, ignoring it. Behind her, Sarah could hear Greville and Amelia starting to bicker again as they all went out into the yard.

'You realise that you will have to marry me now!' Greville was saying, in an exasperated undertone, to which Amelia retorted,

'I would rather walk across hot coals, sir!'

They journeyed to Woodallan in bad-tempered silence.

* * *

Woodallan lay two miles from the turnpike road, in a hollow beside a stream, sheltered by the hills behind and with a glorious vista of rolling country before it. The rain had cleared as quickly as it had come, and the house's golden Bath stone gleamed in the late afternoon sunlight. Next to Blanchland, it had always been one of Sarah's favourite places, and now she felt a lump in her throat as the years rolled back. She remembered walking up the long lime avenue as a child, clutching her father's hand, remembered playing hide-and-seek in the topiary garden, remembered tickling trout in the stream during the hot summers...

The Blanchland and Woodallan estates had marched together and the families been friends since the first Baron Woodallan and Sir Edmund Sheridan had sailed the seas together as privateers under Queen Elizabeth. It had always been a family joke that Frank Sheridan had inherited his wanderlust from his ancestors.

The carriage drew up in front of the main door and Guy jumped down to help her descend.

'Welcome back,' he said, and for a moment it seemed that he had invested the words with a greater significance.

Sarah shrugged the thought aside. It was too dangerous for her to start to feel at home in her childhood haunts, for in a week's time—two at the most—she would have to return to Bath and the life she was accustomed to. Time spent at Blanchland and Woodallan could only be a passing phase, but when she had planned her journey she had not spared a thought for the way in which old memories would be stirred up. She looked at Guy, who was looking up at the house with a half-smile on his lips.

'It must be a great pleasure for you to be home again,

my lord, after so long abroad,' she said spontaneously, and he smiled down at her, and for a split second Sarah was happy.

'Oh, it is, Miss Sheridan, for here I have all the things I most care for.'

Again, Sarah tried not to read too much significance into his words. She turned aside and followed Amelia and Greville up the steps, reminding herself that she was vulnerable to him and must be always on her guard.

The Countess of Woodallan was in the hall to welcome her son home, and, as word of Guy's arrival spread, it seemed that the house was full of beaming servants all wishing to greet him. Sarah and the others hung back until the crush had lessened a little, when the Countess turned and caught sight of her.

'Sarah! Good gracious, what a wonderful surprise! Forgive me for not welcoming you sooner, my dear!' She enveloped Sarah in a warm hug. 'And Greville! Guy...' she swung round accusingly on her son '...you should have told us you were bringing a party!'

Guy, who had been conversing quietly with his father's steward, came forward. 'I'm sorry for giving you no warning, Mama, but it was a spur-of-the-minute decision. Miss Sheridan and her cousin are travelling on in the morning, but I persuaded them to break their journey here tonight.'

The Countess swallowed her disappointment well. 'I am sorry to hear you will be leaving so soon. But perhaps—' she smiled at Sarah '—you will consider visiting us again on your journey back? You could stay for Christmas! That would be most pleasant, for we have so much news to catch up on!'

Sarah smiled a little stiffly. In the warmth of her welcome she had almost forgotten the reason for her visit, and the fact that she would be travelling on to Blanchland almost immediately. The Countess, suddenly aware of an air of constraint about her guests, turned her warm smile on Amelia. Greville stepped forward to make the introductions.

'Lady Woodallan, may I present my fiancée, Lady Amelia Fenton. Lady Amelia is Miss Sheridan's cousin.'

'I am not!' Amelia said hotly, then catching the look of amazement on her hostess' face, stammered, 'That is, I am Sarah's cousin, but I am *not* Sir Greville's fiancée!'

There was an awkward silence.

'I am afraid that Lady Amelia has not quite become accustomed to the idea yet, ma'am,' Greville said easily, ignoring Amelia's fearsome glare. 'I must apologise for imposing on your hospitality like this, particularly when you must be wishing to have Guy to yourselves!'

'You are very welcome for as long as you wish to stay,' the Countess murmured, trying not to stare at Amelia as though she had a lunatic in the house. 'But you look as though you were caught in the storm, my dears! I will show you to your rooms so that you may change, and send word to Cook to increase the covers for dinner. Guy, your father should have returned by then. He has driven over to Home Farm to talk to Benton about the milk yield, but I expect him back at any time!'

'Before you carry Miss Sheridan away, Mama, I should like to speak with her in private,' Guy said firmly. 'There is a matter to be settled between us that cannot wait.'

Sarah blushed scarlet and the Countess frowned. 'But, Guy, Miss Sheridan will be tired from her journey, and is drenched by the rain besides! Surely it can wait a little—'

'Oh, yes, indeed, ma'am,' Sarah added hurriedly, 'there is no urgency!'

'I am desolate to contradict you, Miss Sheridan,' Guy said smoothly, 'but it is imperative that we speak now. I do not wish there to be any further misunderstandings!'

'It seems to me that we have two ardent suitors here and two reluctant ladies!' a voice said, from behind them, and Sarah swung round to see her godfather in the doorway.

The Earl of Woodallan was leaning heavily on his stout ash stick and looked a lot older than Sarah remembered, but the expressive dark eyes, so like his son's, were as sharp as ever. 'Lady Amelia…' he gave as courtly a bow as ever his son could achieve '…and Sarah, my dear! What a delightful surprise! And Sir Greville, too! Well, Guy—' he turned to his son, the sardonic gleam in his eye belied by a smile '—good to see you back again, boy!'

'Sir!' Guy hurried forward to shake his father's hand, and Sarah took advantage of the moment to step back, throwing her godmother a pleading glance.

'If we could be permitted to change our clothes, ma'am—'

'Of course, my love.' The Countess swept up her goddaughter and Amelia, and shepherded them towards the stairs. 'Come along with me! The gentlemen are quite preoccupied and will not notice—'

The Earl's voice stayed them as they reached the half-landing.

'Charlotte, be sure to deliver Miss Sheridan to the

blue drawing-room just as soon as she is ready! Guy will be waiting for her!'

'Like father, like son,' the Countess murmured under her breath. 'I fear that an autocratic nature is in the Woodallan blood!'

It was three-quarters of an hour later that Sarah descended the stairs again. She was clean and dry, dressed in a becoming russet gown belonging to the younger of Lady Woodallan's daughters and with her hair neatly braided into a bun on the top of her head.

'Too austere, Miss Sheridan,' was Guy's comment as he ushered her into the blue drawing-room. 'You are too soft and sweet to pretend to such severity!'

He, too, had changed into clean buckskins, polished boots and an olive green jacket that fitted his broad shoulders to perfection. Sarah, experiencing a traitorous rush of feeling on seeing him, immediately went on the attack.

'By what right do you criticise my appearance, sir? Kindly refrain from becoming too personal!'

Guy grinned, unabashed, and gestured her to a chair before the fire. 'That was precisely the matter I wished to discuss with you, Miss Sheridan—Sarah. May I call you Sarah?'

'I am surprised you trouble to ask, sir!' Sarah said hotly. 'No, you may not!'

'Very well then, Miss Sheridan, I will not provoke you!' Guy sat down opposite her. Sarah, who was feeling quite on edge, resented his assumption of ease. 'I am grateful to you for granting me a hearing. I feared you would not. My behaviour in Bath—' He stopped, and started again. 'After the things I said, I could not blame you if you choose to deny me the chance to apologise.'

'I have promised to hear you out, my lord,' Sarah said coldly. 'Beyond that, I promise nothing.'

Guy grimaced. 'You are not making this easy for me, Miss Sheridan! I wished to apologise to you, both for my actions and my words last night—'

Sarah got to her feet, her face suffused with colour. Her instinct was to flee the room immediately out of sheer embarrassment. Despite herself, she could not prevent a scorching memory of the events of the previous night from invading her thoughts.

Anticipating her retreat, Guy moved swiftly to stand between her and the door.

'Please, Miss Sheridan—you promised me a hearing—'

'I have done so, sir,' Sarah said, as steadily as she could. 'You wished to apologise and I have heard you.'

'And?'

'And, sir?'

Guy gave a sigh of exasperation. 'And do you forgive me? I do not seek to justify myself in any way. What I did was inexcusable.'

Sarah paused. It did seem churlish to reject his apology when he seemed sincere, particularly as he had made no attempt to excuse his actions. She could feel a tiny corner of her heart unfreezing towards him and ruthlessly sought to conquer her weakness. It would never do to allow the spark of that earlier attraction to be rekindled into life. She had burned herself badly enough on that already.

'Very well, sir. I accept your apology.'

'That was not precisely what I asked.' Guy was frowning. 'I wished to know if you forgive me.'

'And the answer is no.' Sarah met his eyes very straight. 'I do not forgive you for speaking to me as you did, nor for believing me a...a woman of easy virtue. That I cannot pardon.'

Guy inclined his head. 'You are very frank and I accept what you say, Miss Sheridan. But there were mitigating factors—'

'Which you said you would not raise to justify yourself!'

Guy gave her a wry smile. 'That's true, but may we not sit down and talk a little more?'

Sarah looked at him for a moment, then reluctantly returned to her seat in front of the fire. Despite the uncomfortable situation, she had to admit that the atmosphere of Woodallan was very restful. The drawing-room, decorated in pale blue and gold, and with the small fire adding a heart of warmth, was most peaceful. The charm of Woodallan went beyond mere wealth or good taste—it was so tempting to relax into it, but Sarah knew she could not afford to do so. She did not belong here.

'You seem unaccountably determined to prolong my discomfiture, my lord,' she observed, knowing that the colour still burned in her cheeks. 'Generosity might prompt you to let the matter go now.'

'Forgive me, there is a reason that I shall come to shortly.' Guy sat forward, resting his chin on his hand. 'I am sorry for listening to groundless gossip and still more sorry for acting on it, as I have said, but I confess I am puzzled as to the truth, Miss Sheridan. What can have prompted you to decide to travel to Blanchland, when you knew that to do so would cause such speculation?'

Sarah hesitated. She was terribly tempted to tell him

the truth, but realised that this was only because she wanted him to think well of her again. Such a motive was hardly a good enough reason to give away the secret. If Guy could not trust her without proof, then she would not oblige him.

'It is a family matter,' she said evasively. 'I am fulfilling a request from my late brother.'

Guy frowned a little. 'Can you not be more specific, Miss Sheridan? I am trying to understand—'

Sarah shook her head. 'I appreciate your concern, my lord, but it is a private matter. I have told no one, not even Amelia.' She looked up and met his eyes. 'She does not know the reason for my quest, but she is prepared to trust my judgement and accompany me, even so.'

'Point taken, Miss Sheridan,' Guy murmured. He got to his feet again and strolled over to the window. 'But you must also take my point. Whilst your motives for travelling to Blanchland may be of the purest, the interpretation put on them will not be. It is inevitable that the world will make its own judgements. Miss Sheridan, if I could only prevail upon you to reconsider your visit? Could not your man of business undertake the commission to Blanchland? You could then stay here at Woodallan for a while and there would be no grounds for scandal…'

Sarah was tempted. The Blanchland visit had already caused so much trouble, and she had not even arrived. And to be able to stay at Woodallan would be blissful. She shook her head slowly. 'Do not press me, sir. There is much appeal in your suggestion, but I cannot. My brother has asked me to undertake this quest personally and I shall do as he wished.'

Guy looked at her for a moment, but she did not

retract her statement. He sighed. 'Then you must also take the consequences, Miss Sheridan. Greville may not have put it most delicately when he told Lady Amelia she would be ruined, but he is in the right of it. Without the protection of his name, she will be reviled. And the same must apply to you.'

Sarah frowned. 'I do not dispute the truth of your words, sir, but I am not surprised that Amelia quarrelled with Sir Greville over it! He was insufferably righteous, and to make an offer in such a manner is to beg a refusal! As for my own situation, I feel it is not as acute as Lady Amelia's. I have no position in society to support—as a poor relation I have no prospects to ruin!'

'You may choose to see yourself in that light, Miss Sheridan,' Guy said quietly, 'but others will think differently. I myself…' he hesitated '…I believe that you should consider… In short, it would give me the greatest pleasure if you would do me the honour of marrying me.'

Sarah stared at him in total disbelief. 'Are you mad, sir, or is this some ill-timed jest?'

Guy's lips tightened angrily, though he was clearly trying to keep control of his temper. 'Neither, madam! I saw it as a way out of your present difficulties—'

'Thank you!' Sarah was on her feet as well now, facing him across the room. 'Despite my lack of prospects, I had not viewed marriage as a solution to my problems!' She was astounded at the strength of her own anger. 'Yesterday you told me that my behaviour suggested that I was some sort of trollop and you treated me as such! Scarcely the conduct of a man prepared for matrimony! Then today you suggest I marry you to provide a way out of an unfortunate predicament! Forgive me, my lord, if I do not fall into your arms with tears of gratitude!'

Guy winced. 'I realise that this is not the way you might have wished it—'

'Very true! I do not wish to hear this at all!'

'Yet you should know that I have already given people to understand that we are shortly to become betrothed in order to protect your good name!'

Sarah looked at him in infuriated silence for a moment before bursting out, 'You take too much upon yourself, my lord! Upon my word, of all the high-handed, arrogant, ill-conceived ideas—'

Guy closed the distance between them in two strides. He seemed amused rather than angered by Sarah's outrage. 'I am aware of your opinion of me, Miss Sheridan, but I believe you are being less than honest. Confess that you like me a little!'

Sarah glared up at him. 'I shall not! Conceited, overbearing…'

She was incensed to see that Guy was actually grinning. He took her hands. 'Come, come, Miss Sheridan, we could be here for some time at this rate! Say you will consider my proposal, at the least!'

Sarah's treacherous heart did a little somersault. The warm touch of his fingers was distracting. 'Certainly not, my lord!'

'Then you force me to be less than chivalrous!' He was drawing her closer. Sarah resisted, feeling her heart start to race.

'It would be more surprising to find you behaving in a gentlemanly fashion, sir!' The words came out more huskily than she intended. His proximity was having a disastrous effect. Sarah was suddenly aware of the intimate heat of the room, the sweet scent of lilies by the fireplace, the sensitivity of her skin beneath his touch…

'Unfair, Miss Sheridan!' Guy murmured in her ear. 'Have I not just behaved in the most gallant manner possible? Alas that you force me to a point of clarification on our discussion earlier.' His lips brushed her hair, causing Sarah to shiver. She desperately tried to step back but found that her limbs would not obey her.

'Clarification, sir?' Her words came out as a whisper.

'Indeed. I wish you to know,' Guy continued, 'that when I apologised for my behaviour that night it was in relation to our argument and the unfounded accusations I made against you.' He looked directly into her eyes. 'I do not intend to apologise for…what came after.'

He was very close now. Sarah's gaze moved involuntarily to the hard line of his jaw, his mouth… She felt herself turn hot all over and wrenched her gaze away, fixing it sternly on a potted palm in a corner of the room.

'And yet I believe, my lord, that you were acting under a misapprehension…'

'In a sense…I'll allow I thought myself deceived and believed you…experienced. Yet my behaviour was very much in accordance with what I had wanted ever since I first saw you, Miss Sheridan…'

Sarah felt smothered by the heated atmosphere and her own emotions. Her heart was beating light and fast in her throat and she knew she had to put some distance between them, but she could not seem to break away from him. She could not be so weak as to fall under his spell again so soon, not when he had traduced her character and shown his lack of faith in her, then compounded his sins by a high-handed proposal that she could only refuse...

Guy let go of her hand, but only to draw her closer still, until their bodies were almost touching.

'Deny that you felt the same way, too, Miss Sheridan. Deny it if you dare!'

'I do deny it!' Sarah wrenched herself free of him and backed away. She was utterly confused by the emotions he could stir up in her. 'Tomorrow I shall leave here for Blanchland and you need not concern yourself with my affairs any further, my lord. It will no longer be any of your business!'

Guy's expression was inscrutable. He made no move to touch her again, but his voice held her still when she would have run away. 'You have made your feelings plain, Miss Sheridan. I must disappoint you, however. I have made this my business and I do not intend to disengage now. You may have as much time as you wish to get used to the idea, but the fact remains—you *will* marry me!'

Chapter Five

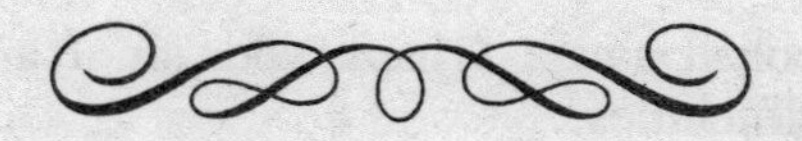

Dinner was a surprisingly good-humoured meal, considering that Sarah was avoiding Guy and Amelia and Greville were evidently not speaking to each other. The Earl and Countess took charge effortlessly, the former charming Amelia and the latter regaling Sarah with tales of her married daughters and their families. Guy and Greville fell to discussing horses, the food was excellent, and the meal passed without incident. It was only later, when the gentlemen rejoined the ladies, that the Earl took a seat beside Sarah and broached the delicate subject. They had chatted for a while about Sarah's life in Bath, reminisced about earlier times and talked about developments in the Woodallan estate, before Sarah had unwisely remarked that the Earl must be glad to have his son and heir restored to him. Lord Woodallan smiled.

'I must admit there were times when I thought I'd never see Guy again! I suppose he had to get rid of his restlessness before he was prepared to settle down. In my youth it was the Grand Tour and these days it is the War, but either way…' He twinkled at her. 'And now

I find that he is all set for parson's mousetrap, but the lady of his choice is not willing!'

Sarah blushed. 'Sir—'

The Earl patted her clasped hands. 'I know I am an interfering old man, but I only wished to say that nothing would make me happier than to see Jack Sheridan's daughter take her place in due course as mistress of Woodallan.'

Sarah looked away. 'Thank you, sir. I am sorry… there are difficulties…'

'I guessed as much,' the Earl said drily, 'but perhaps they will resolve themselves more easily than you might think, Sarah! Just do not keep my scapegrace son waiting too long, I beg you. He may seem a rogue, but he has many sound qualities—I should know, for he inherits them all from me!'

The Earl of Woodallan's study faced southwest, looking across the bowling-green and the formal parterre to the deer park and the Mendip Hills beyond. On this particular evening, the heavy brocade curtains were closed against the night and two lamps burned on the tables each side of the fire. Guy, who had just finished a game of billiards with Greville, found his father sitting in one of the armchairs, perusing a well-worn leather bound book. He invited his son to pour them both a drink.

'Brandy for you, sir?' Guy asked, crossing to the decanter and pouring a generous measure into the two cut glasses that stood there. He took one across to his father, noting the effort it seemed to cost the Earl simply to stretch out a hand for the glass. The Earl managed to conceal his weakness most of the time, but his son could see the changes that illness had wrought in him.

The Earl fixed Guy with his piercing dark gaze and said gruffly, 'I meant it when I said I was glad to see you back in one piece, boy. I must admit there were times in the last four years when I wished you'd had a brother!'

Guy laughed. He sat down opposite his father, stretching his legs out towards the grate. A fire burned there and its warmth was comforting.

'I am here now, sir, and don't intend to go travelling again!'

The fierce black gaze looked him over. 'You look well enough on it, I suppose,' the Earl said. 'A bad business, though. Must have had its nasty moments.'

'Yes, sir, although there were none when I thought I would not see my home again!'

'You were lucky,' the Earl said unemotionally. 'The quacks tell me I shouldn't touch this stuff,' he added, tilting the brandy glass to his lips with evident enjoyment, 'but it makes no odds now.'

'I expect it helps sometimes.'

The Earl gave him a sharp look. 'No fool, are you, boy? You know I'm dying. No...' he made a gesture as Guy shifted uncomfortably '...denials are for the women and the medical men. I know the truth. It's one of the reasons I wanted you back here.'

'Of course. You know that I will do anything in my power—'

The Earl put his glass down with a hand that was not quite steady. 'There is something I have to ask of you, Guy, a particular commission before you can come home for good and settle down. Set up your nursery, perhaps.' There was a glint of a smile. 'It pains me to send you away no sooner than you arrive, but I have no choice.'

Guy made a slight gesture, at a loss. 'Name your commission, sir. I will undertake it.'

'In a moment.' The Earl turned aside, picking a letter from the table at his elbow. 'Tell me, what is the nature of the quarrel between you and Miss Sarah Sheridan?'

Guy met his father's quizzical gaze. 'Forgive me, sir, but I do not wish to discuss it. It is…a personal matter.'

'I see,' the Earl said slowly. 'Can it be anything to do with her intention to return to her home at Blanchland? I take it that that is her destination tomorrow?'

Guy jumped. Some brandy spilled. From early childhood his father had had an uncanny knack of reading his mind and the young Guy had sometimes wondered whether the Earl had supernatural powers. Their eyes met. Guy had always found it impossible to lie to his father.

'Devil take it, sir, how can you possibly know that? I cannot believe that Miss Sheridan would have mentioned it—'

'She did not,' the Earl confirmed with a smile. 'In point of fact, she refused to tell me the difficulties that afflict your relationship. I take it that I am correct in thinking that you wish to marry the lady?'

Guy grinned reluctantly at his father's perspicacity. 'Yes, sir. You mentioned earlier that you wished to see me settle down… Well, almost as soon as I met Miss Sheridan I had such thoughts, for all that I had known her so short a while.' He shifted in his seat. 'They were thoughts quite alien to the lifestyle of a rake!'

'It happens to us all sooner or later,' his father said drily. 'But you quarrelled—over Blanchland?'

Guy shifted slightly again. 'More or less. I thought that her decision to go there reflected ill on her character and judgement. I said some terrible things to her, for which I am truly ashamed. When I had had chance to reconsider, I realised that I might have misjudged her, and apologised. But still she refuses to tell me the reason for her decision—'

'I believe that I may throw some light on that,' the Earl said, surprisingly. 'You had better read this letter now.'

Guy took the proffered sheets with a certain curiosity. He had no notion what to expect, but now he saw that it was in a gentleman's hand and read the signature as that of Francis Sheridan. He remembered Sarah telling him that her quest to Blanchland was in connection with her brother and frowned.

'But Frank Sheridan…'

'Yes, he has been dead these three years,' the Earl agreed readily. 'Unusual, is it not! There was a covering note from the lawyer…' He passed it over.

Julius Churchward's note was brief and to the point. A situation had arisen that had prompted him to send the enclosed letter to the Earl. He was confident that the letter from Lord Sheridan would be self-explanatory, but he felt that he should add that Miss Sarah Sheridan had also been given a letter from her late brother. He remained his lordship's humble servant, etcetera. Guy raised his eyebrows.

'As clear as day!'

The Earl laughed. 'Read the letter, Guy.'

Guy settled back in his chair and scanned the sheets with close interest.

Dear Sir

I am conscious that you will find it most odd in me to be communicating with you from beyond the grave, but I find I must. I am compelled to

> contact you to ask that you do me a service, not for my own sake—I know your feelings on that matter only too well!—but for the sake of my sister, and indeed to aid your own grandchild.

Guy looked up, his gaze suddenly startled, but the Earl's expression was hooded. 'Finish the letter, boy.'

> At the time of writing, Miss Meredith is fifteen years old and attending a seminary in Oxford. She is a pretty, behaved girl who has never caused either myself or her adoptive parents any concern. I have no reason to suppose that she will not progress from her school to make a suitable and entirely respectable marriage in the fullness of time. I only wish I had the means to ensure it. Unhappily I cannot. I am dying and I am aware that that will leave Miss Meredith and her parents without the security that my family has been able to provide, albeit at a distance, for all of her life.
>
> I could think of only one plan. I have instructed Dr Meredith and his wife that if ever their daughter is in great need, they should contact Julius Churchward. They are good people and I am persuaded would only resort to this if the need was genuine and severe. Once Churchward receives any communication from them, he is to contact Sarah and acquaint her with the problem.
>
> I have thought much about asking my sister to go to the aid of my natural daughter. It is most irregular. I should, of course, have made the request to you directly, sir, but the truth is that I did not dare. You made your feelings for me quite plain all those years ago and even now I know that

you cannot forgive me.

But now I am beseeching you, for the sake of the love you bear Sarah as her godfather, to stand her friend. Her innate goodness will prompt her to do what is right, but she may be in need of protection. And I commend Miss Meredith to you as an innocent child who does not deserve to suffer for her father's faults. Forgive me for my presumption. I can only add that if you see fit to answer my request I will be forever thanking you for your kindness.

Francis Sheridan.

Guy put down the pages of closely written words and reached for the brandy decanter again.

'I see,' he said slowly. 'Miss Sheridan goes to Blanchland at her brother's request to aid his natural daughter.' He met his father's sardonic gaze. 'What do you wish to tell me about the detail of this letter, sir?'

The Earl gave a rueful shrug. 'How do you read it?'

Guy's gaze narrowed. 'That you have a grandchild whom, for reasons of which I am unaware, you have chosen not to acknowledge. To say that I am astounded would be to understate the case. And if Frank Sheridan was her father, then who—?'

'You have—you had—three sisters, Guy.'

'Yes, but—' Guy was aware that he sounded incredulous '—you imply that *Catherine* had Frank Sheridan's child? But she was only sixteen when she died… She died of a fever—'

'Childbirth fever,' the Earl said heavily. Suddenly he looked old and tired. 'You had no idea, Guy?'

'Not the least in the world!' Guy put his glass down. His head was spinning. He had only been twelve when his elder sister had died and had never questioned that the family tragedy had hidden a catastrophe of even greater proportions. It seemed incredible.

'I can scarce believe it,' he said slowly. 'But surely…I mean…could they not have married? Sheridan was wild, but he was not an unsuitable match. Surely he would not have abandoned her!'

The Earl shook his head slowly. 'That is at the root of the whole tragedy, Guy. Catherine did not tell anyone until near the end and none of us even guessed. Looking back I cannot believe that we were so blind, but it was so. Oh, we knew that she had a *tendre* for him—Frank Sheridan could charm the birds from the trees—but we had no notion that it had gone any further! Why, she was only sixteen and the sweetest child—' He broke off. 'And by the time we found out, Sheridan had set off on one of his harebrained trips abroad. The babe was born and Catherine died whilst he was away.'

Guy stared into the glowing heart of the fire. 'What happened when Frank Sheridan returned?'

The Earl's face was in shadow. 'There was the most appalling scene, as you might imagine. He stood over there—' the Earl nodded towards the fireplace '—paper-white and shaking, and swore that he had not known, that he would have married her. But, of course, it was all too late. I called him a blackguard and a cad, and threatened to have him horsewhipped from the house. I never spoke to him again, to the day he died.'

'And the child?'

The Earl looked away. 'I am ashamed to say that I allowed Jack Sheridan to take her away and to make all the arrangements. I could not forgive her, innocent as she was, for robbing us of our daughter's life. I knew she was well provided for—Jack made sure of it, but to my shame I never wanted to know more.' He cleared his throat. 'I believe that your mother would have acted differently, had I permitted it, but I was bitter and sick with anger. Even now, when this arrived—' he tapped the letter '—I was in two minds about how to act. I was tempted to burn it and forget about it for another seventeen years!'

'What made you change your mind, sir?'

'Two things,' the Earl said bleakly. 'Firstly, your mother told me plain that it was my bounden duty to help my goddaughter. And then, of course, Sarah arrived here.' He met his son's eyes. 'When I realised that she was prepared to do what I was not, for the sake of her brother's child, I felt ashamed. And also...' a smile warmed his voice for the first time '...she is all the things that Frank Sheridan was not. She is good and true and brave, and I do not believe we should let her go to Blanchland alone!'

Guy got up to put another log on the fire. He stirred it to a blaze before he replied. 'How much of this story do you think Miss Sheridan knows, sir?'

'Very little, I imagine,' the Earl said. 'Jack Sheridan swore that neither he nor his son would ever burden Sarah with the tale, nor do I think they would bring shame on Catherine's name in such a way. And that is why—' he leaned forward, suddenly urgent '—you must find Miss Meredith before Sarah ever sets eyes on her!'

Guy frowned. 'I collect that you do not wish Sarah to be aware of my sister's part in this?'

'Absolutely not! No one must ever know! It must remain a secret!'

Guy shook his head slowly. 'I do not like the sound

of this, sir. You must be more plain. What is it that you wish me to do?'

The Earl brought his fist down hard. 'Find the girl! Buy her off! Persuade her to go away! The difficulties she finds herself in may well be pecuniary and she may be open to persuasion! Do whatever you have to, to keep the matter a secret!'

Guy looked at his father in bafflement. 'You set me a strange task, sir,' he said wryly. 'I have never seen you act in such a way before. Are you sure that this is what you truly want? And as for deceiving the woman I wish to marry before the knot is even tied—it does not augur well for my future happiness!'

'And yet I must ask it of you, Guy,' his father said, fixing him with his fierce, dark gaze. 'It must be done. Catherine's memory must not be despoiled.'

They talked long into the night but Guy was unable to persuade his father to change his mind.

It was impossible to travel on to Blanchland the following morning. The rain of the previous day had frozen in deep ruts overnight, making the roads impassable.

'Another day and the frost will be hard enough for you to travel,' the Countess said cheerfully as she came to Sarah's room to acquaint her with the news. 'Or else it will thaw again and you can be on your way! But for the meantime, Sarah dear, I am very happy for you to prolong your stay!'

Sarah herself had mixed feelings. Having got so close to her destination, the waiting was hard to bear. Then there was the prospect of another day in Guy's company when she would far rather put some distance between them. And then there was the fact, which she would admit only to herself, that although half of her wanted to run away from him, the other half found him all too attractive.

She was spared Guy's company in the morning, however, for the gentlemen had gone out for an early ride and were not expected back before luncheon. Lady Woodallan, recognising a kindred spirit in Amelia, bore her off to inspect the still room, so Sarah was left to her own devices. This did not trouble her. She spent a happy hour reacquainting herself with Lord Woodallan's extensive library collection, then turned her attention to the glass cases containing an assortment of semiprecious stones that he had collected on his travels abroad. Here was the brilliant deep blue of the lapis lazuli that had so fascinated her as a child, the pale green of the peridot and the deep amber of the tiger's eye, flecked with gold.

The walls of the library were furnished with family portraits and Sarah paused on her way out to consider the large family grouping over the fireplace. Here was a younger Earl and Countess of Woodallan, smiling proudly as their four children played about their feet. Guy looked stiff and self-conscious in his child's velvet suit and Sarah smiled a little. His younger sisters Emma and Clara, the latter barely more than a baby, sat on the floor at their feet, but the eldest girl stood shyly by her mother's chair. She must have been a couple of years older than Guy, Sarah thought, and she looked grave but with a smile breaking through. Sarah frowned, trying to remember her name. Catherine. She had died when Sarah was only seven and Sarah had no clear memory of her.

Sarah moved on to pictures of Lady Emma and Lady Clara as debutantes, both fair-haired, brown-eyed and heartbreakingly lovely. The Woodallan looks were very distinctive, Sarah thought. She remembered them both with fondness as having a great sense of fun and thought with regret that it would have been very pleasant to accept Lady Woodallan's invitation and return for Christmas, when both daughters and their respective families were expected.

That, of course, was not the only proposal that had been made to her. And there to remind her was a portrait of Guy in his early twenties. The artist had captured brilliantly the wicked twinkle in those brown eyes and the unconsciously arrogant tilt to his chin. He looked strikingly handsome and Sarah's heart contracted a little.

She went out into the hall, closing the library door quietly behind her. The sun had come out and Sarah decided that she would take a walk before luncheon. She picked up her cloak, donned her boots and went out into the morning air.

A quick tour of the gardens took her through the parterre and downhill towards the fields that bordered the trout stream. Sarah leant over and dabbled her fingers in the crystal clear water, finding it icy. There was no danger of lingering outdoors today, for an easterly wind made Lady Woodallan's predictions of a hard frost seem very likely.

'Good morning, Miss Sheridan.' Sarah turned to see Guy leaning on a five-bar gate a few yards away. He must have moved very quietly; she had not heard his approach. 'Did you fancy sledging down the hill as we did as children?'

Sarah laughed. 'I do not believe there is sufficient snow, my lord! The last time we tried that there were drifts five foot deep!'

'I remember!' Guy pushed the gate open and strode through to join her. 'I borrowed a tray from the kitchen and found it ran faster than the proper sledge!'

'And you finished head down in a drift and Clara screamed and screamed because she thought you were dead!'

They laughed together.

'Perhaps we might try again when you return to Woodallan for Christmas,' Guy said, as they turned back towards the house. 'There is bound to be further snowfall before then. Indeed, I believe we are in for quite a cold snap!'

'So your mother was saying.' Sarah pushed her hands into the fur muff and shivered a little. 'I would not wish you to forget, however, that I have made no commitment to return for Christmas!'

'Of course.' Guy's smile was rueful. 'I am sorry, Miss Sheridan! It was my own hopes that were speaking! I do most ardently wish that you will stay a little at Woodallan after your quest to Blanchland is completed.'

'I shall see,' Sarah said cautiously. 'Shall we walk back, sir? It is too cold to tarry here!'

'By all means.' Guy fell into step beside her as they turned back up the hill. 'What are your impressions of Woodallan after all these years, Miss Sheridan? Does it bring back happy memories for you?'

Sarah paused. They were skirting a huge oak that stood alone in the middle of the meadow. In the summers long ago she had scrambled up into its spreading branches and sat feeling the sway of the tree in the breeze. Clara and Emma had been too scared to climb so high and Lady Sheridan had scolded her daughter for being a tomboy.

'Sometimes it is a mistake to go back, my lord.'

Guy's hand was on her arm. 'But if the past could also be the future, Miss Sheridan...?'

Sarah felt terribly tempted. To regain so much, to return to a place that held such happy memories... But the one thing that she really wanted—Guy's love—was not part of the bargain. His charm and kindness to her were dangerous, drawing her in again, stirring up feelings she wanted to forget, making her vulnerable. Many, more practical than she, would settle for such an advantageous marriage of convenience. Perhaps, Sarah thought, she might have done so herself were her feelings not engaged. But the thought of Guy with another woman in his arms made her feel quite sick. If she bore his name, she could not bear to lose him.

Sarah turned away abruptly and walked on.

'There is something I need to tell you, Miss Sheridan,' Guy said, after a moment. 'It concerns your trip to Blanchland. Would you care to discuss it here, or wait until we are back in the house?'

'Perhaps it would be better to talk as we walk back, my lord.'

'To avoid another uncomfortable tête-à-tête?' Guy gave her an ironic smile. 'Have no fear, Miss Sheridan! Even I am not so lost to all sense of propriety as to try to seduce you in my parents' house! However, if you wish, we shall talk of it now. The cold air is death to strong passion, after all!'

Sarah blushed angrily. 'Did you have some material point to make, my lord?'

'Indeed!' Guy stretched lazily, then drove his hands into his coat pockets. Sarah hastily averted her eyes. Such blatant masculinity at such close quarters was decidedly unsettling.

'I have to tell you that I am to accompany you to Blanchland,' Guy continued. He smiled at Sarah's evident annoyance. 'I am sorry, Miss Sheridan, but my father wills it so and I am sure you would not wish to disappoint him!'

'I thought that you said you would not tell your parents of my destination,' Sarah said crossly. She regarded him with suspicion. 'There is something very strange about this, my lord! Do you care to explain?'

'Very well,' Guy said obligingly. 'I believe that you received a letter from your late brother asking you to offer your aid to a certain young lady. The request necessitated you travelling to Blanchland. My father received a similar letter asking that he offer you all support in your search. Unfortunately he is too ill to undertake the obligation, so he has asked me to do so in his place. So I will be journeying to Blanchland with you, Miss Sheridan!' He held the gate open for her to walk through into the gardens. 'I am sure you cannot be pleased—'

'No, indeed! It is most unfortunate!'

Guy's ironic smile deepened. 'Thank you, Miss Sheridan!'

'Oh!' Sarah caught herself. 'Indeed, I am very grateful to Lord Woodallan for offering me assistance, but truly there is no need—'

'You waste your breath if you seek to dissuade me, Miss Sheridan,' Guy said drily. 'My father is adamant and I must do as he wishes.'

They walked on a little in silence. The winter wind was chill with an edge of sleet to it now.

'If you were to consult your own inclination rather than your duty—' Sarah began.

'Then the answer would still be the same. I am at your disposal!'

Sarah gave an angry sigh. 'Frank should not have burdened Lord Woodallan with such a commission!'

'I agree with you,' Guy said readily. 'I also believe that your brother must have felt he had placed you in an invidious position, not to say an irregular one! He was appealing to Lord Woodallan as your godfather and the person who could offer you protection. Had he known that Blanchland had become a house of ill fame I am persuaded he would never have laid such a charge on you!' He shrugged. 'As it is, I am astonished you accepted the obligation!'

Sarah pulled the brim of her bonnet closer about her face to protect her from the sting of the wind. 'I know it must seem most singular,' she admitted, 'and, to own the truth, I did not wish to do so! But Frank has asked it and the girl is my niece whether I like it or not, so...' Her voice trailed away. She was not sure whether she was glad or otherwise of Guy's support in the matter. Had it been Lord Woodallan, as Frank had intended, she would have accepted his help unequivocally. But Guy was a different matter and now Frank's actions had made it impossible for her to keep him at a distance.

'How do you intend to present your case to Sir Ralph?' Guy asked, watching lazily as doubt and worry chased each other swiftly across Sarah's expressive face. They were approaching the door of the house now. 'Do you intend to reveal the whole to him?'

Sarah bit her lip. Guy seemed to have a talent for hitting on precisely the matters that concerned her. She still had not decided how to tackle that problem, uncertain whether to take Sir Ralph into her confidence or not. Sarah's heart sank as she realised how ill prepared she was for the whole venture. What thoughts she had had since leaving Bath had been all to do with Guy himself and nothing to do with Olivia Meredith at all!

'I have not really decided...' She knew she sounded vague. 'I confess I need more time to fashion a tale... Oh, dear,' she finished, despairing, 'was there ever such an ill-thought-out enterprise!'

Guy's lips twitched. 'My dear Miss Sheridan, can I not persuade you to change your mind, even at this eleventh hour? Despite my reluctance, I am willing to stand your friend and go to Blanchland on your behalf!'

For a moment, Sarah was tempted. To wash her hands of the whole matter was very appealing, but she had not persisted this far in order to turn back now.

'Thank you, sir. It is a generous offer, but I feel I must go myself.'

'You are very obstinate, Miss Sheridan!' Without warning, Guy stopped and took her hands in his. 'Obstinate, difficult, determined to cause a scandal—'

'I will thank you to be quiet, my lord!' Sarah was pink with indignation. She dropped the muff and could not free herself to pick it up again. 'Let me go! Someone will see us!'

Guy shrugged. 'Very probably! I cannot say that the thought disturbs me!'

'Oh!' Sarah tried disengage herself again. Guy refused to let go.

'You yourself,' Sarah said furiously, 'are arrogant and high-handed—'

'I believe you have already told me, Miss Sheridan!' Guy was smiling down at her with the wicked amusement that always made Sarah's pulse race.

'If you are to accompany me to Blanchland, I trust that you will behave with decorum, my lord!'

'I think that that is very unlikely. You had best be prepared for the worst!' Guy turned her hand over and pressed a kiss on the palm. 'Do not forget,' he said caressingly, 'that I still have to persuade you to accept my hand in marriage. I shall be doing my utmost to convince you!'

Sarah wrenched her hands away, knowing she was trembling violently. It was intolerable that he should have such an effect on her!

'Pray do not persist in this ridiculous jest, my lord! We both know you cannot mean it!'

'Never more serious, I assure you, Miss Sheridan! As I said yesterday, you will have time to become accustomed to the idea.' Guy was laughing at her. 'What you will not have is the chance to refuse me!'

Sarah drew breath for a scathing retort but broke off as the door swung open to reveal the butler, his expression as wooden as the door panels. 'Luncheon is served, my lord. Miss Sheridan,' he bowed politely, bending to retrieve the muff, 'allow me, madam—'

But he was talking to thin air. With a fulminating glance, Sarah had stalked off, leaving Guy still grinning as he watched her indignant figure walk out of sight.

After lunch the sleet turned to light snow that lay like icing across the parkland.

'Oh, how pretty!' Amelia exclaimed, as she stood by Sarah in the library and looked out across the hills. 'If it continues like this, I fear we may have to stay some time!'

Sarah looked exasperated. 'It is only five miles to Blanchland, Milly! If the worst comes to the worst, I shall walk there tomorrow!'

Amelia's face fell. 'Would you not prefer to stay at Woodallan, Sarah? It is so pleasant—'

'Of course I would rather stay here!' Sarah said crossly. 'How could I possibly favour Blanchland over this? The fact is that I have lost a week already since the letter arrived and—'

She broke off, remembering that Amelia was not party to the letter's contents. Amelia gave her a curious look.

'Is time a material factor then? I had not realised.'

'No, I am sorry.' Sarah looked shamefaced. 'I did not say…'

Amelia pressed her hand. 'Time enough for you to tell me all about it when you are ready.' She gave Sarah a penetrating look. 'I understand, however, that Lord Renshaw accompanies us?'

Sarah felt the telltale blush creep into her cheeks. 'So I am told. It was not at my instigation!'

Amelia raised her eyebrows. 'On his own inclination, then—'

'No!' Sarah realised she sounded too vehement and tried to calm down. 'That is, he tells me that Frank wrote to Lord Woodallan, asking him to help me in my quest. Unfortunately, the Earl is too ill to accompany us, so…' She shrugged.

'So Lord Renshaw comes instead!' Amelia frowned. 'Are you sure about this, Sarah? It sounds all a hum to me!'

Now it was Sarah's turn to frown. 'Whatever can you mean? Of course I am sure!'

'Only that it seems a little odd. I am not sure why, but…'

'Yet it must be so. Guy—Lord Renshaw,' Sarah corrected herself meticulously, 'knew of the purpose of my visit, and that can only have come from Frank's letter.'

Amelia shrugged lightly. 'As you say, my love. I must surely be making a mystery out of nothing!' She moved across to the writing box. 'Now, since it is not really the weather to go out, I shall write some letters.'

'I'll sit with you and read a book,' Sarah said, selecting one from the shelves. She settled in an armchair beside the roaring fire, and for a time there was no sound but for the pages turning softly and the scratch of Amelia's nib on the paper. Sarah, however, was hardly concentrating. Amelia's words had raised some doubts in her mind, yet she was unsure what it was that disturbed her. Never mind—tomorrow she would reach Blanchland at last and unravel the mystery of Olivia Meredith.

Dinner was another very pleasant meal and was followed by charades and card-playing before bedtime. Lady Woodallan was chatting to Amelia as they ascended the stairs and it was completely by chance that Sarah, trailing a little behind, heard the conversation between father and son in the hall below.

'You have told her that you will go, then,' Lord Woodallan was saying as he lit the remaining candles to see them up to bed.

'I have, sir.' Guy sounded a little grim.

'But not the rest? Not about—?'

'No. It is as you wished.'

'Good.' Woodallan sounded relieved. 'Then you will see to it, Guy. Find Miss Meredith—and make sure that Miss Sheridan does not—'

Guy glanced up at that moment and Sarah shrank back into the darkness at the top of the stairs. Her mind was racing as she puzzled over what she had heard. So what Guy had told her was true, but only up to a point—his father did want him to accompany her to Blanchland, but not simply to give her his aid! Apparently he had his own reasons for wishing to find Olivia, and she was not to be made aware of them…

'Sarah!' Amelia called, a little impatiently. 'Where are you? I am waiting to say goodnight!'

She yawned widely as Sarah hurried up the remaining few steps, then gave her cousin an affectionate peck on the cheek. 'Sleep well, my love!'

But Sarah tossed and turned for over an hour as she tried to work out what connection the Woodallan family might have with Olivia Meredith and, more importantly, why she should not be privy to it. Her musings shed no light, however, and in the end she fell asleep, to dream that she was chasing a fair-haired girl across the park at Blanchland, but, just before she reached her, the girl disappeared.

Chapter Six

Blanchland stood on the top of a rise, surrounded on three sides by a woodland of tall pines. As the carriage drew nearer, all the occupants could see that it was a supremely elegant house of pinkish stone with a small gold cupola on the roof, where Lord Sheridan had once housed the telescope he had used for astronomical observations. In the morning sunlight, with the bright white fields as a backdrop, it looked very beautiful.

Just seeing the house again almost brought tears to Sarah's eyes. She blinked hard to keep them at bay and set her mouth in a determined line.

'I had almost forgot how pretty it is…'

They drove through Blanchland village, huddled at the bottom of the hill, and started the climb to the gates of the house. It was very quiet. The frost glittered in the sun but no one moved in the still landscape. Sarah repressed a shiver.

She knew that Guy was watching her and the sympathy she could see in his eyes made her feel dangerously close to breaking down. As Amelia leant forward to speak to Greville, forgetting for a moment her antipathy to him, Guy bent close to Sarah and touched her gloved hand. The fleeting contact gave her both comfort and confusion.

All had gone to plan that morning. They had left Woodallan early, sped on their way with the Earl and Countess's good wishes and pressing invitations to return for Christmas. The Earl had shaken Guy's hand and wished him luck, and Sarah had searched the face of both men for some clue to Guy's secret errand at Blanchland, but there was nothing. Her doubts gnawed at her and added to her disquiet, but there was nothing she could do until the time Guy chose to tell her—or she dared to ask him.

Now that she had almost arrived, Sarah was prey to mixed feelings. Just seeing her old home again was emotional enough, but she was apprehensive as to what she might find there. Would Sir Ralph have ruined it beyond repair? Would he throw them all out into the snow—or worse, would he be indulging in some loathsome orgy? There was only one way to find out…

The silence, as they drew up on the forecourt, was almost sinister. All the windows of the house were shuttered and nothing stirred.

'Perhaps no one is at home,' Amelia said hopefully. 'It seems deserted. Perhaps we should go back to Woodallan—'

'We only left there a half-hour ago!' Sarah said firmly. She stepped forward and rang the bell hard. They all heard it echo distantly before the silence settled again. The horses stamped impatiently on the gravel and Sarah jumped. Her nerves were on edge and she knew she was not the only one. Greville was looking grim and exchanged a quizzical look with Guy, and Amelia was shivering and peering around fearfully, as though she expected satyrs to jump out of the nearby bushes.

'Oh, good, there is no one here! Let us go at once! Sarah—'

Sarah turned the door knob. The door was not locked and opened with a creak of protesting hinges that sounded loud in the morning quiet. Amelia gave a little shriek.

'Oh, how Gothic! I declare, I will not set foot inside!'

'Then pray wait in the cold!' Sarah snapped, her nerves getting the better of her. 'Gentlemen? Will you accompany me?'

Greville and Guy followed her over the threshold and after a moment so did Amelia, who clearly preferred not to be left alone. Inside the house it was almost as cold as in the open air. Sarah could see her breath crystallise on the air before her.

All the windows were shuttered and the hall was deep in darkness. She could just see the cobwebs that festooned the ornate central chandelier and the thick dust on the tiled floor. There was a stale smell in the air, the scent of dirt and decay. Sarah shivered violently.

'It is scarce welcoming...'

'Most quelling,' Guy agreed. He strode forward and flung open a few doors. 'Hello! Is anybody there?'

His voice echoed strangely around the high ceilings, but there was no reply. Amelia gave a little shriek. 'Oh, my goodness! How disgusting!'

She was staring with fascination at a lewd statue of two entwined lovers raised on a plinth at the side of the hall. Their entangled limbs and suggestive expressions were grossly indecent. Sarah looked away hastily.

'You are fortunate if that is all you find to offend you here, Lady Amelia,' Greville said drily. 'Since you have chosen to come here of your own free will, I beg you not to give way to missish vapours!'

Amelia fired up at once. 'Pray do not be so ungentlemanly, sir—'

Sarah put her hands over her ears. She was not sure that she could stand their wrangling at that moment and evidently someone else felt the same.

'God's teeth!' a voice roared from the top of the stairs. They all spun round. A huge man in straining waistcoat and breeches, a monstrous bedcap still perched on his balding head, was standing staring down on them. He clutched his head and gave a groan.

'Madam, I must ask you to desist from that shrill cacophony! A termagant female is more than flesh and blood can stand!'

Sir Ralph Covell, for it could only be he, did not cut an attractive figure. His embroidered waistcoat strained over an ample stomach and his little blue eyes peered suspiciously from beneath heavy black eyebrows. His complexion was high, suggesting a choleric temperament and his voice loud enough to shake the windows. Sarah, feeling a sudden rush of apprehension, wondered if he was about to throw them all out of the house without another word.

Then, miraculously, Sir Ralph's face broke into a smile of startling sweetness. He hurried down the stairs towards her, arms outstretched.

'Well, if it isn't little cousin Sarah! My, my, child, how you've changed! And what a pleasure to see you again!'

He came forward, enfolding a stunned Sarah in a bear hug. 'I never thought to see you at Blanchland again, my dear, but you are very welcome in your old home!'

Sarah, released with all the breath crushed out of her, found herself struggling to form a suitable response. Only five minutes previously she had been racking her brains to think of a way to explain her presence at Blanchland. She had imagined Sir Ralph unwelcoming at best and most probably downright hostile. This bonhomie was as startling as it was unexpected. She caught Guy's amused gaze on her and realised that he was trying not to laugh. Seeing her lost for words, he stepped forward, holding out a hand.

'How do you do, Sir Ralph? I am Guy Renshaw—we have met in London, but several years back. I must apologise for our intrusion in your house—'

'No intrusion at all, sir!' Sir Ralph had seized Guy's hand and was pumping it energetically. 'My cousin is always welcome here and any friends of hers can only be my honoured guests!' He bustled over to the windows and started to throw the shutters back with gusto. 'That's better! Let the dog see the rabbit!'

His smiling gaze swept round to encompass Greville and Amelia, both of whom Sarah thought were looking as stunned as she felt.

'Greville Baynham!' Ralph beamed. 'Remember you from that club in Bath last year! Now, what was its name...?'

Greville cleared his throat, looking discomposed for the first time. 'Sir Ralph. May I make you known to my betrothed, Lady Amelia Fenton?'

This time, Amelia did not argue with him, but dropped a little curtsy. She was looking quite bewildered. Sir Ralph smiled sunnily. 'Delighted, my dear, delighted! Would be more delighted if you could speak in a slightly softer tone, though! My head this morning, don't you know...' He turned back to Sarah, a slight frown marring his brow.

'Sarah, my dear, you are most welcome to visit, as I hope I have made clear! However, there is one small problem...' Sir Ralph came to an unhappy stop and rubbed his hands together with undoubted embarrassment. A deeper shade of red came over his already puce countenance. He looked like a schoolboy caught out in some unfortunate escapade. He stumbled on. 'You see...you may not be aware... I hold small house parties here every so often...my revels, as I like to call them—'

'Indeed, sir, I am aware.' Sarah tried not to smile as she wondered how her cousin would broach this delicate subject. It was proving extremely difficult to dislike Ralph, for he seemed as eager to please as an overgrown puppy.

'Ah, good.' Sir Ralph looked gratified. 'Good! I rather thought that my parties were getting a name for themselves! How agreeable! But—' he suddenly seemed to recall the problem '—I am not at all certain, however, that they are the sort of affairs for a gently bred young lady! There are gentlemen, you know, and ladies of...ah...' He floundered to a halt.

'Dubious virtue?' Guy supplied, helpfully.

'Oh, you mean Cyprians!' Sarah said heartily. 'Why, yes, cousin Ralph, I have heard all about them!'

Ralph looked slightly winded. 'You have?' He recovered himself a little. 'But perhaps you did not realise—there are masques and plays, and a pagan ceremony to celebrate the winter solstice—'

'I will not regard it,' Sarah said blithely, ignoring Amelia's look of horror and Guy's amusement. 'If you are happy for me to be your guest, cousin Ralph, I will only thank you for your generosity!'

Ralph frowned again. It was obvious that his mind was currently too befuddled to unravel the puzzle before him. 'I find it most singular that you were aware of

Blanchland's reputation yet still chose to come here!' he said at last, clearly puzzled. 'I do not like to criticise, Sarah, my dear, but I do not feel it is at all the way for a young lady to go on! Why, like as not you will find yourself with your reputation in tatters! I do feel you should show a little more concern!'

Sarah dropped a meek curtsy. 'I am persuaded that you are correct, cousin Ralph! Mama always said that I had no decorum! I am so very sorry if I have shocked you!'

Now it was Sir Ralph's turn to appear lost for words. 'I do not expect that you will be staying long…' he said hopefully.

'Oh, no!' Sarah agreed with a blithe smile. 'It is simply that Frank asked me to conduct a little business in the neighbourhood, but I expect that I shall be gone directly! And do not worry that I will disturb you, cousin Ralph! I shall be so quiet you will scarce know I am here!'

She heard Guy laugh and smother it with a cough.

'Well, then…' Sir Ralph seemed a little at a loss, clearly uncertain how to deal with his unorthodox relative. 'Well, then,' he said again, lamely, 'you will need rooms, I suppose, and refreshment…' His shoulders slumped as though the thought of it was almost too much. 'I will call Marvell. Marvell is my general factotum…' he glanced at the clock '…if he is from his bed… Pray excuse me! No way to greet ladies… If you would care to wait in the drawing-room, I shall see you are served with coffee! Join you shortly…' And he hurried off, bellowing for the servants.

'What an odd man,' Amelia said, casting another doubtful glance at the statues as she followed Sarah into the drawing-room, 'but he seems quite harmless! Perhaps we shall find that the Blanchland revels have been quite overrated!'

Sarah would have liked to agree, but she had seen the wry look that had flashed between Guy and Greville, a look that said louder than any words that their troubles were only beginning.

'It's quite disgusting!' Amelia said indignantly later, throwing herself down on Sarah's bed and causing a huge dust cloud to rise into the air.

'I know, Milly—' Sarah sneezed and averted her eyes from the garish painting of naked nymphs cavorting in a stream that hung above the bed '—but you were aware of what it would be like here.'

Amelia looked blank. 'Oh, no, I did not mean the picture! No, the dust! Everywhere! These curtains are filthy and my room cannot have been cleaned for an age! I shall speak to the housekeeper immediately after luncheon!'

'I feel we may be fortunate to have any luncheon,' Sarah said drily. She thought about unpacking her trunk and decided against it. There really was nowhere clean to put all her clothes. 'I doubt that Sir Ralph's guests will arise before this afternoon and I am not even sure that there is a housekeeper here any more! Certainly Mrs Lambert left after my brother died and I do not imagine Sir Ralph finds it easy to keep servants...'

'He certainly does not keep any good ones!' Amelia opined, running her finger along the dust on the bed-head. 'Look at this, Sarah! I would have plenty to say to my servants if this was the state of my house! And as for that undrinkable coffee...'

'It is still a beautiful place, though,' Sarah said, a little wistfully. She was standing at the window, looking out across the rolling Somerset hills. Beyond the ring of woodland, the fields tumbled away towards the village and beyond. It gave one the impression of standing on top of the world.

'Yes,' Amelia said, her tone softening, 'it is indeed a lovely house and it is a crime that it should have been allowed to become so neglected.' She brightened. 'I was wondering what I should do with myself whilst you were about your mysterious quest, my love! Well, now I have my answer! I shall bring order and cleanliness to Blanchland!'

Sarah raised a mental eyebrow at the thought of Amelia sweeping through the house like a new broom. She rather thought that Sir Ralph would be terrified at the prospect.

'You will tell me what all this mystery is about once it is resolved, will you not?' Amelia asked, a little plaintively, tracing the pattern on the bedspread. 'I know it is a personal matter, but I do so dislike secrets!'

'Of course!' Sarah touched her cousin's hand. 'I am sorry to be so secretive, Milly—it is only the fact that the tale is not really mine to tell that holds me back!'

'Sir Ralph did not seem very curious,' Amelia observed thoughtfully. 'I am surprised he did not press you more on the reasons for your presence here!'

'I think he was too embarrassed,' Sarah said, with a giggle. 'Poor Ralph, I believe he thinks we will put a blight on his revels!'

'Well, we may try!' Amelia got to her feet. 'Sarah, I have been thinking about Lord Renshaw's purpose in accompanying us. I know that you said that the Earl decreed it, but are you sure that it is not also because Guy wishes to be near you? It seems to me that his lordship is intent on pursuit—of one description or another!'

Sarah knew that a telltale blush burned her cheek. She was not sure whether it would be worse to tell Amelia the truth about Guy's proposal or distract her by sharing what she had overheard the previous night. But that would involve too many explanations; besides, she knew that Amelia's real interest lay in the romantic aspect of the case.

'Well...Lord Renshaw has made me an offer, Milly, but it is not at all as you imagine!'

Amelia looked understandably bewildered. 'An offer? But not as I imagine? Pray, how do you think I am imagining it, Sarah?'

'No, I mean, it is not at all romantic—' Sarah struggled, aware that she was making a mull of things. 'That is, Lord Renshaw offered me the protection of his name in much the same way as Greville offered for you! Now you understand me?'

'Oh, I see!' Amelia's brow cleared. 'It seems to me that the gentlemen have been suffering an excess of chivalry,' she added, in an acerbic tone. 'What was your answer, Sarah?'

'I told him that he need not put himself to the trouble! I dare say I was not very gracious, but I thought his actions high-handed and arrogant—'

'He was not, then, proposing because of his behaviour to you the night of the ball?' Amelia asked delicately. 'If he realised that he had mistreated an innocent girl—'

Sarah blushed vividly. 'No! He did mention the... incident, but said...' she hesitated '...that he regretted all the things he had said, but he did not regret what he had done!'

'Well, that's honest at least!' Amelia laughed. 'Why did you not accept him, Sarah? You know you have a *tendre* for him—'

'I do not!' Sarah said hotly. She met her cousin's amused gaze and added, a little shamefacedly, 'I'll admit that he is a prodigiously attractive man and I might have had a small partiality for him before, but that is quite at an end! Why, there are a dozen reasons to refuse him! I think him altogether too presumptuous and sure of his own charm! And you of all people should understand, Amelia, for Greville's overbearing behaviour did not find favour with you!'

Amelia pursed her lips, distracted as Sarah had intended her to be. 'No, indeed! To announce to all and sundry that we were betrothed! It quite puts me out of patience! And it is very out of character!'

'Yes.' Sarah regarded her cousin thoughtfully. 'Yet it is odd, for you have been always blaming Greville for being too courteous! It seems he cannot do right in your eyes!'

Now it was Amelia's turn to look away in confusion. 'Well, you must allow that he is generally a very amiable gentleman! I thought him so amiable that he was almost dull!'

'Yet for all your protests I believe you find this display of autocratic behaviour rather attractive,' Sarah said shrewdly. 'You had best be quick if you wish to stake your claim, Amelia! I believe some of the ladies at this houseparty might find him attractive, too!'

Luncheon proved to be the disappointment that Sarah had suspected. There was only herself and Amelia present, for the gentlemen had apparently gone out for a ride and Sir Ralph's guests had still not put in an appearance.

'I dare say they have ridden over to Woodallan for a square meal!' Amelia said darkly. 'It is the outside of enough! First they force their company on us and then they promptly disappear!'

They rang the bell several times and finally a slatternly maid appeared who seemed amazed to be asked to provide some food. An inordinate amount of time later, she returned with a plate of stale bread and smelly cheese, slapped it down on the table and strode out again.

'Monstrous!' Amelia said, two bright spots of outrage burning in her cheeks. 'The sooner I take matters into my own hands, the better!'

Sarah nibbled a crust of bread, forced down a little of the cheese, then went to fetch her cloak. She had resolved to set off immediately on her quest to find Olivia and, as Guy was out of the way, it seemed a good opportunity. She did not want him dogging her footsteps, and if she was able to steal a march over him, so much the better. Perhaps, if she was really lucky, she would find Olivia at once and they could all escape from this awkward situation.

The path down to Blanchland village was muddy where the sun had melted the snow. Water dripped from the bare branches of the overhanging trees and Sarah picked her way with care, huddling in her cloak against the cold. She had walked that path many a time when she was a child and enjoyed passing all the sites she remembered from then: the hollow tree where she had played hide-and-seek, the stile over the hedge into Farmer Burton's field, where once she had been chased by a bull, the old tumbledown gatehouse... Sarah sighed over her memories, picked up her skirts where the mud was an inch deep, and entered the main street of the village.

She noticed a change at once. Blanchland village was only small, one main road with houses on either side, but it had always been a bustling community. Now, however, half of the cottages looked either empty or neglected, the land overgrown with weeds and the retaining walls tumbling into the street. There was no sign of life except for the smithy, from where the clang of hammer on iron could be heard.

The doctor's house was the only residence of any size in the village, set back a little from the road, with a modest carriage sweep before it and neatly tended gardens all around. Sarah rang the bell, but there was no answer. She had hardly expected to find Olivia Meredith at home, but hoped that her mother or even a servant might be present to give some information. However, the house had a closed and shuttered air very similar to Blanchland and there was something watchful about its silence. Sarah tiptoed through the shrubbery and round the back, and peered in at the scullery window, but there was no sign of life. Then, something moved behind her. She saw the reflection on the glass and spun round with a gasp of alarm. An old man, clutching a garden hoe in a vaguely threatening manner, was standing right behind her.

'B'aint no one 'ere, miss, so it would be best that you go…'

'I am looking for Mrs Meredith,' Sarah said haughtily, feeling embarrassed at being caught prying. 'Pray tell me, will she be home soon?'

'No,' the old man said. He offered no further information and waggled the hoe at her. 'Best to leave, ma'am!'

Sarah raised her eyebrows at the threatening tone and the fierce light in the man's blue eyes. Somehow his antagonism made her want to stand her ground. 'And Miss Meredith? Is she at home?'

'No,' the man said again. 'Powerful many folks looking for Miss Meredith these days!' He shifted slightly. 'Now then, ma'am, I'm sure you would not like me to call the constable—'

'I should like it above all things,' Sarah said crossly, 'so that I may tell him how unwelcoming you are to visitors here in Blanchland! Why, in my father's day no one would have spoken thus! What has happened to turn this place so unfriendly?'

The old man lowered his hoe slowly, peering at her from beneath his thatch of white hair. 'And who might you be then, ma'am?' He took a step forward. 'Never Miss Sarah come back to us!'

Recognition struck Sarah at the same time. 'Tom! I am so sorry! I did not recognise you! Why, it must be fifteen years—'

'Fourteen and a half,' the old man said, 'since I left Blanchland. And two since I came back. Aye, and a mistake that was good and all!'

Sarah sat down on the garden wall and gestured to him to join her. Tom Brookes had been the head groom at Blanchland when she had been a little girl, but had left when Sarah was nine years old to join his brother in running an inn down in Devon. Evidently the venture had not worked out.

'What happened to the inn, Tom?' Sarah asked sympathetically. She knew that he had sunk all his savings into it.

'Locals didn't like the competition,' Tom said morosely. 'Lot of trouble, Miss Sarah, so in the end I came home. Went to the big house, but Sir Ralph wasn't taking on staff, not even those who'd worked for the family before. No horses anymore, neither.' He spat on the path. 'Begging your pardon, Miss Sarah, but the house ain't the same as it used to be. No one takes care of it—no one wants to work there neither, with the things that go on! Shocking, it is. No…' he shook his head '…it was the worst of all times when the old lord died.'

'The village seems as bad,' Sarah said. 'Why, it is deserted! I would scarce have recognised it! What happened to the school, Tom?'

'Closed. I misremember when. But it's a bad business…'

'And Mrs Meredith—has she left, too? I know that the doctor died a few years back, but I thought that his wife and daughter continued to live here?'

Tom was watching her thoughtfully with his very blue eyes. Sarah had the suspicion that he was nowhere near as simple as he was pretending to be.

'Mrs Meredith's gone to stay with her sister near Glastonbury,' he said, in his thick Somerset burr. 'I don't know when she'll be back, Miss Sarah, and that's a fact.'

'And Miss Meredith?' Sarah persisted. She had a feeling that there was something he was not telling her. 'You said that lots of people were looking for her?'

'Aye.' Tom threw away the piece of grass he had been chewing and straightened up. 'Powerful few. And all of them gentlemen. Always gentlemen asking after Miss Olivia! First some young gentleman that's staying at the big house, then a lord that's a friend of Sir Ralph…' he looked as though he was about to spit again, but thought better of it '...and today a mighty fine gentleman with his London clothes and his gold...'

A small shiver went down Sarah's spine. 'A gentleman from London?'

'Oh, no, Miss Sarah! London clothes, London manners, but...' Tom hesitated. 'Mrs Anthrop said as he was from Woodallan, and she should know, for her daughter's in service there now that there's no work at the big house!'

Sarah frowned. So Guy had already been asking questions in the village! In fact, he had deliberately misled her by telling her he was going out riding when he was actually looking for Olivia. Sarah's eyes narrowed. She had been right to be suspicious last night. Lord Woodallan and his son were pursuing some secret quest of their own!

Sarah stood up and shook out her skirts. She could not afford to lose any time in the hunt, or Guy would get there first!

'Gave me some money,' Tom was saying, with a disparaging sniff, 'and told me to tell no one he was asking. But as it's you, Miss Sarah...'

Sarah smiled. 'Thank you, Tom. Miss Meredith must be very pretty, I suppose,' she added, 'to be so admired. She was a lovely little girl—'

'Aye,' Tom said grudgingly, 'a proper lady is Miss Meredith! And well to a pass, like you, Miss Sarah! How comes it that you're not married?'

'I fear I am too particular,' Sarah said, and heard the old man laugh for the first time. 'Well, I had best be going if Miss Meredith is not at home. But, Tom—' She stopped, suddenly struck by a thought. 'If you see her, pray tell her that I was looking for her.' She gave him a very straight look. 'And if she is in any need of help, please let her know that I will stand her friend. Indeed, I am here for that very purpose!'

The old man touched his cap. 'I'll be sure and do that, Miss Sarah. If I see her.'

Sarah nodded. 'Thank you. Good day, Tom!'

The old man watched her walk away though the shrubbery, but when she was gone, he did not return to his hoeing.

Out in the main street Sarah hesitated, but could see no other purpose than to return to Blanchland. It was dispiriting, for she had hoped for some clue to Olivia's whereabouts, but it seemed that there was nothing further she could learn. And yet she had really learned quite a lot. She walked slowly along the village street, thinking. She now knew that Olivia was pretty and much sought after. Could that be the source of her problems? If one of the gentlemen from the house had taken a fancy to her, it could spell trouble for a provincial doctor's daughter, especially one with no male relatives to protect her. Sarah frowned. Tom had said that there was a young gentleman and a lord at the house who had both been asking after Olivia. No doubt they were both Ralph's guests and she would meet them later.

And she had also learnt that Guy had been asking questions—and paying for silence... As though in answer to her thoughts, she saw the familiar bay stallion tied up outside the smithy and, as she watched, Guy's tall figure emerged into the street. He turned for a parting word with the smith and some money changed hands, which the smith slid hastily into his apron. Sarah hesitated, in two minds as to whether to avoid him, but it was too late. He had seen her.

'Miss Sheridan! Taking an afternoon stroll?'

'Lord Renshaw.' Sarah knew she sounded cold. She

could not help it, harbouring the suspicions she did. Guy raised an amused eyebrow.

'Dear me, have I done something to offend you, Miss Sheridan? Something else?' He looped the reins over his arm and fell into step beside her. 'Have you had any success in your enquiries?'

'No,' Sarah said. She looked him straight in the eyes. 'Have you, my lord?'

'Ah.' A rueful smile curled Guy's mouth. 'It seems you have had *some* success, Miss Sheridan! You know, for instance, that I have been making enquiries of my own!'

'Indeed! Money buys much, my lord,' Sarah said sweetly, 'but old loyalties are worth more!'

'So it seems!' Guy still seemed rueful. He looked down at her and the expression in his eyes made her heart skip a beat. 'I can understand why you command such loyalty, Miss Sheridan! Do you not trust me, then?'

'No,' Sarah said, surprised and disturbed to find that it was true.

Guy laughed. 'You may do so. I swear that I would never do anything to hurt you, Sarah!'

'That is not the point, my lord,' Sarah objected, trying to ignore the fact that he had addressed her by her given name, and in so caressing a tone that she found it difficult to concentrate. 'You have not answered my question! Why have you been asking after Miss Meredith?'

Guy shrugged. He gaze was clear and untroubled. 'I thought to spare you some effort! If I were to find her first, you would have no need to make enquiries and we could all go home! That is all!'

There was a silence. Sarah did not believe him and

she felt hollow with hurt at his duplicity. She had given him the chance to confide and he had deliberately chosen not to do so…

'Penny for your thoughts, Miss Sheridan,' Guy said lightly.

'Oh—' Sarah looked away in confusion '—they are not worth half that, my lord! I was merely reflecting on the differences in the village since my father's time.'

Guy did not challenge her although she had the uncomfortable feeling that he did not believe her. Sarah knew that they both felt that the other was withholding something, but they fell to talking about Blanchland, a topic that lasted all the way back to the house and which both of them knew was assumed over more important preoccupations.

There was a different smell in the entrance hall at Blanchland when they got back, a mixture of beeswax and fresh flowers. Sarah stopped and stared. The terracotta-and-black-tiled floor was shining and the white marble pillars, no longer festooned with cobwebs, glowed softly in the light. Guy whistled.

'What a remarkable transformation! And so quickly! Your handiwork, Lady Amelia?'

Amelia was standing by the stairs, sleeves rolled up to her elbows, an old apron over her dress. Beside her was a small maid, clutching a polishing cloth and looking terrified. Amelia smiled.

'That's very good, Mary.' She turned to Guy and Sarah. 'I have only made a start on a few of the rooms, but Mary tells me she has two sisters who can come in to help tomorrow! And it does look much better, does it not?'

'The flowers?' Sarah questioned, wondering where

her cousin had found such luscious blooms in the winter.

Amelia beamed. 'Why, they are from your father's hothouses, Sarah! Of course, it is all going to rack and ruin, but Mary tells me an old man called Tom comes in to tend to them sometimes—'

From the staircase came the tread of someone descending. Amelia looked up, closed her lips in a straight, disapproving line, and whisked the small maid through the door to the servants' quarters without another word, rather in the manner of a fairy godmother. Sarah raised her eyebrows.

'Well, well! What have we here?'

The voice was oily. When Sarah looked up at the man standing on the half-landing, she thought there was something altogether too unwholesome and greasy about him. Tall and thin, he was dressed all in black, with a quizzing glass on a gold chain about his neck. She guessed that he was about forty years of age, but the look in his eyes, at once knowing and weary, suggested that he had seen enough for a lifetime. This, then, must be the first of Sir Ralph's guests, and perhaps even one of Olivia's suitors.

'The Honourable Miss Sheridan, I presume!' the man said, smiling in a somewhat predatory manner. His pointed chin jutted like the beak of a bird of prey. He reached the bottom of the stairs and bowed. 'We heard of your arrival. Delighted to meet you, my dear! Edward Allardyce, at your service.'

Lord Allardyce stepped forward and raised Sarah's hand to his lips. His mouth was wet against her skin. His black, knowing eyes appraised her thoroughly. 'Such a pleasure to meet unsullied innocence after a stay in this house!'

Sarah felt Guy stiffen beside her. His face looked as though it had been carved from stone. He gave the slightest of bows, so slight it was almost an insult.

'Allardyce.'

'Renshaw!' Lord Allardyce did not appear to have noticed Guy's frosty tone. 'A pleasure to see you again, old fellow!' He shot a look at Sarah. 'I believe you had that delicious opera singer in keeping when last we met in London! Good to see that your taste has improved!'

Guy's mouth tightened. 'Miss Sheridan is my father's goddaughter and I am here in his place to assist her in some family matters,' he said tightly. 'I do not anticipate that Miss Sheridan will wish to remain any longer than is absolutely necessary!'

'I should think not!' Allardyce gave an affected shudder. His black eyes gleamed. 'The place is filthy and the food atrocious! Assure you, I was about to leave myself when Miss Sheridan's arrival made everything so much more interesting!'

Guy took a step forward. Sarah could feel his tension, tight as a bow about to snap.

'I don't believe you heard me, Allardyce—'

For a moment the other man hesitated, then he laughed. 'I heard you, Renshaw. The irreproachable Miss Sheridan is out of bounds—to both you and I!' He turned and strolled away with deliberate provocation. 'Too bad! But there is plenty more sport in this house, when all is said and done!'

There was an expression of almost murderous fury on Guy's face. He took a step after the departing figure, but Sarah put her hand on his arm to restrain him.

'Do not! It is not worth it!'

For a second Guy looked so angry Sarah thought he

had not even heard her, then his expression softened and he covered her hand with his for a brief moment.

'I beg your pardon, Miss Sheridan. I wish you had not had to hear that.'

'It is nothing, my lord,' Sarah said a little shakily. 'I believe I shall have to hear worse if I remain at Blanchland!'

'Yes—' Guy's expression was brooding '—that may well be true! But I do beg you to be careful of Allardyce, Miss Sheridan. He is…' Guy hesitated '…a deeply offensive man and not one with whom you should ever associate!'

Sarah wondered whether that was why Amelia had hurried the little maid away so abruptly and, as she went up the stairs to prepare for dinner, she could not help but speculate again whether it had been Lord Allardyce who had been asking after Olivia. She shivered, remembering his unctuous voice and greasy manner. And Allardyce was only the first of Ralph's guests that they had met! She could not help but wonder what on earth the others would be like.

Amelia's influence had not yet reached the food and dinner was an unpalatable meal redeemed only by the quality of the wine. It had quickly become apparent to Sarah that Sir Ralph's guests could only visit for two reasons—the Blanchland wine cellar and, presumably, the entertainment Ralph provided with his revels. Neither was a good enough reason to draw her to Blanchland, but his guests were a different kettle of fish.

The houseparty were an oddly assorted mixture, a group who apparently had only their interest in the revels in common. Sir Ralph himself appeared to be directing his amorous attentions towards a Mrs Eliza Fisk, whose husband was also present but seemed to be asleep most of the time. Mrs Fisk was decidedly fat and past the first flush of youth, but Sir Ralph evidently liked plenty to get hold of.

There were two other ladies, of dubious age, status and virtue: Lady Tilney, who had transferred her attentions from Lord Allardyce to Greville Baynham with alacrity, and Lady Ann Walter, a statuesque blonde, who was eyeing Guy with feline speculation. Lord Allardyce did not seem unduly disappointed by Lady Tilney's defection, for he was seated next to Sarah at dinner and was making a great fuss of her. His attentions made Sarah feel faintly sick and very wary. Amelia, meanwhile, was busy charming a young man who looked barely out of leading reins and was quite obviously dazzled by her.

'Young Justin Lebeter,' Allardyce said, following Sarah's gaze. 'He has a doting mama, a lazy trustee and more money than sense, which accounts for his presence here! It is shocking to see the young fall into such bad company!' The malicious twist to his thin mouth suggested that he really found the corruption of innocence rather amusing. 'Perhaps Lady Amelia may save him—she is rather high in the instep, is she not?'

Sarah chose not to reply. She was already feeling decidedly vulnerable in this disreputable company. There was nothing openly licentious about their behaviour, but an unpleasant undertone to the conversation, an innuendo that could not be ignored, made the whole experience very uncomfortable. Added to this was an air of suppressed excitement, as though it was only a matter of time before the façade of civility cracked to reveal the lechery beneath.

Sarah applied herself to the mock turtle soup, but it

was stone cold and tasted of little but salt. It was impossible to force it down. Her eyes seemed drawn by some curious magnetism to the frieze of nude characters that cavorted around the room. Everywhere one turned there were images of lewdness in the worst possible taste, with some truly shocking cartoons framed on the wall. Sarah felt the colour rising to her cheeks and hastily looked away.

Lord Allardyce viewed her discomfort with amusement. He allowed his appreciative gaze to linger on Sarah's figure, taking in the demure high-necked evening gown, the neatly coiled hair and the modest shawl. His smile broadened.

'My dear Miss Sheridan, you could not be making more of a statement if you spoke it aloud! Whatever can have prompted a pattern-card of rectitude such as yourself to come to this nest of reprobates? Why, you will surely be ruined, if not in deed, at least in word!'

Sarah's eyes narrowed at the turn the conversation was taking. 'I have family business here at Blanchland, my lord.'

'Ah! The mysterious family business!' Allardyce sat back, his button-black eyes bright with speculation. 'It must be pressing indeed to bring you to this house! Have you not heard of Sir Ralph's revels? Naked orgies and cavorting in the snow—'

An obsequious footman dressed all in black removed Sarah's untouched bowl of soup and placed a plate of steaming mutton before her.

'Cavorting in the snow?' Sarah said, deliberately indifferent. 'It all sounds rather cold, my lord! One must be careful not to catch a chill, I should think!'

For a second Allardyce looked taken aback, then he smiled in appreciation of her tactics.

'Very sensible, Miss Sheridan! I can see you are a lady not easily shaken! But is your practicality proof against the black arts?'

Sarah looked up, startled. 'Against witchcraft? Surely not even Sir Ralph would indulge in such foolish practices!'

Lord Allardyce's smile was positively vulpine. 'There is a little temple in the woods where—'

'Oh!' Sarah smiled brightly, cutting him off before he should have the chance to go any further. 'You mean the grotto! I used to play there as a child! There is a spring in the rocks—it is indeed a charming place!'

Allardyce looked put out. He was not accustomed to both his compliments and his intriguing hints falling on such stony ground. He gave up temporarily and applied himself to his mutton. Mr Fisk appeared to have fallen forward into his. Further down the table, Sir Ralph was feeding mutton stew to Mrs Fisk in a coquettish manner that made Sarah feel faintly nauseous. Sir Ralph looked up, caught her eye, and put his fork down with an abashed expression.

Next to him, Lady Tilney was pouring Greville some more wine, leaning forward to display her rampant cleavage and running her fingers along the back of Greville's hand. Greville did not look as though he minded in the least. Sarah knew that Amelia had also seen and that the slightly brittle gaiety she was showing young Lord Lebeter was a direct result. Lebeter was at least enough of a gentleman to behave with propriety, and his youthful face showed some embarrassment at the increasingly uninhibited behaviour of the company.

Sarah reflected ruefully that Guy and Greville both seemed remarkably at home in such scandalous surroundings. She knew enough of Guy's reputation to be unsurprised, but a dull weight seemed to settle on her stomach that owed nothing to the greasy mutton. It did not matter how much she told herself to disregard it—it seemed his behaviour still had the power to disturb her.

There was a roaring log fire in the room and the heat was growing all the time. Sarah fanned herself surreptitiously and noted the reddening faces of the other diners. Guy was the only one who still looked cool, immaculately sophisticated in his evening clothes, as though he were in a London drawing-room rather than amidst a raffish houseparty. As Sarah watched, Lady Ann Walter rested one white hand on Guy's shoulder as though to emphasise a point she was making, then raised it to caress his tumbled fair hair in a gesture so intimate that Sarah almost caught her breath out loud.

'I believe that Lady Ann and Lord Renshaw were acquainted before,' Lord Allardyce said slyly in her ear. 'I fear you may have lost your beau, Miss Sheridan…'

Guy was laughing now at whatever Lady Ann was whispering in his ear. Sarah stared transfixed at the strong, brown column of his neck, the thick fair hair curling over his collar, the flashing white smile. Lady Ann was also watching him, with hunger in her gaze. Sarah felt an extraordinary jealousy twist inside her, so strong that she had to look away.

'You quite mistake the case, my lord,' she said coldly, aware that Allardyce was watching her avidly. 'Lord Renshaw accompanies me on behalf of his father, no more and no less. I have no claim on him.'

Allardyce looked unconvinced. 'Is that so? It would be interesting to see whether Lord Renshaw feels the same way, ma'am. Perhaps a taste of his own medicine would do the trick…'

For a moment Sarah was tempted, but she knew that she would be playing into Allardyce's hands. Besides, she had just claimed to be unconcerned by Guy's behaviour and was not about to show that the reverse was true. Still, the idea had held brief appeal. To make Guy jealous...if only she could! A small smile curved her mouth at the thought; at that moment, Guy looked up and straight at her. The amusement died from his dark eyes as he saw Sarah's smile and Allardyce bending close to her, one hand on her arm. Sarah felt as though she was pinned in her seat by the intensity of his stare and wondered if she imagined the anger she had read there. Then Allardyce laughed softly and the spell was broken. Sarah looked away, the colour mounting in her cheeks.

'That's the spirit, Miss Sheridan! That is all it takes!'

'I do not care for this conversation, sir!' Sarah snapped. 'Pray let us change the subject!'

'Very well,' Allardyce murmured, 'by all means let us discuss the weather if you wish it, Miss Sheridan!'

The mutton had congealed on Sarah's plate. The obsequious footman removed the covers and brought in a raspberry mousse. There were murmurs of appreciation, but not for the skill of the cuisine. The dessert wine, one of the late Lord Sheridan's finest, was circulating the table and the giggles and uninhibited behaviour was becoming more strident.

Sarah caught Amelia's horrified gaze as Lady Tilney dipped a finger into the dessert and held it out for Greville to lick, a lascivious glint in her eye. It seemed that Mrs Fisk was intending to use the mousse even more creatively, for she was encouraging Sir Ralph to dip his spoon into a bowl balanced on her magnificent bosom. Mr Fisk snored before the fire. Sarah felt as though she was getting hotter and hotter. Wherever she turned, it seemed there were images of wantonness.

'Excuse us, Sir Ralph—' Amelia's icy tones cut across the growing raucousness '—I believe it is time for the ladies to retire.'

Sir Ralph leaped up like a scalded cat, sending the bowl of mousse flying from Mrs Fisk's chest. 'Lady Amelia! Of course, ma'am! Pray retire! Ladies—' he looked hopelessly at Ann Walter and Lady Tilney '—perhaps you would be so good as to wait for us in the drawing-room.'

Lady Tilney giggled, trailing her fingers down Greville's cheek. 'Don't be so silly, Ralphie! We want some port…'

Lady Ann was feeding Guy grapes from the burgeoning fruit bowl. Sarah watched her pop them into his mouth and felt physically sick.

'As I said,' Amelia said pointedly, 'the *ladies* will retire…'

She got haughtily to her feet, raising her eyebrows when neither Guy nor Greville stood up. Lord Lebeter hurried to hold her chair, whilst Allardyce gave Sarah his arm to the door. Sarah's last image of the dining-room was of Greville with Lady Tilney sitting squarely on his knee and Guy twirling one of Lady Ann's blonde curls about his finger. Then the door was closed firmly in her face and almost immediately a burst of wild laughter could be heard on the other side of the panels.

Sarah could feel Amelia shaking like a leaf as they made their way up the stairs, but could not tell whether it was from anger or misery. She felt little better herself. Although she had told herself that life at Blanchland would contain some aspects she found distasteful, being confronted by the reality was both more shocking and more painful than she had imagined. In her heart of hearts she had expected that both Guy and Greville would act as gentlemen and defend her and Amelia from the harsher realities of Ralph's revels. The proof had shown them to be less than gentlemen and more than inclined to throw themselves into the spirit of the place. Never had Sarah felt so alone. When her father had died she had at least had Frank to provide some comfort and when he, too, had gone, Amelia's companionship had been solace. Here, both of them were in a completely unfamiliar situation and had nowhere to turn.

As soon as the door was closed, Amelia threw herself onto the bed and burst into angry tears.

'How dare he! How dare he profess to love me and then behave like that with that common little trollop! I hate him!'

Sarah sat beside her and stroked her shoulder tentatively. 'Milly! Please don't cry! Ten to one Greville is doing it to make you jealous—'

Amelia's pointed little face looked like an angry cat. 'Jealous! I would not have him now if he begged on bended knee! That vulgar strumpet was all over him—it was disgusting! I could not tell whether it was the food or the behaviour that revolted me more!'

'It was truly repellent,' Sarah agreed, with a shaky smile. 'That mutton—'

'Never mind the mutton! Did you see the way that that woman behaved with him? Licking her fingers, indeed! I dare swear—' Amelia broke off, gave an infuriated squeak and pummelled her pillow hard.

'Well,' Sarah said, struggling to be even-handed, 'Guy's behaviour was almost as bad. I know he is reputed a rake, but I did not wish to witness the evidence! Lord Allardyce told me that he and Lady Ann Walter—'

'Allardyce!' Amelia gave a disgusted snort. 'He is more unwholesome than the rest put together! I do beg you to be careful there, Sarah!'

'There is no need,' Sarah said, pressing her hands together. 'We shall not stay. I see now that it is impossible! We shall leave at first light!'

Amelia stopped punching her pillow and stared at her cousin. 'Leave? But you have yet to accomplish your quest!'

'It is of no consequence. Churchward may act as my agent here. When I think of what we have endured—'

'But we cannot go now!' Amelia, with a complete change of heart, stood up and started to pace about the room. 'Why, those wretched creatures downstairs would believe that they have chased us away! I could not bear them to triumph!'

As if in confirmation, there was the sound of running feet in the passage outside, followed by giggles and growling sounds. Sir Ralph—Sarah devoutly hoped that it was he—was becoming amorous.

'Let us play hunt the squirrel!' she heard one of the ladies shout. 'Greville darling, you may hide in here with me...'

A door closed along the passage. Sarah wrinkled up her nose with distaste. 'Good God, I thought we were rid of them—'

'Oh, Lord Renshaw,' a melting female cooed outside, 'I fear I shall be easily caught if you are doing the hunting...'

Sarah found that she was about to laugh hysterically. It was all so dreadfully like a bad melodrama and she had to stuff her hand into her mouth to stop the giggles erupting. Amelia's face was buried in the pillow again and her shoulders were shaking, but Sarah suspected that her affliction was laughter, not tears, this time. So it proved. When the growls, murmurs and titters outside the door had subsided, Amelia raised her head and said, 'Oh, Sarah, what are we to do?'

Sarah met her cousin's quizzical gaze. She was astonished to find that she was inclined to be angry, not afraid. 'We will not run away!' she said stoutly. 'I could not bear those odious creatures to win! They do say, Amelia, that revenge is very sweet. I have an idea...'

Chapter Seven

It was much later when Sarah left Amelia's bedroom and ventured across the darkened landing to her own room. She was feeling weary but still buoyed up by the plan that she had hatched with her cousin. The urge to laugh at the ridiculous antics of Sir Ralph's guests had fled now, but the flame of revenge that had taken hold of both herself and Amelia still burned very brightly. Sarah thought it unlikely that she would sleep, despite her tiredness.

Instead of retiring to her room, she tiptoed down the stairs to the library in search of a book to help her calm herself. The hall was in darkness now and it seemed that whatever revelling was still going on was probably taking place behind closed doors upstairs. Sarah refused to think about it. She opened the library door tentatively and was relieved to find it all in darkness.

Sir Ralph had sold many of Lord Sheridan's books upon inheriting Blanchland, but the old oak shelves still held a few volumes, steeped in dust and smelling strongly of damp. Sarah climbed the little wooden step-ladder and selected a couple of her old favourites. It did not seem as though anyone had touched them since she had last been at Blanchland. She curled up in an old armchair and turned the pages slowly, enjoying the rediscovery, and relaxing as silence took over the house.

The door opened suddenly and the candle flame scuttered in the draught. Sarah jumped violently and the books fell from her hands. For a moment the shadowed figure in the doorway was unrecognisable, and then Guy Renshaw stepped forward into the circle of candlelight and Sarah let her breath go on a long sigh. Not Lord Allardyce, then, but possibly just as dangerous. It had definitely been a mistake to go wandering after the lights were out.

'Good evening, my lord. Could you not sleep?' Sarah was proud of the steadiness of her voice and even prouder that she sounded so uninterested. She picked her books up and stood looking at him with polite indifference.

At some point in the evening Guy had removed his jacket, and his linen shirt revealed rather than concealed the ripple of taut muscles beneath the fine material. His cravat was undone, giving him a slightly dishevelled air that Sarah could not deny was attractive. The important point, she reminded herself sternly, was that Guy's rumpled look was no doubt the result of some activity she did not really wish to dwell on. His fair hair was tousled, probably by feminine hands, and there was a glitter in his dark eyes that was deeply disturbing.

'I have not yet attempted to sleep,' Guy said smoothly, 'being too occupied with other activities. But you, Miss Sheridan—I had thought you retired hours ago.'

Sarah felt a rush of fury at the Guy's casual reference to his recent debauchery. She gave him a cool little smile.

'I wonder that you had time to notice, my lord! You were...somewhat occupied! '

A smile that was not reassuring curled Guy's mouth. The flickering candlelight made him look very tall and gilded his skin with a bronze sheen. 'Oh, I noticed, Miss Sheridan. I noticed that Lord Allardyce was most attentive and that his compliments were not unwelcome to you!'

Sarah shrugged indifferently. 'His lordship was amusing.'

'I see. You did not consider my warning worth heeding?'

'I considered your judgement faulty, my lord,' Sarah said coldly, 'as demonstrated by your own choice of company.'

'I see,' Guy said again. He took a step forward, until he was close enough to touch her. She could sense the tension in him. 'Do you then object to the company I keep?'

'I have no opinion,' Sarah said, neatly sidestepping the trap that had been laid for her, 'other than that of any gently bred lady who does not wish to see the amorous affairs of others displayed before her!'

Guy put his hand under her chin and tilted it up to force her to meet his eyes. 'You have no personal feelings on the matter? Even though I have given you the right to an opinion?'

It cost Sarah a huge effort to meet his gaze so calmly. 'You may remember that I declined your offer of marriage, my lord,' she said steadily, 'and with it the privilege to a hold an opinion on your behaviour.'

She saw the flash of some emotion in his eyes, vivid as lightning, before his expression was veiled once more.

'Indeed. I do recall that.' His fingers brushed Sarah's cheek, sending shock waves tingling through her. It was terribly difficult to concentrate and even harder to remain indifferent to him when her whole body was responding to his touch. 'Is it possible to make you change your mind, Miss Sheridan?'

'I doubt it. But I have observed that you do not repine too much, my lord!' Sarah stepped back, her books clutched to her chest like a shield. She wished this had never started. The mockery in that intent dark gaze suggested that Guy was not going to let it go easily. 'Excuse me. I am tired and must retire.'

'In a minute.' The challenge in Guy's tone was more apparent now. 'I thought you were down here reading because you were unable to sleep, Miss Sheridan?'

'That was a half-hour ago.' Sarah took a wary step sideways. He moved negligently to block her path to the door.

'And now you find you are conveniently tired? I was hoping that you would indulge my curiosity and tell me why my offer of marriage was repugnant to you.'

Sarah frowned, aware of the quicksand at her feet. She did not wish to get involved in this conversation when she was tired and her emotions were worn to a thread. She felt intensely vulnerable, all too aware of this man and the power he could exert over her senses.

'I believe that that discussion must await a better occasion, my lord,' she said, a little huskily. 'It is late—'

She broke off as Guy took the books out of her hands and placed them very deliberately on the table beside her. He held her gaze with his. Sarah knew what was about to happen and knew also that he was giving her plenty of time—time to run away, time to make an excuse, any excuse, to leave before it was too late. She did not move. She felt breathless, incapable of anything other than standing there and watching him as he watched her. She could see a pulse beating in the hollow of his throat and felt a shocking urge to press her lips against the skin there... She tore her gaze away, but only to trace with her eyes the hard line of his jaw, the curve of his mouth...

Sarah was never sure which of them moved first. Guy's arms closed around her and it felt confusingly right to be there. This was a softer and sweeter kiss than the one at Amelia's ball and for a moment she freed herself a little.

'My lord, you mistake your companion—'

'Certainly not!' She felt Guy smile and it made her weak with longing. 'I could never mistake you for anyone else, Sarah. And if you think that I would ever let Allardyce touch you—'

His lips returned to hers before Sarah could reply. The last vestiges of common sense were draining from her mind, leaving her pliant in his arms. He was so gentle, but there was a current that ran hot beneath the tenderness. Sarah felt the tension uncoil within her. It was easy to forget that she did not trust him, that only an hour before he had probably held Lady Ann Walter in his arms... Jealousy, sharp and shocking drove through her like a knife. She stepped back and Guy released her at once. In the shadowy library it was impossible to read his expression.

'I must go.' Sarah knew she sounded breathless. 'Good night, my lord.'

Guy did not try to stop her, but she knew he watched her from the doorway as she made her way upstairs, and for some reason the knowledge made her want to cry.

* * *

The morning brought more snow, drifting white over ground that was already frozen hard. No one was stirring when Sarah donned her pelisse and boots, and went for a walk. She had not waited for breakfast, correctly assuming that there would be none. Later, when Amelia started to put her plans into practice, the food would definitely improve, but for now Sarah did not relish stale bread and cold coffee.

Close to the house lay the formal gardens, bare of colour now, the snow transforming the empty branches into ice sculptures. Sarah wandered beyond the rose garden and out into the park, her feet crunching on the frozen ground. At a little distance from the house, she turned to look back at the elegant façade of Blanchland, sitting serenely within its ring of trees. Sarah sighed. Was everything as deceptive as the view before her? Blanchland looked exactly as it had done ten years before, and yet the happy days of her childhood there were gone forever. Sir Ralph had turned the house into something unrecognisable, yet it looked just the same on the outside…

Sarah turned her back on the view before she became too melancholy. She did not want to think about the home she had lost, nor to think about Guy, to whom her thoughts inevitably turned. Her instincts told her to trust him, but at the same time a contradictory conviction suggested that he was hiding something from her. Perhaps he was as deceptive as the view.

The woodland closed about her and the dead leaves were crisp beneath her feet. Here, sheltered from the wintry breeze, was the little grotto that Lord Allardyce had referred to the night before. It had always been one of Sarah's favourite places.

She stooped to enter the mouth of the cave, then

straightened up and looked around. It was just as she remembered it. The faint light reflected off the shells that lined the interior, giving it a ghostly glow. In one corner, a natural spring bubbled softly over stones into a pool. It was very peaceful and made a nonsense of Allardyce's suggestions of black magic. Sarah sat down on the stone bench beside the pool and trailed her fingers in the icy cold water.

A shadow darkened the entrance and Sarah jumped, feeling relief as she recognised the newcomer. Perhaps Allardyce's stories had made her more nervous than she had realised.

'Tom! Good gracious, you startled me!'

'Sorry, Miss Sarah!' Tom Brookes touched his cap diffidently. 'Saw you walking this way and waited to catch you on your own.' He glanced over his shoulder and the very secrecy of the gesture made Sarah shiver a little. 'I've a message for you from Miss Meredith. She sent this for you.'

He fumbled in his pocket and took out a small package, wrapped in brown paper. Sarah looked at it curiously. 'But is there no letter, Tom?'

The gardener looked awkward. 'Don't know, ma'am. This was all I was given. From a friend of a friend, if you know what I mean…'

'And Olivia—where is she now?'

The gardener looked awkward. 'Can't say, ma'am, to be sure! At this very moment she could be in any number of places…'

Sarah smiled, understanding him. 'Very well. I shall not ask any more questions!' She put the little package in the pocket of her pelisse. 'Thank you, Tom. If I need to find you—'

'I'll be in the greenhouses, ma'am, trying to find flowers for Lady Amelia.'

Sarah smiled. 'A hard task in December! Amelia is a household tyrant, I fear! But I thank you, Tom.'

The gardener turned his cap around in his hands. 'Lovely job, ma'am,' he said, and the old West country phrase made Sarah smile again. She waited until she heard his footsteps crunch away from the grotto, then took the parcel out once more. Her fingers were a little clumsy with the cold, but eventually she managed to remove the brown paper and dropped the contents into the palm of her hand.

It was a locket.

Sarah gave an exclamation of surprise. The locket looked very old, for the pattern chased in the gold was worn and smooth beneath her fingers. The clasp opened with a tiny click to reveal the portraits inside. Sarah held it up to the light.

On the left was a lady with chestnut ringlets, sparkling brown eyes and a wide smile. She looked as though she would have been fun to know and Sarah's own smile widened in response to the obvious happiness that the painter had captured. She also looked a little familiar. The picture on the right... Sarah almost dropped the locket on to the stone floor. It was Guy's face that looked back at her from its setting in the golden frame: the thick fair hair, tied back here in an old-fashioned queue, the striking dark eyes, the high cheekbones and firm line of the mouth. The painted gaze seemed to mock Sarah's astonishment.

She looked back at the other portrait again. The lady was in a low-cut gown with one ringlet resting in the creamy hollow of her throat. Little of her dress was visible. But in Guy's picture the artist had at least included the bottle-green frieze coat that fitted those broad shoulders so well... Enlightenment came to Sarah in a blinding flash. The locket was old and the pictures were also antique, from at least fifty years before. The gentleman in the picture had to be Guy's grandfather.

Once Sarah had thought of this, the differences rather than the similarities seemed clear. The gentleman in the picture had the same unconsciously arrogant tilt to his head that Guy had, but none of Guy's easy humour was perceptible. The man's eyebrows were more heavily marked, adding to the air of aloofness, the dark gaze hooded. Sarah shivered a little. It was becoming cold in the grotto, and whilst the realisation that the man in the picture could not be Guy Renshaw brought some reassurance, it also raised questions she needed to consider. She got to her feet a little stiffly and turned towards the entrance.

Immediately, her foot scuffed a tiny scrap of paper that had fallen unnoticed from the locket when first she had opened it. Sarah bent to pick it up.

Miss S

Please meet me at the Folly Tower at twelve tonight.

Yours, O.

Sarah wrinkled up her nose. It seemed that Miss Meredith had a penchant for melodrama, for why else choose a midnight rendezvous at the ruined tower? In winter! Sarah shivered a third time at the thought and made for the pale sunshine she could see outside.

Once out in the daylight she carried on walking away from the house, all the while trying to make sense of the locket. Had Olivia Meredith sent it just to hide the note, or in an attempt to give her another, coded, message? More importantly, how had it fallen into Olivia's possession? It could hardly be a coincidence, so what was her connection with the Earls of Woodallan? Once again, Sarah remembered the mocking dark gaze of the portrait, the arrogant lift of the head. Finding such a trinket in Olivia's possession underlined the sinister role Guy seemed to be playing. Sarah remembered the conversation she had overheard between the Earl and his son. It had been important to find Olivia first, and Guy had been making enquiries, offering money… Sarah tried to make sense of the ever more complex pattern.

There was no reason to doubt that Olivia was Frank Sheridan's daughter, for her brother had told Sarah that himself. It seemed, however, that Olivia also had a connection with the Woodallan family that was not so clear. Sarah frowned as she remembered Guy assuring her that Frank had written to Lord Woodallan asking for his aid. That was probably true, although Frank's reason for asking now seemed more complicated than had first appeared. It could not be solely because Sarah was the Earl's goddaughter. Woodallan himself must also have some link with Olivia. Sarah shook her head over the questions with no answer. She could always ask Guy directly, but for some reason she hesitated over from such a course of action. His secretive behaviour had created a barrier between them.

'Miss Sheridan!'

Sarah jumped as the voice penetrated her thoughts. She had been walking almost aimlessly through the woods and now found herself back on the south side of Blanchland, where the frozen lake sparkled in the early sun. Coming towards her, a large brindled wolfhound at his heels, was Guy Renshaw himself.

Sarah blushed, aware of a feeling of guilty embarrassment. She was not sure whether it was her recollection of the previous night or her suspicions that were making her feel so uncomfortable, but facing Guy in the cold light of day was proving difficult. She said the first thing that came into her head. 'Good gracious, my lord, wherever did you find that dog?'

Guy laughed. He was looking as casually elegant as ever, his resemblance to the gentleman in the locket very pronounced. It made Sarah feel very self-conscious.

'I believe he has adopted me! He is Sir Ralph's pet and of a wholly gentle disposition!'

Sarah watched dubiously as the hound ran off to sniff excitedly amongst the reeds. 'He seems very happy to have some exercise! I doubt Sir Ralph is prone to taking long walks!'

Guy fell into step beside her, glancing at her with a look of such evident admiration that Sarah was once again forcibly reminded of the scene in the library. A deeper shade of colour crept into her cheeks that she hoped could be attributed to the chill morning air. She quickened her step towards the house. Some thirty yards ahead of them stood the Folly, a small tower built by Lord Sheridan in a position that gave a superb view of the surrounding countryside. It immediately brought Olivia to the forefront of Sarah's mind again.

'Perhaps we could all go skating this afternoon,' Guy was saying thoughtfully. 'The ice looks thick enough to be safe. Did you skate here as a child, Miss Sheridan?'

Sarah wrenched her mind away from the mystery of Olivia and her locket and answered him slightly at random. 'Skating? Oh, yes, it was great fun! I have not tried for years, but I believe I would not have lost the skill.'

'You sound as though you were thinking of something else, Miss Sheridan,' Guy observed acutely, giving her a searching look from his very dark eyes. 'Perhaps it is Miss Meredith who occupies your thoughts? Do you have any plans to continue your search today?'

Sarah mentally damned him for his perception. 'I had not thought of it,' she lied, evading his eyes. 'Since I made little progress yesterday, I am at a loss to know what to do next. And you, my lord?' She recovered her poise sufficiently to look straight at him. 'Do you have any plans in that direction?'

Guy shrugged easily. 'I think not. I am, however, entirely at your disposal if you wish me to escort you—'

'Oh, no,' Sarah said, too quickly, 'I should not put you to that trouble, sir! That is, if I should decide to make further enquiries…'

'Of course.' Guy rescued her smoothly from her floundering. His perceptive gaze swept over her once more. 'If you should change your mind, Miss Sheridan—'

'Oh, I shall not!' Sarah said hastily. 'I feel too tired today to go venturing far!' The locket and the note seemed to be burning a hole in her pocket and she turned her face away to hide her confusion.

'The consequence of your late night excursion to the library, I expect!' The mockery was back in Guy's tone. 'I trust you found your way back to your bed safely, Miss Sheridan!'

Sarah could feel herself blushing. 'Of course! I am not afraid of Blanchland after dark, my lord! I grew up here! Now, if you will excuse me, it grows cold and I would wish to be indoors.'

Guy bowed slightly. 'I will see you later then, Miss Sheridan! If you are fortunate, you may find that your cousin has brewed some coffee and provided breakfast! I know she was working on it as I left the house!'

Sarah watched his tall figure stroll towards the lake again, the dog trotting eagerly at his heels. She did not believe him when he said that he had no interest in pursuing his search for Miss Meredith any further. There was a lump in her throat that felt like unshed tears and the hard outline of the locket scored her fingers. With a sigh, Sarah turned to ascend the steps to the terrace. She knew she was as bad as he, for she had lied, too. The sad fact was that she did not trust him, but now the deceit was becoming intolerable.

When Sarah got back to the house she found not only coffee and fresh bread in the breakfast room, but what appeared to be a whole army of maids cleaning the dining-room under Amelia's watchful eye.

'I simply could not bear to eat another meal in such disgustingly dirty surroundings,' her cousin greeted her. 'I have high hopes that this afternoon we may start to tackle the bedchambers, for I fear there may be fleas and worse—'

Here she broke off as the crashing of moving furniture became too loud to sustain a conversation. When matters quietened down again she added mischievously, 'Lady Tilney and Lady Ann are in the morning-room should you wish to avoid them, my dear! They were both much put out to be disturbed by all the noise!' Amelia gave a little giggle. 'I fear Lady Tilney looks quite raddled in the daylight and Lady Ann is much the worse for too little sleep! I offered them my rose petal cream to rejuvenate their skin, but they declined!'

Sarah tried not to laugh. 'Amelia—'

'Oh, I have only just begun,' her cousin said, understanding perfectly Sarah's unspoken question. Her eyes sparkled. 'There is no end to the commotion I can cause when I try!'

'And Greville? Have you seen him today?'

Amelia's smile became positively angelic. 'Poor Greville! I believe he has a headache this morning! I have mixed him a concoction of raw eggs, tomato extract and liquorice!'

'Oh, Amelia!' Sarah started to laugh. 'Almost I pity him! And how does Sir Ralph take this transformation of his house?'

'Oh, Sir Ralph is most impressed!' Amelia said blithely. 'He told me I was a spirited little filly and that I had a free hand to do whatever I wished! So…' She picked up a duster and started to wield it industriously.

'Maybe he will not feel so happy when he discovers the keys to his wine cellar are lost,' Sarah mused.

'Maybe not,' Amelia confirmed with a smile, 'but by then it will be too late!'

It was a day of irritating inactivity. Sir Ralph's guests all declared themselves too exhausted by their early rising to even think of skating that afternoon, and they whiled away a few hours in the library with Sir Ralph's prized collection of erotic French lithographs. When Sarah went down to the lake she discovered that the ice was too thin to risk going out and later it began to snow in earnest, huge flakes falling from a pewter sky, so she retired to her room with a book. She tried to ignore the ribald laughter and conversation that floated up the stairs.

Guy had disappeared at some point in the afternoon

and did not reappear until dinner and, despite her attempts to think on other matters, Sarah could not but wonder where he had gone. The rendezvous with Olivia weighed on her mind. It seemed a long time until midnight.

Dinner was a meal quite unlike the previous night. It soon became apparent that Amelia had taught the cook some simple but nutritious recipes, for the first course was a delicious vegetable soup, followed by trout in a white wine sauce. The eyes of all the guests lit up as they took their first tentative mouthfuls, and even Mr Fisk woke up with the words, 'Food! Excellent!'

Mrs Fisk looked somewhat discontented by the fact that her spouse stayed awake for the entire meal, but this was nothing to the emotions of the others on finding that there was no wine. At first, when a large jug of ice-cold water had been brought in, no one had commented, but as the meal progressed and the famous Blanchland wines were not forthcoming, Lady Tilney could not contain herself.

'Turned puritan, Ralph?' she asked coyly, fluttering her lashes at him. 'Or are you trying to reform us all?'

Sir Ralph looked discomfited.

'Lady Amelia—' he began, to break off at once, clearly unable to criticise Amelia after she had magically produced such delicious food. Sarah, knowing that the responsibility for the absence of wine lay firmly at Amelia's door, waited with amusement to see what would happen next.

Her cousin had been conversing with Justin Lebeter and looked up at the expectant pause.

'The wine? Oh, dear, I was hoping that you would not ask…' She cast her eyes down modestly. 'I fear the key was lost when we did our cleaning today. The maids swear that they have scoured the house for it, but it cannot be found…'

There was an outcry, but it came mainly from the ladies.

'No wine? How dreadful! How shall we survive! Sir Ralph, pray do something!'

Guy caught Sarah's eye with a quizzical lift to his eyebrows, but she kept her expression to one of limpid innocence. She was not going to give Amelia away.

'Surely there is wine in this exquisite sauce?' Greville Baynham said, his gaze challenging Amelia's across the table.

Amelia sighed. 'Oh, yes, but that was the last of yesterday's bottles. And I do feel that too much wine can dull the palate. Do you not agree, Lord Lebeter?'

Justin Lebeter looked as though he was about to agree with anything Amelia would care to say. Lady Tilney gave a snort of disapproval.

'I am happy for my palate to suffer in a good cause!'

'Indeed!' Amelia said sweetly. 'I suspected that your taste was already jaded, Lady Tilney!'

Sarah thought she heard Greville smother a laugh.

'You promised me a bath in the vintage champagne, Ralphie,' Mrs Fisk grumbled petulantly from further down the table. 'You said it was one of the specialities!'

'Damned waste!' her husband grunted. Mrs Fisk glared malevolently.

'Did you know anything about this, Miss Sheridan?' Lord Allardyce asked with a sly smile. 'You are deep in your cousin's confidence, after all!'

Sarah returned the smile very pleasantly. 'I knew the keys were lost, of course,' she admitted, 'but then I realised that there was this refreshing spring water to replace it! Have you tried it, Lord Allardyce? It comes from the spring in the grotto and is so very bracing!'

Allardyce wrinkled up his nose with distaste. 'I thank you, but no, Miss Sheridan! Water is for the peasants!'

'You will become quite thirsty, then!' Sarah said, applying herself to her food.

There was an ill-tempered silence for a while.

'You must send to Bath for more wine tomorrow, Ralph!' Lady Tilney said stridently. 'This is really not to be borne!'

'The roads are so bad that I imagine it will take several days for the wine merchant to reach us,' Amelia said, smiling brightly.

'Perhaps Lord Renshaw will take pity on you and send to Woodallan for supplies!' Sarah put in, with a quick sideways look at his lordship. 'For myself, I could drink the spring water for days!'

'I cannot imagine that it could be good for us!' Lady Ann Walter shuddered. 'There may be so many noxious substances that have drained into it! Why, it could be quite poisonous!'

'But perhaps quite improving for the skin, Lady Ann,' Amelia suggested blandly.

Her ladyship flushed angrily.

Something seemed to have happened to the spirit of the house party, Sarah thought, as they all turned back to their food again and the silence became prolonged. It could not simply be the wine, but there was an atmosphere of near gloom in the dining-room. Amelia, eating heartily, seemed quite unaware of it. Even Lord Allardyce, so suggestive the previous evening, confined his conversation to platitudes about the weather. Once the meal was ended, no one lingered at the table and, as there was no port to circulate, the ladies and gentlemen all retired for a game of whist. It was, Sarah thought, one of the few vices still left to them.

At fifteen minutes to midnight that night, Sarah donned her cloak and boots and slipped out of her room. Since dinner, she had watched the clock and found herself unable to settle to doing anything to pass the time.

There was a light still showing under the drawing-room door as Sarah crept across the hall, and she tried to open the front door as silently as possible. The snow had stopped and the sky was clear with a bright white moon. It was an eerie but beautiful scene. Sarah hesitated. Her footsteps would be all too clear in the snow, visible to anyone who chose to look. She could only hope that no one would be abroad that night and that more snow would fall before morning.

She set off at a brisk pace, keeping in the moon shadows and taking as much cover as she could from the trees. The night was very quiet, though every so often some snow would tumble from the branches, making Sarah jump. Despite telling Guy earlier that nothing at Blanchland frightened her, she was distinctly nervous and wishing that Olivia had suggested a meeting in a nice warm parlour instead of a lonely tower. It seemed most sensible to keep the meeting as brief as possible, and suggest another appointment in the daylight—unless Olivia's situation was so extreme that she needed help at once. Sarah paused to consider the possibility. She had no idea what she would find at the Folly Tower and felt woefully unprepared.

She had just crossed a clearing deep in snow when a scuffling sound behind her made Sarah freeze and spin around. She could see no one lurking under the trees, but some sixth sense told her that she was not alone, and, whilst she hesitated over whether or not to call out, a dark figure detached itself from the shadows and hurried forward. Sarah's instinctive squeak of alarm died unheard and she let out her breath on an angry sigh.

'Amelia! What the—what on earth are you doing here?'

'I heard you leave the house and I followed you,' her cousin said, somewhat out of breath. 'What are you doing here, Sarah?'

'Never mind what I am doing!' Sarah gave Amelia's arm a shake. 'How could you be so foolish, Milly? Why, you could have got lost, or fallen into danger—'

'All the more reason why you should not be wandering around on your own, then!' her cousin replied with spirit. 'Where are you going, Sarah?'

'I am going to the Folly to meet Miss Meredith,' Sarah said crossly. In the distance she heard the faint chimes of the Blanchland church clock. 'There's no time to explain now, for I am late as it is! I suppose you had better come with me!'

'Who is Miss Meredith?' Amelia enquired, trotting along behind Sarah through the wood. 'And why are you arranging a meeting in the middle of the night?'

Sarah smiled despite herself. She was amazed at how much better she felt to have some company. 'Miss Meredith is my niece and the reason I came to Blanchland. As to why—'

'Your niece!' Sarah marvelled at Amelia's instinct for gossip even under such circumstances. 'You mean that she is Frank's daughter? But Frank never had a child—'

'This is no time for a rehearsal of the Sheridan genealogy,' Sarah hissed back. She almost stumbled over a tree root and put out a hand to steady herself. 'Oh, this is ridiculous! I wish the wretched girl did not have such a sense of the dramatic!'

They were reaching the crown of the hill and came out of the trees to see the dark bulk of the tower looming before them. Amelia clutched at Sarah's cloak.

'Sarah, are you sure about this? Why can you not meet up in daylight? I do not like this!'

'Nonsense!' Sarah knew that one of them had to be bracing or they would both run away in a fit of panic. 'We are going to meet a seventeen-year-old girl, not a monster! Pray go back if you do not wish to stay with me!'

Amelia shuddered. 'I will not walk on my own through the wood! Where is the girl, then? There is nobody here!'

Sarah pushed open the tower door and peered into the interior. It was pitch-black. The Folly Tower had been built by her great-grandfather and on a fine day one could see three counties and the sea from the top, but tonight Sarah could not even see in front of her nose.

'Olivia?' It came out as half-whisper, half-croak. Sarah cleared her throat and drew breath to call again. The words were never spoken. Something soft and smothering pressed down over her head and she was grasped in an iron grip. Beside her, she heard Amelia start to scream and then someone dropped her hard on the stone floor of the tower and all hell seemed to break out around her.

The confusion resolved itself so quickly that Sarah could almost have imagined it. Within seconds, Amelia's screams had died away and the suffocating cloth was removed from Sarah's face. She struggled to sit up and found herself cradled in gentle arms that held her firmly but surely. A lantern had been placed on the stone floor and cast a small pool of light about them. Sir Greville Baynham was standing behind the lantern and Amelia was kneeling and peering into Sarah's face with so fearful an expression that her cousin almost burst out laughing.

'Oh, Sarah, are you much hurt? He dropped you with such a jolt I was sure you had broken some bones!'

Sarah moved a little gingerly and the restraining arms that held her loosened their grip very slightly. She did not need to turn her head to know that it was Guy who held her; the feel of his arms was familiar and the warmth of his body against hers was reassuring, but she had to break the contact.

'I am very well,' she said a little shakily, gratefully accepting Greville's help to ease her to her feet, 'but whatever happened? Someone attacked me—I was certain they were about to carry me off!'

'Most probably they would have done had we not arrived in time!' Guy said drily. He was still holding her with a steadying hand under her elbow. Both he and Greville were dressed in dark cloaks and the snow was falling off their boots onto the floor. 'Somebody ran out of the tower as Lady Amelia started to scream, but they were lost in the darkness before we could see them. We did not pursue them, for our first thoughts were for the two of you. It is fortunate that we arrived when we did.'

Sarah thought it fortunate, perhaps, but also deeply suspicious. How had Guy and Greville come to be wandering about the wood at precisely the time she had arranged to meet Olivia? And where was Olivia now? Someone in addition to herself had obviously known of the rendezvous. It would be better to keep very quiet on the subject of her own activities. Aware that some difficult questions were about to be asked, Sarah avoided Guy's too-perceptive gaze and made a business of brushing the dirt from her cloak.

'Well, I am grateful to you both,' she said guardedly. 'Some poacher taken by surprise, I expect! There is no harm done!'

'The point in question is how the devil did you come to be taking a walk at this time of night, Miss Sheridan?' Guy said forcefully. 'Have you taken leave of your senses?'

Sarah glared at him. She only just managed to swallow the retort that sprang to her lips, aware that he could provoke her into a response all too easily and that she might give something away.

'Perhaps Lady Amelia would care to answer that question,' Greville said smoothly, stepping forward into the light. 'I have noticed that where your cousin leads, you are not far behind, ma'am! Or is it the other way about?'

Sarah and Amelia exchanged a quick glance. Amelia gave a careless little shrug.

'Why, it is no great matter, Sir Greville! Sarah could not sleep and, as I had not yet retired, we decided to take a short walk. The snow looks very pretty in the moonlight!'

'Not from inside a darkened tower!' Greville said grimly. 'Next you will be telling me that you thought to climb to the top to look at the view! What nonsense is this?'

Amelia's lips were set in a mutinous line. She picked up the lantern. 'Let us not stand about here in the cold! Poor Sarah will be wanting her bed!'

'At the least, it will have cured her insomnia,' Guy

said, with an ironic lift to his eyebrows. 'A persistent affliction, Miss Sheridan! Can you improve on Lady Amelia's version, ma'am? It lacks something in originality!'

Sarah did not meet his eyes. 'It is as Amelia says, my lord. We thought it would be pleasant to take the air!'

'Cut line, Miss Sheridan,' Guy countered derisively, 'and spare us the tales of moonlit views, fresh night air and the like! I never heard so thin a tale!'

Sarah looked at both of them. Guy was planted foursquare before her, his expression unyielding. Greville was beside the door, giving the impression that they were unlikely to be allowed out until they came up with the truth. The flickering lantern cast huge shadows up into the vaulted roof and gave the whole scene an appearance of unreality. Sarah gave Guy a challenging glance.

'Very well, my lord! If you don't like my tale, perhaps you can offer an alternative!'

Their gazes locked, Sarah's defiant, Guy's thoughtful. He shifted slightly.

'A midnight rendezvous seems most likely, Miss Sheridan!'

Sarah's eyes narrowed. How far would he go to discover the truth? She knew that he had things to hide, just as she had, but she judged him eminently capable of calling her bluff. There was no doubt that this was very awkward.

'I am not in the habit of arranging night-time trysts, sir,' she snapped. 'No doubt the atmosphere of Blanchland is affecting your judgement!'

'I was not suggesting that you were creeping away secretly to meet Allardyce,' Guy said pleasantly, 'for you have your cousin with you! Although, perhaps, knowing his tastes—'

Sarah blushed bright red and it was Amelia who threw herself into the breach.

'I see that your observations are as offensive as ever, sir! If it comes to that, how do you explain your timely but somewhat questionable arrival?' She turned sharply on Greville. 'Perhaps Sir Greville would care to answer? Is Sir Ralph holding one of his bacchanals in the woods tonight?'

Greville started to laugh. Amelia looked so furious at this inappropriate response that Sarah was glad she was holding the lantern and unable to set about him with her bare hands. Now that her temper was up, there was no stopping her.

'By what right do you question us anyway, Sir Greville?' Amelia demanded hotly. 'Even if we choose to go *dancing* in the woods all night long, it would be none of your affair! Kindly mind your own business!'

Greville gave her a derisive little bow. 'My dear Amelia, I only question your behaviour as I fear you are setting your cousin a bad example! You, an older woman, should take it upon yourself to act responsibly—'

'Monstrous!' It sounded to Sarah as though Amelia was about to explode. The lantern wavered dangerously and she took it out of her cousin's wayward grip, then wondered if she should have done so when it appeared Amelia was about to slap Greville. He caught her arm in a negligent grip and turned towards the doorway.

'Fascinating as this encounter is, Lady Amelia, I feel we should be taking up your suggestion and returning to the house. Miss Sheridan, could you light the way?'

'Allow me,' Guy said, taking the lantern. 'I should

not like to be at the mercy of your somewhat dubious sense of direction, Miss Sheridan!'

Sarah was beginning to feel as annoyed as her cousin, who was arguing with Greville in a furious undertone. Before she could frame a blistering reply, however, another figure stumbled out of the trees and into the circle of light at the folly entrance.

'Renshaw?' a voice said incredulously. 'Baynham? What the deuce—'

It was Lord Lebeter who came towards them, blushing suddenly as he saw Sarah and Amelia. 'Ladies! I beg your pardon! I thought—'

It was evident to Sarah exactly what Lord Lebeter was thinking. In a place like Blanchland, where no activity was apparently too outlandish, he must have thought he had stumbled into some new entertainment.

'Evening, Lebeter,' Guy said laconically. 'Do you suffer from sleeplessness also?'

'Oh…' Justin Lebeter looked self-conscious. 'A short stroll before I turn in… Thought I saw a light up here…'

'We were just returning,' Sarah said helpfully, as his words ground to a halt. 'Would you care to walk back with us, sir?'

Nobody spoke as they trudged back through the snow and it seemed to Sarah that a distinctly awkward atmosphere had settled over the group. The presence of Justin Lebeter at least ensured that neither Guy nor Greville persisted in any awkward questions, but Sarah knew that they would scarcely give up so easily. Once they got back to the house, both Sarah and Amelia made sure that they divested themselves of boots and cloaks so quickly that the gentlemen had no further opportunity to interrogate them.

As she mounted the stairs, Sarah's mind was full of

all the unsolved issues. To the question of the locket was now added the reason for Guy and Greville's presence at the tower, the absence of Olivia, the mystery attacker… And what had Lord Lebeter been doing strolling about the woods at midnight? Matters were becoming all too complicated…

Sarah pushed open her bedroom door and set the candle down on the bedside stand. A movement in the corner of the room caught her eye and she spun round with a muffled gasp.

In a chair by the wall was a slender young lady, watching her with huge, apprehensive brown eyes. As Sarah recoiled, she said hastily, 'Miss Sheridan? I do beg your pardon for intruding in such a way, but it was my only chance! I am Olivia Meredith, and so very happy to make your acquaintance!'

Chapter Eight

Miss Olivia Meredith bore a startling resemblance to both the portraits in the locket and also to the current Viscount Renshaw. Sarah stared, and reflected that there could now be no question over her relationship to the Woodallan family. Here was the same thick blonde hair, tied in long braids in Miss Meredith's case, and the deep brown eyes that provided such a striking contrast to her fairness. Olivia's face was the oval shape of the lady in the locket, but her other features were discernibly from the Sheridan side of the family, and it gave Sarah a curious feeling to see the fusion. Here was an example of what a child might look like if it had herself and Guy for parents.

Sarah realised that she was staring and that Olivia, huddled deep in the armchair, was looking even more apprehensive than before.

'Forgive me, Miss Meredith,' she said hastily, 'it is just that you remind me—' Sarah broke off, suddenly remembering that Olivia might have no idea of her parentage.

'I am sorry if I startled you, ma'am,' the girl said quickly. 'I could think of no other way of meeting you in private! It was Tom's idea—Tom Brookes, you know—for he and his family have been hiding me.'

'I see,' Sarah said slowly, coming forward and taking off her cloak. 'Then the meeting at the Folly Tower—'

'Oh, it was all a ruse! Tom knew that if he let a few rumours drop that I would be at the Folly, Lord Allardyce would leave the house and the coast would be clear for me to seek you out here!'

'I see!' Sarah said again, grimly. 'I must remember to congratulate Tom on his strategy! Having us all tripping about in the snow must have afforded him considerable satisfaction!'

Olivia let out a peal of laughter, then clapped her hand hastily to her mouth. 'Oh, dear, how dreadful! I am so sorry, Miss Sheridan, but you see, we had to thwart Lord Allardyce at all costs!'

The fire had burned down and Olivia was shivering a little, though whether from cold or the thought of Allardyce, Sarah could not guess. She stirred it to a glow, then sat back on her heels to survey her niece.

'Is Lord Allardyce the reason you wrote to Mr Churchward? You must tell me how I can help you, Miss Meredith. But first—are you hungry or thirsty? I can always send to the kitchen for some food—'

But Olivia was shaking her head. 'Oh, no, thank you, Miss Sheridan. Mrs Tom feeds me very well! I will not keep you from your bed for long, but if I could just explain my difficulties...'

'Of course,' Sarah said. She sat down opposite. Olivia's head was bent, a shade of colour in her cheeks. She played nervously with a pleat of her skirt.

'Tom Brookes told me that you had come to help me,' Olivia said, in a rush. 'When I wrote to Mr Churchward, I scarce expected that he would ask you to come here yourself—' She broke off, looking confused, to start again, a deeper pink colour now in her pale face.

'I think you should know, Miss Sheridan, that my mother—my adoptive mother,' she corrected herself carefully, 'told me of my connection with your family a few years ago. Believe me, I have no wish to push myself on your notice, but I had nowhere else to turn!'

Sarah smiled at her niece's anxious face. 'There is no question of you putting yourself forward, or being unwelcome, or anything like that, Miss Meredith! You know now that I am your aunt, and I am very happy to have found you!'

Olivia smiled back a little tremulously. 'Thank you. I must own that it is strange to find I have another family and I am sorry—' her face fell '—that I never knew your brother, my...father.'

'Yes.' Sarah hesitated, trying to think of something both true and complimentary to tell Olivia about Frank Sheridan. 'I was very fond of Frank. He was...a most interesting and charming man and I am sure he would have liked you, Olivia. I may call you Olivia, may I not?'

'Oh, please!' Olivia had started to look a little happier.

'And you must call me Sarah, for I cannot bear to be called 'Aunt'! It makes me feel far too old!'

Olivia giggled. 'I cannot believe that you are many years older than I, Miss—Sarah! It will be like having a sister!'

'Excellent! We must talk much more, but perhaps the most pressing matter is for you to tell me how I can help you, Olivia. Your letter to Mr Churchward suggested that you were in either grave danger or dire need;

as I have already met Lord Allardyce, I can perhaps imagine—'

The light fled from Olivia's face, leaving it looking pinched and cold again. Sarah leant forward and instinctively touched her hand. 'Come! It cannot be so bad—'

'I am sorry,' Olivia said in a rush. 'It is such a silly matter, but I did not know where to turn. Oh, I am not explaining myself at all well—'

'Start at the beginning,' Sarah counselled, settling back in her chair. 'You were away at school in Oxford until recently, I believe?'

'Oh, yes! I came back to Blanchland only a few months ago. Mama was worrying about what I should do here, for I know she wishes to see me respectably settled and there is so little society hereabouts! Until recently I believed that she hoped I might go to Bath for a season, but there were insufficient funds. I believe Father had not invested wisely and when Mama became ill—' Olivia shrugged prettily '—all our remaining money had to go on medicines. I did not repine, for I was sure that matters would resolve! The family of one of my school friends offered to help me find a position—a governess or companion would have done, I should not have minded! But then…'

Olivia stopped and looked away into the fire. 'Then Lord Allardyce came here, to Blanchland.'

Sarah had been quite still during Sarah's rehearsal of the events that had led to this point. She could imagine Mrs Meredith's hopes and fears for her daughter, the unlucky investment of the money given by Lord Sheridan, the difficulties as Olivia's prospects shrank with the loss of fortune. She had seen it herself—without money it was always a struggle. Sarah knew that she had been lucky to have both a family name to ensure her position in society and a rich cousin willing to help her. Olivia had had neither, but had still determined not to call in the debt owed by her father's family. Not until Lord Allardyce had come to Blanchland…

'I first met him in the village and he was most attentive,' Olivia continued. 'He took to calling on us and Mama was most excited—I believe she thought I might catch an Earl! But I did not like him, nor did I believe that his intentions were at all honourable!'

Remembering Allardyce's penchant for the pure and innocent to refresh his jaded palate, Sarah could well imagine why Olivia would appeal to him. Not only was she young and beautiful, but she had an utterly unspoilt quality.

'Then, one day, he called when Mama was from home and although I refused at first to see him, he insisted. He asked me—' Olivia looked up, caught Sarah's eye, blushed and looked away. 'In short, he proposed that I should become his mistress. He promised me all manner of comforts to ease my life, but at such a price! Believe me, Miss—Sarah, I was not even tempted!'

'I believe you,' Sarah said truthfully. There was something so transparently innocent about Olivia that Allardyce's proposal could not help but be repugnant to her. 'But I do not suppose that Lord Allardyce took his dismissal lightly?'

'No, indeed! He pestered me for days until I scarce dared step outdoors! And then he came to us one day, all triumphant, to tell us that he had purchased the lease of the house from Sir Ralph and that he would throw us into the street unless I agreed to his demands!'

Sarah sighed. It was so simple when one had the means. Allardyce would barely have noticed the price of a lease and it was just the lever he needed. Mrs Meredith, whose health was not strong in the first place, would have been almost beside herself with worry.

'What did you do, Olivia?'

Miss Meredith sat up a little straighter. 'Why, I set off straight away to come here to see—'

'Sir Ralph?'

'No…' Olivia looked momentarily confused '…Lord Lebeter!'

For a moment Sarah wondered whether she had been listening properly. The sudden introduction of Justin Lebeter into the situation threw her briefly, until she reflected that, with a young lady as lovely as Miss Meredith, there would surely be a welcome suitor as well as a villainous one. It probably explained Lord Lebeter's surprising appearance at the Tower earlier that evening. He, too, must have heard the rumour that Miss Meredith would be there, and had gone to find her.

'Are you then already acquainted with Lord Lebeter?' Sarah asked carefully.

'Oh, yes!' Where Olivia had been cast down before, her eyes now sparkled very brightly indeed. 'Lord Lebeter is the brother of one of my school friends, you see, and I met him originally at her house. Then, when my circumstances changed, I did not believe that I should ever see him again. Imagine my feelings when I saw him riding through Blanchland village one day!'

Sarah raised her eyebrows. In the face of this dewy-eyed bliss she suddenly felt a very old aunt indeed.

'Of course,' Olivia added, blushing, 'I was a little cast down to think of him staying here, for Sir Ralph's parties have such a shocking reputation! But he is so truly the perfect gentleman that I cannot believe—' She stopped, overcome by natural delicacy.

'So when you were in trouble, you naturally turned to Lord Lebeter,' Sarah prompted.

'Oh, yes! But the terrible thing was that he had just that morning left Blanchland to visit in Devon, and when I approached the house I was met instead by Lord Allardyce! I was so afraid of what he might do that I ran away, which was how Tom found me, and the rest you know!'

Sarah felt slightly breathless at the dash through the events that had led to Olivia's disappearance. 'I am sorry to appear a slow-top,' she said, 'but if I could just clarify a few points—'

'Oh, of course!' Olivia said obligingly. 'What is it that you wish to know?'

'Well, firstly, how did you come to write to Mr Churchward?'

'Oh, Mama suggested that as soon as Lord Allardyce started importuning me! But I thought to turn to Lord Lebeter first!'

'Of course. And when you ran away from Lord Allardyce, Tom helped you—'

'Yes, for he found me hiding in his greenhouse!'

'I see. And he has been hiding you ever since?'

'We thought it was a good idea,' Olivia explained. 'Lord Allardyce has been looking everywhere, but of course he did not think of the servants! And, as Tom works here, he was able to watch Lord Allardyce and make sure that he did not get too close.'

'I see,' Sarah said again. 'Were you not tempted to seek Lord Lebeter's help once he returned here?'

Olivia's eyes sparkled again. 'I was, but Tom and Mrs Tom thought it a bad idea. They were afraid that Lord Lebeter might be as bad as Lord Allardyce, and though I knew that could not possibly be true, I could see that such a course of action would not be at all respectable! Besides, I had written to Mr Churchward by then and Tom advised me to await his reply. When he saw that you had come to help me, Sarah, he said that everything would be all right and tight and that, if Lord Allardyce kicked up a fuss, you would set your cousin on him! Is she very fearsome, Sarah?'

'Very!' Sarah said, lips twitching at the thought of Tom's description of Amelia. 'But I am sure that she will like you, Olivia! She is your relative, too!'

Olivia looked very struck by this, but also rather apprehensive. 'Well, I hope she may like me, for I wish to meet her above all things! So, what do we do now, Sarah?'

Sarah sat back. 'I think, perhaps, that you should come back to Bath with us, Olivia, and your mama, too, of course. I shall speak to Amelia in the morning. Lord Allardyce will not trouble you once he sees you have friends to help you, and once we are in Bath we may consult Mr Churchward over the lease of your house, and speak to Amelia's man of business about the investments, and make lots of plans! How does that suit you?'

Olivia's eyes had regained their sparkle. 'Oh, may we indeed? You are so kind! Why, I think that would be the most exciting thing in the whole world!'

'And, of course,' Sarah said with a twinkle, 'we shall give Lord Lebeter your direction in case he wishes to call! Now, can you be ready to travel tomorrow?'

Olivia's face fell a little. 'I fear that Mama is not very strong at present and will not be well enough to go for a day or two, although such good news will lift her spirits! I am so sorry, Sarah!'

It was bad news, but Sarah swallowed her disappointment. Her instinct was to take Olivia away from Blanchland as soon as possible, but it was clearly unfeasible to do so without Mrs Meredith's presence at her daughter's side. That left the dilemma of what to do with Olivia in the meantime, for Sarah had no illusions as to the lengths Allardyce might go to thwart her plans. It was essential to prevent him from finding her niece and every delay meant danger.

'Can Tom continue to hide you, Olivia?' she asked cautiously. 'He seems to have been most adept at it so far, and we must be careful until we have you well away from here. I should not like Lord Allardyce to find you—'

'No, indeed!' Olivia shuddered. 'I am sure that we may stay with Tom a little longer. I am sorry for the delay, Sarah, but I am sure Mama will be recovered directly.'

The grandfather clock in the hall struck one. Olivia was yawning and Sarah felt quite exhausted. She stood up. 'I should not keep you any longer, Olivia, for you look quite done up! Oh, but there is something I must return to you!'

Sarah reached across for her cloak and dug deeply into the pocket. Olivia's note and the locket were still there. Sarah took it out and handed it to her niece.

'You will be wanting this back, for it is very pretty. Do you know where it came from, Olivia?'

Olivia wrinkled her brow. 'I thought...that is, I have had it since I can remember and I rather thought that it was a present from my father, but—' She broke off, uncertain, watching Sarah's face. 'Am I mistaken, then? It is just that I look so very like him—like the man in the picture!'

Sarah hesitated. It was understandable that Olivia

would think the locket a gift from the Sheridan side of the family, but she knew that it had never been one of their heirlooms. On the other hand, so strong a resemblance to the Woodallans could hardly be by chance. Sarah took a deep breath.

'I wondered whether the locket was from your mother,' she said carefully.

The colour flooded Olivia's face in a huge wave. 'Oh! I cannot believe so! I do not know who my mother was, but I understood her to be a servant or—' she stopped, and finished poignantly '—I hoped you might be able to tell me, Sarah!'

Sarah did not think twice but went across and hugged her. 'I do not know who told you that she was a servant, Olivia, and even were it true it would not matter! We know your father was my brother, and that makes you a Sheridan, but now I have seen the locket, I may be able to find out who your mother was as well. Be patient—I will do what I can!'

Olivia hugged her back hard. 'It is enough that I have found you, Sarah! More than enough, for I cannot believe my good fortune!'

Sarah swallowed the huge lump in her throat and let her go. 'It is nice for me to have family, too! Now, does Tom have some cunning plan to spirit you out of the house again?'

Her niece wrapped herself up in her cloak once more. 'I must go down to the servants' door and he will be waiting!' The spark of excitement rekindled in her eyes. 'This is all very dramatic, is it not?'

'Very,' Sarah agreed, wondering if it was her age that left her preferring a slightly more mundane existence. 'Surely Tom does not expect you to descend the main stair, though? I am disappointed in the man! I had pictured a far more ingenious scheme!'

She moved towards the door. 'I will go first and check that the coast is clear. Keep well hidden over the next few days, Olivia, and if you have need of me, send word by Tom. As soon as your mama is well enough to travel, we shall be away to Bath!'

She kissed her niece on the cheek. 'Now, take care and I will see you soon, for we have much to discuss!'

She watched as her niece sped away down the stairs and was swallowed up in the shadows. The servants' door closed behind her with a soft click and Sarah turned back to her room. It seemed very quiet without Olivia's bright presence. Sarah sighed. She had a lot to think about, but she was too tired to make sense of it now. Wearily she prepared for bed, and was almost instantly asleep.

Sarah woke late, roused only by the tap on her door as Amelia came in bearing a breakfast tray.

'You are very wise to stay in your room, my dear!' she greeted her cousin cheerfully. 'Sir Greville has already been quizzing me about last night's escapade and I thought Lord Renshaw would dispense with the proprieties and march in here to demand an explanation!' She saw Sarah's look of alarm. 'Oh, I have told him nothing, but the tale of insomnia is wearing a little thin and anyway...' she put the tray down on the end of the bed '...I wish to know myself what is going on! Do try this fresh bread,' she added, pushing a plate towards her cousin. 'I have taught the cook bread-making and this is her first attempt! Not bad, I think!'

Sarah sat up and pulled the tray toward her. There

were rolls with butter and honey and the most delicious-smelling cup of chocolate.

'What do you wish to know, then?' she asked with her mouth full.

'Why, everything!' Amelia looked affronted. 'You have an unknown niece whom you were to meet at the Folly Tower last night! Tell me about that, for a beginning!'

Whilst she ate her breakfast, Sarah slowly recounted the whole of Olivia's story, from Churchward's visit to the surprise of finding her waiting in her room the previous night. The only part she left out was her suspicions of Guy's conduct and Olivia's speaking resemblance to the Woodallan family. That felt too personal to share, even with Amelia, but Sarah was beginning to realise that she would have to sort the matter out with Guy, and soon. When she had finished, Amelia gave a heavy sigh.

'That loathsome man, Allardyce! Can we not spirit Miss Meredith away from here at once, Sarah?'

Sarah shook her head slowly. 'I wish we could do so, Milly, but Mrs Meredith will scarcely entrust her daughter to strangers! I fear we must just wait patiently for a few days, difficult as it is!'

Amelia stood up and picked up the tray. 'Well, I have my tasks to complete to help me pass the time! We hope to finish cleaning the bedrooms today.' She looked around and wrinkled up her nose. 'I wonder that you can breathe in here for all this dust, Sarah!'

After her cousin had gone, Sarah got up and dressed slowly, thinking about what she should do next. Frustrating as it was, she felt inclined to say nothing to Guy about Olivia. The fewer people who knew that she had met Miss Meredith, the better. She did not like the concealment, but it was better than risking Allardyce hearing of Olivia's whereabouts. Eventually, of course, she would have to speak to Guy. As soon as anyone saw Olivia they would realise that she must be related to the Woodallan family, and Sarah needed to know the truth before that happened. Her heart was heavy when she thought of confronting him.

Sarah was determined that she would not spend the enforced wait in moping about the house. It was a bright morning with crisp snow and she walked down to the lake, finding Tom Brookes in the old tumbledown summerhouse that sat by the shore.

'Morning, Miss Sheridan!' he greeted her cheerfully. 'Is all well?' He was cleaning a pair of skates, evicting a family of spiders that had evidently taken up residence inside the boots, and polishing the steel runners to a shine.

'All's well with me,' Sarah said with a smile. 'And your own family, Tom? Your extended family?'

Tom gave her a shrewd look. 'Some improvement this morning, I'm glad to say, ma'am! I don't think it will be long—' He broke off as Guy Renshaw came through the door. 'Good morning, my lord! These will be ready for you directly!'

Sarah found herself blushing, and shrank back a little into the hut's shadowy interior. She was uncertain whether it was guilt or nerves that prompted the reaction, or simply the fact that Guy always seemed to have this regrettable effect on her. He noted her presence with a quick lift of the eyebrows.

'Miss Sheridan! Did you intend to go skating as well, ma'am?'

'That would be very pleasant,' Sarah said primly. 'It

is too fine a day to stay indoors!' She turned to Tom Brookes. 'Perhaps you would be so good as to polish my own skates when you have finished Lord Renshaw's, Tom? They are old, but I hope they will still fit!'

'And in the meantime, you could come tobogganing with me, Miss Sheridan!' Guy said persuasively. 'Tom has already made the sledge shipshape and I am inclined to try it on the long hill beyond the house!'

He picked the sledge up with a word of thanks to Tom, and stood aside for Sarah to precede him out of the hut. The sun was bright on the snow. Sarah blinked a little.

'Tobogganing is all very well when one is a child of ten, my lord—'

'But for a lady of your advanced years it is quite beneath your dignity?' Guy grinned at her. 'For shame, Miss Sheridan! I thought you had more spirit than that!'

'It is not that!' Sarah hesitated. In truth the thought of the enforced intimacy of the small sledge and the exhilaration of the flight downhill was quite exciting, but she could hardly explain that to Guy.

'I should enjoy it, I am sure, but—'

'But it is scarce ladylike!' Guy was shaking his head in mock dismay. 'It is a pity to see you so trammelled about with rules and conventions! Take a risk, Miss Sheridan!' He gave her a teasing look. 'You are willing enough to do so under other circumstances!'

Sarah knew that he must mean her midnight rendezvous with Olivia and a rush of apprehension caused her steps to falter. She had known it would only be a matter of time before he challenged her on last night's activity and she dreaded it. The necessity of lying—or at least omitting certain facts—was quite alien to her nature.

However, it seemed that Guy did not intend to quiz her just yet. They had reached the top of the long field that tumbled down the hill towards Blanchland village and he put the toboggan down and gave it an experimental push. The polished runners slid across the snow with a smooth hiss.

'There! That seems to work well enough! And if you will not join me, Miss Sheridan...' Guy shrugged, folded his long body inside the little sleigh, and pushed himself off down the slope.

Sarah found that she was laughing spontaneously as she watched his progress down the hill. At the bottom he stood up, dusted some stray snow off his jacket and picked the sledge up as calmly as though he were walking into some drawing-room. Sarah was still laughing as he reached her side, barely out of breath from his climb.

'Oh, that looks prodigious good fun, my lord, if a little dangerous! If the London hostesses could see you now, your sophisticated reputation would be quite undone!'

'I trust you to tell no one!' Guy agreed. His fair hair was tousled by the breeze and his eyes were bright with laughter. 'You see how much I am in your power, Miss Sheridan! Come now, admit that you would like to try it, too!'

'Well...' Sarah hesitated. It was very tempting. She glanced round. Blanchland Court was all but hidden by a dip in the hill and the village looked very far away.

'No one would see you,' Guy continued, reading her mind. 'Besides, what do you care for the foolish rules of society? If one cannot enjoy oneself...'

'You are very persuasive, my lord!' Sarah's eyes were sparkling at the prospect. She felt reckless, as though she was behaving like a naughty child, and it was very stimulating.

'I will steer,' Guy went on, 'and you may sit before me and admire the view!'

Sarah drew back a little. 'But surely there cannot be room for both of us in that little toboggan! And it would be so—'

'So enjoyable!' Guy agreed, with a wicked smile. His dark eyes challenged her. 'Well, Miss Sheridan? Do you join me or not?'

He climbed into the sledge, holding out a hand to help Sarah sit in front of him. She was surprised to find that he was correct; the sledge was quite roomy and she could curl up, tucking her skirts about her in a way that was almost decorous and soothed her fears about preserving the proprieties. She had just started to feel better, when Guy put his arms about her.

'What on earth—'

'I cannot steer unless I reach about you, Miss Sheridan,' Guy said innocently. 'For shame, to suspect me of other motives!'

Sarah hesitated. She could hardly draw back now, but the small space that she had managed to preserve between their bodies was now to no avail. After a moment she tentatively allowed him to slide his arms about her waist, whilst still trying to lean forward and away from him. Guy laughed.

'Very modest, Miss Sheridan, but hardly effective! Move a little closer to me so that I may steer properly—I promise not to accuse you of compromising me!'

Sarah edged closer to him. The material of his coat brushed her hair and she was astounded at the urge she suddenly felt to snuggle closer still and press herself against him. She could smell the mingled scent of fresh air and Guy's lemon cologne and it was decidedly intoxicating. Alarmed by her body's peculiar reaction, Sarah was about to pull away when they set off down the hill.

It was breathtaking. The speed built up quickly and the wind burned her cheeks with an icy chill. Sarah almost cried out with the exhilaration of it, her excitement given an edge by the thought of how very badly she was behaving. Then, suddenly, the bottom of the hill rushed up towards them and they skidded into a snow drift and overturned. Winded, dazed for a moment, Sarah lay still and looked upwards through the bare lacy branches of a tree at the blue sky overhead.

'Sarah?' Guy's fingers were icy on her cheek, his expression concerned as he leaned over her. 'Are you much hurt?'

Sarah drew a shaky breath. 'I think not.' Her gaze took in the snow all over his coat and a smile started to curve her mouth. She raised a hand to brush the powdering of white out of his ruffled hair. Guy caught her hand in his. The concern had died from his eyes, leaving an intensity that was far more disturbing.

'Sarah, you have snow in your eyelashes…'

Sarah's eyes fluttered closed as he bent over and gently brushed the ice from her face. A second later, when he took her mouth with his, she felt as though she were melting in exactly the same way as the snow. A shaken sensation swept over her that had nothing to do with her abrupt descent into the snowdrift. Her fingers grazed the rough stubble of his cheek, then tangled in his hair.

Neither of them noticed the discomfort of their surroundings. Sarah knew enough now to realise that Guy was exercising considerable restraint in his kiss, and paradoxically, the knowledge made her want to provoke him into losing his control. She wriggled further beneath him, pulling him closer, pressing her body against his. A groan broke from his lips and he raised his head to look down into Sarah's eyes, his own glittering with a barely repressed desire.

'Sarah…'

Sarah knew that she had incited this ruthless passion and she revelled in the knowledge, giving him back kiss for kiss. It was only when a fall of snow tumbled from the branches above that Sarah was recalled to reality by the ice slipping down her neck.

'Oh!' She sat up and tried to brush down her coat. Guy had got to his feet and was viewing the scuffled snow with rueful amusement.

'I must choose somewhere more comfortable next time!'

Sarah blushed. 'Do not presume that there will be a next time, sir!'

Guy gave her a quizzical look. He picked her up easily and set her on her feet, keeping an imprisoning arm about her. Sarah struggled.

'Let me go!'

'You were not so eager to escape a moment ago!'

'Oh!' Sarah blushed even more with vexation. 'You are so—'

'I know.' Guy kissed her hard on the mouth and let her go. 'There! Let me help you rub that snow away. You look as though you have been rolling on the ground!'

Sarah gave him a fulminating look. 'I think it best if you escort me back to the house now, my lord!'

'Certainly, if you wish all Sir Ralph's guests to draw the same conclusions,' Guy said agreeably. 'I thought it unlikely I could persuade you to another descent of the hill!' He smiled at her. 'Admit that it was enjoyable, though!'

Sarah felt an answering gleam tug at her mouth. 'It was—quite exhilarating, my lord!'

Guy held the field gate open for her and they started to walk along the tree-lined path back towards the house.

'And yet you still refuse to marry me,' he mused. 'You have an unusually obstinate disposition, Miss Sheridan!'

Sarah looked at him. 'When I spoke of enjoyment I was referring to the tobogganing, my lord!'

'And the rest?'

There was a disquieting gleam in his eyes. Sarah looked away. 'A strong...physical attraction is hardly a good basis for marriage, my lord!'

Guy nodded. 'Well, surprisingly I would agree with you, at least in the sense that I believe it is only one important part of a good marriage! There are other qualities—a like-minded approach to life, perhaps, an enjoyment of similar interests—that may sound less exciting but are equally rewarding.'

Sarah sighed. Once again he had not mentioned love, which only served to prove to her how right she had been in refusing him. She felt hollow with disappointment.

'There are other things I would look for in a husband,' she said, more hotly than she had intended. 'Honesty and trust—'

Guy's glance was suddenly bright. 'Brave words! So, Miss Sheridan, what were you doing at the Folly Tower last night?'

Sarah stopped, neatly hoist by her own petard. She

had been thinking of Guy's secret quest to find Olivia first, and had given no thought to her own actions. She bit her lip.

'Well, Miss Sheridan?' Guy's tone was scrupulously polite. 'Surely you do not advocate qualities in others that you do not espouse yourself?'

Sarah realised how badly she had miscalculated. Guy's demeanour was generally so agreeable that it was easy to forget the core of steel that lay beneath the even-tempered exterior. Now, however, she was forcibly reminded. He was looking singularly intractable.

'I went to the Folly Tower to meet with Miss Meredith,' she said candidly.

'I see.' Guy pushed his hands into his coat pockets. His expression was inscrutable. 'So that farrago of nonsense you enacted last night was all for our benefit?'

Sarah did not allow that to provoke her. 'I had not explained the whole matter to Amelia and I assumed—' she shot him a quick look '—that Sir Greville was not party to the situation. I could not see the benefit in rehearsing the whole there and then!'

Guy let that pass. 'How did Miss Meredith contact you?'

'She sent me a note.'

'How was it delivered?'

Sarah cursed him. 'Tom Brookes delivered it,' she said reluctantly. 'Miss Meredith's message asked me to meet her at the Folly Tower at midnight, so I went to meet her.'

'But she was not there?' Guy's scrutiny was relentless. Sarah could only be grateful that he had not yet asked her anything that would require a direct lie.

'As you saw,' she said woodenly. 'Miss Meredith was not there, but someone else was.'

'Yes.' Guy turned away, to consider the view of Blanchland through the curtain of trees. The Folly Tower could just be seen in the distance.

'Strangely, I had heard a rumour that Miss Meredith would be at the Folly Tower—a rumour that proved to be false. I wonder if your mystery assailant was also aware of that rumour?'

'Very possibly,' Sarah said carefully.

'Yet you do not know who he was?'

'No, I do not know—'

'But perhaps you might hazard a guess…'

Sarah pulled a face. 'You question me hard, sir! To what purpose?'

'I am testing your veracity,' Guy admitted easily, 'for, despite your apparent openness, I believe you are hiding something, Miss Sheridan!'

Sarah flushed and hoped that it could be attributed to anger, not guilt. 'I have answered your questions quite truthfully, my lord!'

'Sins of omission, not commission,' Guy murmured. 'Tell me, Miss Sheridan, do you think that the note and the rumour were laying a deliberately false trail?'

Sarah chose her words with care. 'In the light of what happened, I believe it must be so, my lord.'

'And Lord Lebeter's part in all this? What can that be? These woods were damnably crowded last night, were they not?'

Sarah saw with relief that they were about to emerge onto the carriage sweep at the front of Blanchland.

'Lord Lebeter claimed to be suffering from insomnia,' she said.

Guy laughed. 'I heard him! A common complaint! So, do you intend to try to seek Miss Meredith out again?'

'No,' Sarah said truthfully, 'I shall wait for her to contact me. Excuse me, my lord, I must change out of these damp clothes.'

Guy bowed slightly. 'Very well, Miss Sheridan. You have managed not to tell me a word of a lie, but even so...'

He sauntered off towards the games room, leaving Sarah standing on the gravel and feeling a mixture of relief and guilt. Just how much he knew she could not tell, but it could only be a matter of time before he pressed her for the whole story. Yet if anyone could be accused of withholding information, it had to be he, for he had as yet breathed no word of his own purpose in searching for Olivia.

Sarah ran hastily upstairs to get changed before anyone saw her. Further down the corridor a veritable army of maids was dusting and scrubbing, and Sarah could hear Amelia's voice calling instructions and exhortations. She dived into her room before her cousin could remark on her dishevelled state, and did not emerge again until the bell rang for luncheon.

In the afternoon, Amelia was persuaded to abandon her cleaning efforts for a while and join Sarah, Greville and Justin Lebeter on an expedition to go skating on the lake. The other members of the house party declined with expressions of horror, except for Sir Ralph, who somewhat surprisingly chose to join them. The thickness of the ice was tested to the full when Sir Ralph lumbered onto it, but he proved surprising agile on his skates and even performed an elegant skaters' waltz with Amelia.

This time, Sarah kept well away from Guy and gave him no opportunity to speak with her alone. The look of amusement he cast her showed that he perfectly understood her attempts to avoid him and left her with the unsettling impression that he was only biding his time.

A small bonfire was burning by the greenhouses as they made their way back to the house, and Amelia stepped aside for a quick word with Tom Brookes, who was industriously feeding the flames with what appeared to be old books and papers. Sir Ralph, deep in conversation with Greville Baynham, did not appear to notice the conflagration until a stray breath of wind whirled a fragment of paper into his path. He bent absentmindedly to pick it up, cast it a vague glance, then stopped abruptly in the middle of his sentence.

'My lithographs! My books!'

Everyone stared at the bonfire, where one of the books was shrivelling, its pages curling and turning dark brown. Nearby ashes gave mute testimony to the demise of other volumes. One last edition fell open as it succumbed to the flames, revealing the saucy cartoons inside. Sir Ralph was wailing and appeared to be about to rake through the ashes with his bare hands.

Amelia put a consoling hand on his arm.

'I am so sorry, Sir Ralph. They had the woodworm and smelled quite unpleasant besides! It is the library, you know—I suspect you may have a problem with the drains...'

Sarah looked at Sir Ralph's stricken face and privately wondered whether Amelia had gone too far this time. There would be no more cosy evenings in the library for Sir Ralph and his guests, tickling their appetite with erotic prints.

'Did you sort through the volumes yourself, Lady Amelia?' Greville was asking, with a speculative look. 'What a selfless act!'

Sir Ralph's shoulders slumped and he trudged off alone towards the house. Sarah was about to follow her cousin indoors, but at that moment Justin Lebeter caught up with her.

'Miss Sheridan—may I have a moment of your time? In private?'

Sarah stood back to allow the rest of the party to pass them, and waited for him to speak. Olivia's beau was tall and fair, with a rather earnest expression and bright blue eyes. He fixed these pleadingly on Sarah's face.

'I am sorry to approach you like this, ma'am,' he stammered, a little red in the face. 'Indeed, it is only my concern for...that is, I am anxious to find a certain young lady, and I had heard—' He broke off self-consciously.

Sarah raised her eyebrows. 'Yes, sir? You had heard...'

'That you came to Blanchland to see Miss Olivia Meredith!' Lord Lebeter said in a rush. 'I would not listen to gossip, but I am anxious to see the young lady myself—'

'I see,' Sarah said drily.

Justin Lebeter flushed an even brighter red. 'Oh, no, I would not wish you to misunderstand me, ma'am! Miss Meredith is an old school friend of one of my sisters and I had an invitation for her to visit—' Here he broke off again at the somewhat sceptical look in Sarah's eye. He squared his shoulders. 'The point of the matter is that Miss Meredith seems to have disappeared and I am worried about her! I wondered whether you had seen her, ma'am?'

Sarah relented of her teasing. It seemed that Lord Lebeter was made of sterner stuff than first appeared and he did seem sincerely concerned about Olivia. She wished that she could reassure him, but that was impossible whilst Olivia was still in danger.

'It is true that I came here to meet with Miss Meredith,' she said, wishing that she did not always need to choose her words with such care, 'but I have found that she is from home at present. I am sorry, Lord Lebeter—I really cannot help you.'

Lebeter's eyes narrowed thoughtfully, and for a moment, Sarah had the feeling that he knew far more than he had said.

'Forgive me, ma'am,' he said again, 'but I was under the impression that you had actually met with Miss Meredith.'

Now it was Sarah's turn to feel uncomfortable at being forced into a direct denial. 'No, indeed,' she said, a little too quickly, 'you are mistaken, sir.'

'I see,' Lebeter said. He looked both embarrassed and awkward, as though he wished to accuse her of something but could not quite find the words. After a moment, he bowed abruptly and walked on ahead of her into the house. Sarah, aware that Guy had seen the exchange from the doorway, followed with her face averted. The whole incident had been disconcerting because she hated the deceit and knew that Lord Lebeter was genuinely worried about Olivia. She also had the distinct impression that Lebeter had not believed her, and wondered why. And if Lebeter should express his doubts to Guy—what then?

Chapter Nine

Sir Ralph was still sunk deep in gloom at dinner. The loss of his beloved lithographs and his prized collection of erotic books was a blow that he could hardly bear and he ate his way through the first course in a stolid silence. The food was excellent once again, and it appeared that Sir Ralph's guests were beginning to resign themselves to the lack of wine, some of them even grudgingly complementing the spring water on its purity. The fish course, a fine salmon in anchovy sauce, was followed by a syllabub brought in by the black-clad footman whom Sarah now knew to be the obsequious Marvell. Amelia had made no secret of the fact that she disliked him, but her clean sweep of the servants had so far failed to dislodge him.

Marvell delivered the syllabub with an ingratiating smile, whispering something in Lord Allardyce's ear as he did so that brought an arrested look to the peer's eyes. Allardyce's pensive gaze travelled from Amelia to Sarah, where it lingered in blatant appraisal before he applied himself to the dish before him. Sarah turned her shoulder, uncomfortable as always with his scrutiny.

Amelia and Greville, having spent an afternoon without bickering, were actually sitting next to each other at the table, which meant that Sarah had Greville on one side of her and Justin Lebeter on the other. Despite their difficult encounter that afternoon, Lebeter proved pleasantly attentive and was far more comfortable company than Allardyce. For once, Sarah began to relax and actually to enjoy the meal.

The syllabub tasted of lemon, but with a curious aftertaste that was so sweet as to be almost cloying. Sarah paused to consider the flavour and noticed that Guy was the only one not eating, having waved away the food that Marvell had offered him. She took another thoughtful spoonful, almost certain that she did not like it and wondering what Amelia would think. This would certainly not be one of her recipes. Her cousin, however, seemed oblivious to the food, for she was leaning close to Greville and seemed utterly absorbed in what he had to say. Sarah smiled, thinking how pleasant it was to see them in accord for once. Almost without thinking, she took another mouthful of syllabub, then pushed the bowl away, repelled by the taste.

A huge haunch of beef followed the syllabub and everyone applied themselves with enthusiasm. After a while, Sarah observed that a curious change of mood appeared to have come over Sir Ralph's guests. They were chatting and laughing as freely as though the wine had been circulating for hours, rediscovering the uninhibited enjoyment that had characterised the first dinner Sarah had experienced at Blanchland. Mrs Fisk leant forward and playfully stuck her tongue in Sir Ralph's ear. Lord Allardyce was trailing kisses along Lady Tilney's bare shoulder, but his eyes met Sarah's across the table, wide with mockery and lust. Sarah looked away hastily, suddenly anxious to escape. This was much worse than the first night. Sir Ralph's guests seemed totally unrestrained, their expressions glazed as they neglected their food for more exciting pleasures.

Sarah was about to get to her feet when something even more strange occurred. Lord Lebeter leaped up and rushed from the room without a word, the door slamming violently behind him. No one except Sarah appeared to notice. She turned to look at Amelia, about to suggest that they retire, and experienced a dreadful shock. Amelia's hand was resting on Greville's thigh and, as Sarah watched in utter amazement, she leant forward and pressed a lingering kiss on his mouth.

Sarah gave a little squeak, part-dismay and part-disbelief. How could Amelia, so proper, so much a high stickler for convention and good behaviour, have succumbed to the gross conduct of Sir Ralph's party? It was impossible and yet, before her very eyes, Greville and Amelia rose from the table and went out of the room, entwined in each other arms. They paused frequently to embrace each other, playfully and lovingly kissing and stroking until Sarah thought her eyes would fall out with shock.

There was a movement beside her as Guy slid into the seat vacated by Justin Lebeter. Unlike the rest of the company, his gaze was steady and his voice held a note of emphasis that immediately caught Sarah's attention, despite her agitation.

'Listen to me, Miss Sheridan. We do not have much time. How much of that syllabub did you eat?'

Sarah gazed at him in bewilderment. 'Only a few spoonfuls. I did not care for the taste. What—?'

'The syllabub contained an aphrodisiac, Miss Sheridan.' Guy's gaze was urgent. 'Do you understand me? It held some kind of drug that increases the sexual appetite.' He gestured at the others. 'That is the explanation for what you see before you. And if you ate any at all, you will soon feel the same.'

Sarah could feel the blood draining from her face. 'But I only ate a few mouthfuls! And I feel perfectly well—'

'No matter.' Guy leant towards her, his face set. 'It takes longer to work on some than others, and it may be that the lesser dose will have less severe an effect, but we cannot stay here discussing it! You must come with me—'

'No!' Sarah got to her feet, suddenly terrified. Everywhere were scenes of the most shocking debauchery as Sir Ralph's guests threw themselves wholeheartedly into the orgy. The lurid pictures on the wall, the statues, the romping nymphs on the frieze, all seemed to mock her with their knowing eyes. She gave a little moan of terror.

Guy's hand closed about her wrist so hard that the pain cut through her hysteria. He was already on his feet and pulling her towards the door.

'Listen to me, Sarah,' he said again. 'You *must* stay with me. It is the only way that you will be safe. I promise—'

And then it happened. They were out in the hall, in the flickering candlelight. Sarah felt a curious feeling steal over her, a weakness that left her warm but trembling. An irresistible urge to touch Guy came over her, and she raised her hand to stroke his cheek. The skin felt smooth beneath her fingers, deliciously cool. She brushed her fingers across the curve of his mouth, wishing she could pull it down to meet hers. Her heightened senses were full of him—the smell and the touch, the need for more…

She saw him smile as he gently took her hand and restrained her caresses.

'This is where matters become rather difficult,' he said, and even through the fever in her blood, Sarah thought she heard a note of regret. It did not matter, however, for he had already swept her up into his arms and was carrying her up to her room. Sarah turned her face against his neck and pressed little kisses into the warmth of his throat, and felt very happy. In the heat of her desire, alone with Guy was precisely where she wanted to be.

Sarah woke to pale darkness. Her mind felt as shadowy as the room, floating, insubstantial. She blinked, and the light came into focus. The candle beside the bed was burned so low it was almost out, but beyond it the grey shade of dawn was creeping into the room. Sarah turned her head very slowly.

Guy was lying beside her, and very deeply asleep. The cold morning light cast shadows across his face, highlighting the tension there, the hollows and lines of exhaustion. Sarah jumped as though stung, and immediately his eyes flew open and he reached across and grabbed her.

'Oh! Let me go! What are you doing here?' Sarah's words came out in a muffled scream.

She lay quite still, staring up into his face in horrified incomprehension.

Guy's dark eyes searched her face for a moment, then he let her go and sat up. 'You do not remember anything?'

'Remember what? I...' Sarah's voice trailed away and she frowned. Vague memories flickered through her mind, vivid dreams... She could see the dining-room and images of debauchery wherever she looked; she could remember a feeling of confusion when Amelia disappeared; she saw Guy, speaking to her urgently; recalled a feeling of intense frustration and thwarted desire… And always his voice, speaking to her soothingly, his arms holding her gently but with none of the passion that she desperately wanted and had begged for…

'Oh, no!' Sarah's eyes were wild. 'It was not a dream?'

'It was not a dream.' Guy took her hands in a steadying clasp. 'Sweetheart, listen. It is all over and you are quite safe. Nothing happened, I promise you—'

'But I remember!' Sarah said desperately. 'The things I said—what I did! Oh!'

She tried to free herself, but Guy refused to let go. His voice was very calm and quiet.

'You were not responsible for your actions. I swear you came to no harm, Sarah!'

Sarah burst into tears. She could not have stopped herself even had she wanted to. As it was, the flood of tears was a welcome relief from the horrors of night, the shock and the shame. She cried, and Guy held her trembling body in his arms, murmuring endearments and holding her gently until she calmed at last and fell quiet.

'I dare say that you will be wanting to change your clothes, and have some food and drink,' Guy said, very practically, when at last he let her go. 'I will go to fetch something from the kitchens. Do not open the door whilst I am gone.'

His matter-of-fact tone had the desired effect. Sarah moved almost mechanically to strip off her dress, wash her tearstained face and find some fresh clothes. All the time, her words and actions from the previous night flashed through her mind like some terrible play. She had repeatedly tried to entice Guy, rubbing herself against him in an utterly shameless way and begging for his kisses. She had tried to pull off her own clothing, never mind his! It seemed impossible, unbelievable, and yet... One thing she did remember with utter clarity was that Guy had repeatedly refused her, and the worst thing was that she was so confused that she did not know whether to be glad or sorry...

A knock at the door recalled her from the dreadful nightmare, and she went to let Guy in. Whilst she pulled back the curtains and tidied the room, he coaxed the fire into life, then drew Sarah over to sit beside it. She noticed that he had had a chance to change, but not to shave, and that there were shadows as well as stubble darkening his face.

'How are you feeling now?' he asked, his tone still carefully neutral.

Sarah hesitated. 'A little better.' She met his eyes directly. 'I would not like you to think that I am without proper feeling, my lord, for the experiences of last night were hideous. Nevertheless, I do believe that I owe you my thanks. Matters...must have been very difficult for you.'

There was a pause, then Guy's expression lightened considerably. 'It relieves me that you have not fallen into a fit of the vapours or an irreversible decline, Miss Sheridan, despite so shocking an experience!' He smiled ruefully. 'And, yes, it was very difficult for me. To have you begging me to do all the things that I have wanted to do for some time—and then to resist!' He shook his head slowly. 'I surprised even myself!'

Sarah blushed rosily and poured a cup of tea to try

to distract herself. 'How could such a thing happen? I had grossly underestimated the dangers that might befall us here at Blanchland....'

Guy grimaced. 'I can only suppose that Sir Ralph habitually resorts to such stimulants to arouse the jaded appetites of his guests. It is not to be expected that you would even imagine such a thing, Miss Sheridan. How could you? But that was one of the reasons I was so concerned to think of you coming here alone! An innocent abroad, with no idea of the perils that awaited you!'

Sarah shuddered. 'How dared that man Marvell do such a thing? I saw him whispering to Lord Allardyce as he served the syllabub, but I had no idea—' She broke off. 'It is truly disgusting!'

'I saw it, too,' Guy said heavily, 'and cursed myself that I made no connection until it was too late! As it was, I only refused the dish myself because I do not care for cream!' His gaze swept over her with repressed amusement. 'Had I eaten it, Miss Sheridan, the outcome would have been much different, I assure you!'

Sarah sighed, wondering how she would have felt if she had woken that morning under other circumstances. What had happened was dreadfully shocking and a true lesson against wandering unprepared into unfamiliar circumstances. Blanchland had plumbed the depths of depravity and nothing in her past experience could have helped her begin to understand such things. She was not a green girl, being well aware that a seamier side to life had always existed—but for one who had grown up and lived in relatively sheltered circumstances, such knowledge as she now had was deeply distressing. Had Guy and she both succumbed to the lure of the aphrodisiac...

Sarah took a comforting mouthful of tea and viewed

Guy across the rim of her cup. She was sensible enough to realise that that would have been far preferable to some of the things that might have happened, and despite the fact that the aphrodisiac effect had now worn off, she was forced to admit that it might have been rather exciting…

Sarah replenished her cup, turning her thoughts aside from such matters. She had learned a great deal about herself, as well as others, in the past twelve hours.

'I must commend your quick thinking, my lord!' she said ruefully. 'Once you had realised what was happening you acted very swiftly. I realise how much I owe you—'

Guy sat back in his chair, relaxing a little. 'I hope you understand, Miss Sheridan, that what I did was solely for your protection. I had to get you away from the others as quickly as possible, but I could not have risked leaving you alone. You might have become ill, or wandered off and fallen into some trouble…I am deeply sorry for all the distress this must have caused you. It is truly appalling.'

Sarah made a slight gesture. 'Please, let us not speak of it any more. I have learned a great deal that in my foolish naïvety I did not know…'

'There is nothing foolish about your innocence, Miss Sheridan,' Guy said, a little roughly, 'and I am glad that not all of it has been dispelled this night…'

'Is anyone else awake yet?' Sarah asked hastily, anxious to change the subject. She had not really given much thought to anybody's situation, but suddenly wondered what other disasters the aphrodisiac had wrought.

Guy shook his head. 'The house is quite still. I believe they all took far more syllabub than you, so will be feeling the effects both more strongly and for longer—'

'Amelia!' Sarah suddenly put her teacup down with a clatter that sent the remaining liquid cascading onto the hearth. 'Oh, no.' Her wide-eyed gaze turned back to Guy, imploring his reassurance. 'Did I imagine... surely she did not...?'

A shadow touched Guy's face. 'Miss Sheridan...you force me to be frank with you. You did *not* imagine that your cousin and Sir Greville...' he hesitated '...they did indeed leave together.'

Sarah pressed her hand to her mouth. 'Then they... Oh, no...'

Guy fixed her with a very straight look. 'There is nothing you can do, Miss Sheridan. There would have been nothing I could have done either. Both of them were under the influence of the drug.' His gaze was watchful. 'Forgive me, but it will be less of a shock for Lady Amelia than it would have been for you...'

Sarah looked away. She knew what he meant. Amelia was a widow and therefore more knowledgeable of the ways of the world, but even so...

'I believe,' Guy continued in the same measured tone he had used earlier to reassure her, 'that Lady Amelia and Sir Greville sincerely love each other, for all their wrangling. I am certain that all will be well. It may not be very conventional, but there are times when matters might be so very much worse.'

'I know.' Sarah groped for her handkerchief, finding that the realisation of Amelia's situation had made her cry again. How foolish and naïve they had both been, to think that they could come to Blanchland and escape unscathed! Yet how right Guy was to point out that both of them could have woken in far more terrible circumstances that day. If it had been Allardyce, or Ralph Covell… Sarah shuddered. She had to look beyond the hypocritical rules of society and realise that both she and Amelia were, if not fortunate, at least safe…

Sarah dried her tears and stood up, walking across to the window and looking out over the cold white landscape. She rested one hand on the thick velvet curtain. They would have to leave Blanchland now. There was no other way. That, of course, meant changing her plans with regard to Olivia, for whom she had not spared a single thought in the last few hours, and for the moment she was too tired to make any plans.

Guy had also stood up and now came to stand behind her at the window. 'It is a beautiful place but blighted, Miss Sheridan,' he said softly. 'You have to let it go.'

'I know,' Sarah said. She turned back to him. He was watching her with great gentleness in his eyes.

'Forgive me for pressing you at such a time,' he said with constraint, 'but you must also know that you have to marry me now. Whatever your previous doubts…'

Sarah swallowed hard. She wanted to tell him that she loved him, but the words seemed to stick in her throat. Her previous attraction to him, so sudden and violent, had grown swiftly into love as she had observed how fine a man he was, and she was sure that even the difficulties over Olivia could be overcome if only they could speak of it. She just needed a little time to prepare…

When she did not reply, a slight shadow seemed to touch Guy's face and he turned away.

'There is still the issue of Miss Meredith to be resolved, of course,' he continued. 'Before all last night's events began, Justin Lebeter asked me to speak to you about her.' Guy looked at Sarah thoughtfully. 'He is certain that she is in grave danger and is almost as certain that you know her whereabouts! What do you say, Miss Sheridan?'

Sarah caught her breath. This was sudden, if not unexpected, and she felt woefully unready. To give herself time, she walked over to the bed stand and poured herself a glass of spring water. It was exactly as she had feared the day before—she did not know how Lebeter had guessed her complicity; whether it was simply an instinct, or whether he had seen or heard something, she could not tell. It was the worst piece of luck that he had not believed her denials and had chosen to go to Guy with his suspicions, for now she would have to discuss the subject of Olivia with Guy, and she did not really know how to approach it.

She sat down again in one of the armchairs before the fire, but Guy remained on his feet, evidently preferring to stand. It was extraordinary, but the intimacy of their previous exchange appeared to have completely vanished. Sarah felt her heart sink. She knew that Guy could reasonably expect her to trust him after all he had done to help her, and here she was, apparently demonstrating her lack of confidence in him. Her silence was going to cost her dear.

Guy was waiting for her reply with perfect courtesy, but the expression in his eyes was cold.

'Lord Lebeter is mistaken in thinking that I know Miss Meredith's whereabouts,' Sarah said truthfully. 'I did not lie to him, precisely—'

'Indeed? In the same way, perhaps, that you did not lie to me when we spoke of it?' The sudden contempt in Guy's voice cut across Sarah like a whiplash and she flinched. 'What a talent you have for being sparing with the truth, Miss Sheridan! I should tell you that Lord

Lebeter saw Miss Meredith leaving this very room! He even suggested to me that you may have been involved in procuring your niece's services as mistress to Lord Allardyce!'

The deliberate insult touched Sarah on the raw. She jumped to her feet, her eyes blazing. All the tension and distress of the previous night caught up with her. She did not even stop to think how they could have moved from intimacy to opposition so quickly.

'How *dare* you suggest such a thing, Lord Renshaw? I have never heard anything so immoral! Why, Olivia is my niece! And leaving that aside, I am hardly likely—'

Guy shrugged laconically. He seemed untouched by her fury. '*I* did not suggest it, it is simply what others are saying! And they have grounds for suspicion. Perhaps you view Miss Meredith as an unwelcome addition to the family? Relatives have been known to connive at such solutions!'

'If I thought that you had insulted me once before,' Sarah said, her voice shaking, 'that was as nothing to this! You will leave at once—'

Guy's only reply was to stroll over to the bed, toss the key onto the table beside it, and lie down with his hands behind his head. Sarah stared in speechless outrage.

'What do you think you are doing? You cannot stay there!'

Guy gave her an unrepentant smile. He sounded completely unconcerned. 'Can I not? But you see I am doing so! I have been here all night, after all, so what difference can a few more hours make? This is a comfortable way of waiting until you decide to tell me what I want to know.'

'But...' Sarah was not sure if it was bewilderment or rage that would win out inside her. 'This is quite preposterous! Surely it need not come to this! If we could only speak sensibly...'

Guy turned his head on the pillow and gave her a derisive look. 'I am perfectly willing to do so, Miss Sheridan—but on my terms! It seems to me that I did you a great service last night, but now, for reasons that only you understand, you are refusing repay me with your trust! Well, I cannot force you to tell me about Olivia, but I may stay here until you do!'

Sarah saw red. 'The reason that I do not trust you is because I know you are hiding something from me!' she said furiously. 'I heard you speaking to your father at Woodallan—I know you have some reason to find Olivia first! Oh, I cannot bear this! If you will not leave, then I will be the one to go!'

She snatched at the key, but Guy was too quick for her. His hand closed around her wrist and he pulled hard. Caught off balance, Sarah tumbled down beside him on the huge bed.

Before she could say a word, she found herself pinioned beneath him, with Guy's face a heart-stopping few inches from her own. Sarah's heart began to race.

'Now,' Guy said softly, 'what do you think that you owe me for my forbearance last night? Your provocations were enough to try the patience of a saint, yet I did not succumb!'

'Then pray do not undo all your good work now!' Sarah gasped. She knew that matters had slipped far beyond her control. There was a furious glitter in Guy's eyes and it was only now, when it was too late, that she realised just how far she must have pushed him the previous night. It must have cost him a great deal to keep himself from touching her when she had begged him to make love, and all that frustrated energy and desire had still to be defused. His anger and his passion sprang from the same source.

For an agonising second their eyes locked, then his mouth came down on hers in an emphatic demonstration of his mastery. The desire flared instantly between them and a searing warmth leapt through Sarah's blood, leaving her weak and trembling, yet alive to every sensation.

She opened her eyes and met his gaze, heavy with heat, before his mouth returned to hers with a feverish compulsion that left her gasping. Anger was banished, replaced by an urgent need. Of their own volition, Sarah's hands slid under his jacket to feel the hard warmth of his body beneath the linen shirt. Guy raised himself on one elbow, leaning over to place a kiss on the corner of her mouth, then another in the hollow of her throat. Despite his gentleness there was an insistence in his touch that made Sarah give a soft moan of pleasure.

'Guy, please…'

'Please…what?' His voice was husky and she could hear the smile in it. His fingers were easing her dress from her shoulder, so that he could move his mouth to where it had rested, pressing soft kisses against her skin.

'Are you conscious this time, Sarah?' Guy whispered. He slid a finger under the curve of Sarah's gown and she felt it slip down, revealing the flimsy chemise beneath. Just the brush of his hand against the soft swell of her breasts set her trembling afresh, a feeling of exquisite need in the pit of her stomach. She felt Guy slide the material down with deliberate slowness, exposing her breasts as the chemise slipped lower. She waited in an agony of anticipation to feel his touch against her naked skin, and her lashes flickered open to see him looking at her with such intense, concentrated desire that she could not move or speak. Their eyes held for a long moment of tension, then Guy lowered his head to take one taut nipple in his mouth and such slow, sweet pleasure shot through her that Sarah thought she would scream out loud.

'Do you surrender?' Guy's voice was ragged with emotion. He slid a hand across her bare stomach and Sarah arched against him.

'Yes…' She would have agreed to tell him anything. Olivia, Lord Lebeter, Allardyce, were all forgotten, irrelevant. 'Please…'

Guy bent his head to her breast again, teasing and tormenting her with his lips and tongue until Sarah writhed with need.

'So you will marry me?'

Through the desire that clouded her mind, Sarah dimly realised that this was the wrong question. Surely he was supposed to be asking her about Olivia… Her mind sheered away as Guy bit gently at her satin skin.

'Yes, yes, I will. Of course.'

For some reason she expected him to stop now that he had achieved his aim and when she felt his hand on the silken softness of her inner thigh, her eyes opened wide. 'But I thought…'

Whatever she had thought was never expressed, for Guy was caressing her with a tender urgency that made her cry out and just when she thought she could bear it no more, her whole body exploded in the most intense rapture.

It took Sarah some time to recover herself, but when she did so, she found that Guy had discarded her somewhat superfluous clothing and wrapped her in the bedclothes. She was curled in the crook of his arm, with her head resting against his shoulder and, as it seemed a little too late for embarrassment, Sarah chose instead to snuggle a little closer. Her body felt drugged with pleasure and she was very sleepy, but at the back of her mind was the nagging doubt that something was wrong. She raised herself a little and placed one hand on his chest.

'Guy…'

'Sarah…' She felt his breath stir the tendrils of hair about her face as he leaned over to kiss her. 'Are you well?'

'Yes, very…' Sarah smiled. 'But you…I may not know a great deal about love, but it is not fair—'

She felt him laugh against her hair. 'Much as I appreciate your sense of fair play, sweetheart, I fear that that must wait!'

'But—'

'Don't tempt me,' Guy said, a little roughly. 'It is by the nature of a miracle that I was able to stop at all!' His voice warmed. 'After all, that is the second time I have resisted you—'

Sarah moved slightly and the sheet slipped. Seeing Guy's downward gaze and the sudden heat that leapt to his eyes, she felt her own body suffuse with fire once more.

'Get dressed,' Guy said abruptly. 'Please get dressed, Sarah! I want to talk to you and I will never achieve it at this rate!'

He turned his back as Sarah scrambled for her clothes, and when she had rather haphazardly dressed herself again, gestured to her to join him in the armchairs by the fire. The daylight was stronger now, but still the house had not stirred.

'You accused me earlier of withholding information from you,' Guy began, 'and it is true that I did keep something back. I wish to God that I had told you sooner, Sarah, but—' He broke off. 'There are complications. However, I wanted you to know that Olivia Meredith—'

'Is your niece as well as mine?' Sarah suggested.

Guy stared. 'How the devil did you know that?'

Sarah burst out laughing. 'Because I have seen her! And as soon as I saw her…' Sarah shook her head, a rueful smile on her lips '…well, if you had told me that she was *not* related to you, I would not have believed you! I would even have believed that she was your daughter, were it that I could not think you steeped in debauchery quite so young!'

Guy gave her a look that brought the blood up into her face. 'Thank you! The resemblance is then so strong?'

'A speaking likeness! She also has in her possession a locket that depicts your grandparents, or so I believe. But she has no notion of her mother's identity, knowing only that Frank was her father. I must own myself surprised…that Catherine was her mother.'

Guy gave her a searching look. 'You have deduced that yourself?'

'It seemed the only explanation.' Sarah hesitated. 'Unless I have read it wrongly—'

'You have not. Were you shocked?'

Sarah met his gaze very candidly. 'How could I be, after what almost happened just now? I have learned a lot…I cannot judge or blame. Only…I am surprised at

Frank. He was a scoundrel, but he would not have abandoned an innocent girl…'

Guy sighed heavily. He leant forward, resting his chin on his hand. 'He did not know. Catherine never told anyone until it was too late and your brother abroad. She died in childbirth and my father was so racked with anger and grief that he refused to have anything to do with the child, leaving it all to your family to dispose.'

'Poor little girl,' Sarah said softly, 'and poor Catherine. She can have been no more than sixteen.'

'Yes, the whole thing has been the most appalling tragedy. My father—' Guy stopped, his face sombre. 'He cannot bear for Catherine's disgrace to be known, Sarah. That is the reason he asked me to find Olivia first, and to tell no one, not even you, that I sought her. I am sorry.' He ran his hand through his hair, further disordering the already dishevelled locks. 'It must appear that I did not trust you, but it was only that I had given him my word…'

Sarah was frowning. 'But I do not understand, Guy. Supposing you had found Olivia first—what were you to do? What did your father ask of you?'

For a moment, she thought that Guy was not going to answer her. He got up and threw another log onto the fire. The shower of sparks that shot upwards illuminated his grim expression.

'He asked me to pay Miss Meredith off. His plan was to make it worth her while to disappear. You were never to know.'

Sarah was shocked into silence for a moment. She stared at Guy's averted face whilst anger and outrage warred within her.

'I suppose he is ashamed of Olivia's existence—' she began, in a voice that shook.

Guy looked at her. There was grief and pity in his face. 'My father wished to protect Catherine's memory. He acted from the best of motives. You must remember that Miss Meredith is nothing to him, whilst his daughter's honour and reputation is everything—he could not bear for her memory to be disgraced. I told him that I thought him misguided, but he is a proud old man...'

Sarah was struggling with her feelings. 'Olivia is my niece, too! He had no concern for my opinion! Why, I thought that he had asked you to accompany me to Blanchland to give me support and protection, not to undermine and deceive!'

She jumped to her feet, unable to sit calmly discussing so great a betrayal. 'I cannot believe that, all the time, you were planning to trick me! And then to have the audacity to accuse me of being sparing with the truth—'

Guy came swiftly to her side. He caught her hands in his. 'Sarah, listen to me!' His tone was forceful. 'I had no intention of falling in with my father's plan—'

'Olivia would never have agreed to it!' Sarah said wildly, bursting into tears. 'She has the integrity that other members of her family seem to lack!'

'I am sure you are right.' Guy had gathered her into his arms and was stroking her hair gently. 'It was an ill-conceived plan! We will go to my father and find another solution, I promise you!'

He said no more as Sarah wept uncontrollably into his jacket. After a little while, as her sobs abated, he drew her down to sit next to him on the bed.

'Oh, why can I not stop crying?' Sarah wailed. 'This

is of all things the most intolerable! I am truly sick of it!'

Guy pressed a kiss against her hair. 'It is scarce surprising. You have had a shock, one way and another. Sarah, I wish to say that I am sorry for the things I said earlier. I knew you were concealing matters from me and it made me angry that you did not trust me. Fine words, I know, from one who has just confessed to the same fault! May we start afresh, sweetheart?'

He got no further, for there was a sudden loud shout from the bottom of the stairs. They looked at one another. Even this, it seemed, had failed to rouse the household, for no one stirred.

'I must go and see what is the matter,' Guy said reluctantly, retrieving the keys and unlocking the door. 'There may be some emergency.'

Sarah followed him out onto the darkened landing and down the stairs. Tom Brookes was standing in the entrance hall, his strained face breaking into relief as he saw Guy.

'My lord! Thank God it's you! There has been a messenger from Woodallan. Your father—'

Sarah clutched Guy's arm. 'Oh, no, Tom! Is it—he is not…?'

'No, ma'am,' the gardener said reassuringly, 'but I believe he is taken quite poorly.' He turned to Guy. 'He asks that you return at once, sir. I've your horse already saddled—'

'Thank you.' Guy pressed Sarah's hand, where it still rested on his arm. 'I must go, Sarah. Listen, this is what you must do. Pack your bags, and I shall either return or send a message later. Do not do anything until you hear from me, but keep safe and tend to your cousin.' He kissed her briefly. 'Tom—' the gardener was waiting patiently '—pray keep Miss Sheridan—and Miss Meredith—safe until I return.'

'Olivia!' Sarah said suddenly. 'I never told you—'

'It will have to wait.' Guy kissed her again and ran for the door. Sarah stood on the steps beside Tom Brookes and watched as he rode off into the snow. She felt miserable and bereft, worried about the Earl's illness and wanting to be with his son. But deeper than that, some instinct told her that something was very wrong, and she was afraid.

'The most dreadful aspect,' Amelia said later, plucking at her bedcovers, 'is that I cannot remember a single moment of the whole experience! To be ravished by Greville, and yet to forget it all—it is most extraordinary.'

A delicate shade of colour came into her face. 'I knew at once this morning, of course. Forgive me, Sarah, for speaking to you of such things! I am just so very grateful that you are unharmed...'

'Oh, do not worry about me!' Sarah placed a comforting hand on her cousin's arm. She had managed to reassure Amelia of her own safety very successfully, mainly because her cousin was still so wrapped up in what had happened. 'Milly, what will happen?'

'Oh, do not fear,' Amelia said hastily, breaking into a radiant smile. 'It is no doubt very improper of me to say so, but all will be well. Greville and I have talked...' her colour deepened '...and we are to marry as soon as he may procure a special licence! I have been so foolish, Sarah, for I love him very much, and...' Her voice faded away and she lay back on the pillows, closing her eyes. Sarah realised that the effects of the drug must have been very strong indeed and blessed once again the chance that had led her to eat only a few spoonfuls.

Outside the window the snow was falling from a leaden sky. Sarah thought of her plans for them all to remove to Woodallan, and felt a pang of concern. The weather was poor and it now seemed that Amelia would not be fit to travel. She had not heard a word from Tom, whom she had sent to relay a message to Olivia. With all her heart, Sarah wished that Guy had not had to leave them.

'Apparently all Sir Ralph's guests have awoken with the wrong person,' Amelia said dolefully. 'I changed all the rooms about when I was arranging the cleaning—I thought it might be amusing! And now look what has happened!'

'The important thing to remember,' Sarah said staunchly, 'is that you and I woke up with the *right* person. Sir Ralph and his guests can take care of themselves!' She paused to consider how extraordinary it was that she could be speaking so openly on such delicate topics, but a short space of time had wrought a great change. She sought to inject a lighter note. 'Mr and Mrs Fisk are very happy, at any rate! Apparently they awoke to find themselves together and are so taken by their rapprochement that they plan a second honeymoon!'

The cousins caught each other's eye and started to laugh. 'Oh, dear,' Amelia said, between giggles, 'this is dreadful! At least I have been married and could be expected not to be too missish, but you, Sarah! I was supposed to be looking after you!'

'Lord Renshaw did that very successfully, I thank you! He was the perfect gentleman!'

Amelia gave her cousin a speaking glance and they

both collapsed into fresh laughter. 'I can well imagine!' Amelia said. 'Or rather, I cannot imagine it at all!'

Sarah stood up abruptly and went to the window, watching the dizzy swirl of snowflakes falling.

'Alan was never faithful to me, you know,' Amelia said quietly after a moment, clearly following some train of thought of her own. 'Oh, he was handsome and charming and such fun to be with, but he did not see the need to confine his attentions to one woman—especially the one he had married! It hurt me so deeply I could not bear to think on it! Which is why—when Greville first asked me to marry him…'

Sarah turned back to look at her. She had never seen Amelia's pretty face so creased with distress.

'I thought that you refused Greville because you claimed to find him dull…'

'I know. I appeared not to value his excellent qualities, but in fact I was just afraid, I suppose. Now I shall have to trust him.'

'And you could not commit yourself to a better man,' Sarah said warmly, coming back to the bedside. 'Greville loves you and has done so for a long time now.'

'I know,' Amelia said, a contented smile curving her lips. 'I am indeed truly fortunate! Oh, if only I could remember—'

'Yes—' Sarah gave her a naughty smile '—I can see that it must be very annoying for you. But never mind, you will have plenty of opportunity to find out!'

'Sarah!' Amelia's eyes flew wide open. 'Blanchland has wrought quite a change in you, and not one that is at all proper!'

'I know.' Sarah continued to smile. Her eye fell on yet another painting of cavorting nymphs. 'I suspect it is the influence of these dreadful pictures!'

'It is to be hoped that Guy will make a respectable woman of you, Sarah,' Amelia murmured. A slight frown touched her brow. 'You will marry him, won't you?'

Sarah turned her face away. 'Of course I will—now. Even I can see that some sort of conventionality must be observed after all that has happened!'

'Not because of that!' Amelia's hand pressed hers urgently. 'Because you love him! I know it, Sarah! Oh, if only I were not so tired I would soon make you admit it!'

Amelia slept for most of the day and Sarah stayed beside her. Greville Baynham, recovering from the effects of the drug more rapidly than his fiancée, had checked that Sarah was prepared to be left alone to await Guy's return, then had ridden off at once to purchase a special licence. Sarah suspected that part of his alacrity was to reassure Amelia, but thought that this at least was unnecessary. At last her cousin seemed utterly content and certain of Greville's love.

Sarah felt even more lonely without Greville's comforting presence, but consoled herself with the thought that Guy had said he would return shortly. In the meantime, there was still Justin Lebeter to protect them. The young peer, who had rushed from the dining-room the previous night, had apparently locked himself in his chamber and thrown away the key whilst the aphrodisiac took effect, not wishing to compromise his love for Olivia. When he had regained consciousness that morning he had had to beat on the door until Sarah, with the help of Tom Brookes, had let him out.

The Fisks had departed in a honeymoon glow early in the day, and Sarah had no wish to see either Sir Ralph or the remainder of his guests. She sat at Amelia's bedside, fretting over the difficulties of returning to Woodallan with the Earl very likely on his deathbed and his unwanted granddaughter in their party. Feeling restless, Sarah paced across to the window and sat for a time watching the snow, but its hypnotic swirling gave her no peace.

It was late afternoon and growing dark when Sarah left her cousin sleeping soundly and went downstairs for a breath of fresh air. She watched the daylight fade over the gardens and reflected that Guy would probably not be returning that night after all. Sarah let herself back into the house via the conservatory. The snow falling on the glass overhead made a brushing sound, soothing and soft. It was strangely light and the scent of fruit and summer flowers contrasted oddly with drifts of snow outside. Sarah walked through both hothouses, then sat for a while beside the pond, wondering why her troubled mind would give her no rest. Whatever problems she was facing would surely be resolved once Guy was back by her side. Even so, she felt alone and uneasy. Suddenly the Gothic horrors she had dismissed previously did not seem so foolish after all.

Chapter Ten

Sir Ralph was lurking in the entrance hall when Sarah went back in from the conservatory. He looked nervous and distressed, and cast her the sort of wary glance one reserved for a dangerous animal.

'Cousin! Are you well?' He peered into her face, clearly trying to discern any signs of ravage.

'I am very well, thank you,' Sarah snapped, 'but infinitely regretting the quest that brought me back to my home! I wish I had never set foot here!'

'It was Marvell's fault,' Sir Ralph said pitifully, wringing his hands. 'Marvell and Edward Allardyce! I have turned the man off, and Allardyce is to leave at first light! It was never my intention that you should suffer, Sarah! There will be no more revels now, or ever! Oh, this is a tragedy!'

He wandered off, still mourning. Sarah watched him go, half-exasperated, half-pitying. Sir Ralph had never been accepted by the *ton*, who had considered him beneath their notice even before he had established his repellent revels. Now, it seemed that even the purpose he had found for himself was ruined.

Sarah went slowly upstairs to check that Amelia was

feeling better, then moved softly to close all the curtains and shut out the night. The house was very quiet and of Justin Lebeter there was no sign. Sarah shivered a little, resolving to lock herself in with Amelia until Guy returned.

The snow was still falling, but gently now. Sarah was about to pull the long landing curtains, when she saw torches flaring through the trees as they illuminated the way to the grotto.

So Sir Ralph had decided to hold his solstice revels after all, and only a half-hour after he had told her otherwise! Sarah frowned crossly. Perhaps it was too much to expect a leopard to change its spots, but she was surprised that Ralph's guests had any energy left to join in. She closed the curtains with an angry swish.

The door from the servants' quarters opened with something of a crash.

'Miss Sarah!' It was Tom Brookes who was staggering into the hall and even in the dim light, Sarah could see the livid bruise to his temple. She hurried down the stair and grasped his arm as he almost lost his balance.

'Tom! What on earth—?'

'Hit on the head,' Tom was saying, and Sarah could hear his disgust even through the chatter of his teeth, 'lying in the snow I dunno how long, and Miss Olivia gone—'

'Olivia?' Sudden fear sharpened Sarah's tone, but when Tom looked at her blankly, she guided him over to the stairs and helped him to sit down. 'There, Tom. You stay there and I'll call one of the maids to bathe your head. Steady… Now, you say that Olivia has gone—'

She broke off as Mrs Brookes came dashing through the door with what looked like half a dozen maids in tow, their faces registering everything from fright to excitement.

'Oh, Miss Sarah! There he is! As soon as he heard Miss Meredith had gone, what did he do but go rushing off to find you! I couldn't stop him! I said there was no difficulty because it was you as sent the message and…' She ran out of breath and stopped as she saw the look on Sarah's face. 'Lordy me, never tell me it wasn't you as sent the message to Miss Olivia—'

'It wasn't me,' Sarah said.

Amelia was emerging from her room now, evidently curious about the uproar, and Justin Lebeter appeared from the direction of the games room. It was clear that Amelia was feeling better for it took her only a moment to take charge.

'Susan, please fetch a bowl of warm water and some bandages. Lord Lebeter, could you help Tom upstairs? He needs to lie down and have absolute quiet. Keep back everyone! Give him some air!'

'My!' Mrs Brookes said, impressed, as Tom allowed Lebeter to haul him to his feet and support him slowly up the stairs. 'That cousin of yours, Miss Sarah! Proper cowed, my Tom is! I've never seen anything like it!' She looked more sharply as she saw Sarah pulling outdoor boots and a cloak from the cupboard.

'Where are you going, Miss Sarah? On a night like this with the snow…' she wrinkled up her nose '…and those pagan revels! Wait 'til Lord Lebeter is done, then he can go looking for Miss Olivia—'

'I fear there isn't time for that, Mrs Brookes,' Sarah was pulling on her boots as she spoke. 'At what time did the message come for Olivia?'

'We found it near on an hour ago.' Mrs Brookes was starting to look worried. 'There was a note pushed under the door. I assumed…Miss Olivia said that it was from you—that you wanted to meet. Oh, lordy!'

'Never mind,' Sarah said, feeling as though she was within an inch of throwing up her hands in despair herself. 'You had best get upstairs and make sure that Lady Amelia is not terrifying your Tom!' She paused. 'I don't suppose you know where Olivia was going for our assignation?'

'No.' Mrs Brookes bit her lip. 'I tried to persuade her against it—told her it was a dirty night to be out, but she said she was not going far! Oh, Miss—'

'Pray explain to Lady Amelia and Lord Lebeter when you may,' Sarah said rapidly, her hand on the door, 'and do not worry. All will be well!'

'Her poor mother—' Mrs Brookes began, but Sarah stayed to hear no more. Pulling the door wide, she slipped out into the snow.

The sky was clear and the moon rode high on ragged clouds. From the depths of the wood came the sound of chanting, most unearthly in the black-and-white landscape. Sarah shivered and furiously told herself to stay calm—it could only be Sir Ralph's foolish antics. She had once thought that they could harm no one, but after the previous night she was not so sure. Sarah remembered that, some sixty years previously, Sir Francis Dashwood had supposedly founded a club based on devil worship, where members dressed as monks and nuns and held licentious orgies. No doubt Sir Ralph modelled himself on that example. She took a deep breath. She knew she could not allow herself to become frightened.

Sarah tried to think clearly as she ran through the wood. Olivia had been lured from hiding by someone using her name, and she was certain that it had to be Lord Allardyce. Ralph had said that Allardyce and Marvell were in league, so possibly the servant had discovered Olivia's hiding place. One or other of them must have dealt Tom a blow to keep him out of the way, and now Allardyce meant to use the revels as a cover to carry Olivia off…

Dodging between the trees, Sarah drew nearer to the grotto and tried to keep in the shadows. Torches flared about the entrance and the chanting was much louder now, eerie in the quiet night. Sarah's skin crawled. She could see a brazier burning in the centre of the grotto and a curious smell, sweet and woody, was floating towards her. It made her head spin but it was too late to go back now.

Sarah crept around the outside of the grotto and approached the entrance with extreme caution. She was about to peer in at the door when several figures in long flowing robes came running from the entrance and began to scatter throughout the wood, shrieking and screaming in evident enjoyment. It was impossible to identify the masked revellers, but Sarah recognised a slender wraith that could only be Lady Ann Walter, being hotly pursued by a man in black robes. Catching her about the waist, he tumbled her into the snow and the two of them rolled about in evident and amorous excitement. Sarah drew back in disgust.

A sudden sharp sound from inside the grotto made her jump. She edged forward and tried to see around the corner of the entrance without giving herself away, but the curve of the walls blocked her view. The smell of the brazier was much stronger now, making her eyes water and her head feel dizzy. If it was another of Ralph's noxious aphrodisiacs… There was a scraping sound, followed by silence. Sarah hesitated, barely breathing. She knew that someone must still be inside the grotto. Perhaps Sir Ralph, as high priest of whatever ceremony had just taken place, had stayed after the others to prepare the next stage of the revels... Sarah paused. She had to find out if Lord Allardyce had brought Olivia here.

Sarah drew herself up. Even if Sir Ralph were still in the grotto, he would hardly hurt her. And if it was Allardyce, or Marvell, or both... She shut her mind to that. Once he knew that everyone was alerted to his plan, Allardyce would surely not persist in his abduction of Olivia.

Sarah stepped forward, suddenly resolute, and as she did so a cloaked figure crossed her view, walking directly towards the entrance of the grotto. He put his hood back as he approached and the torchlight gleamed on his fair hair. Sarah caught her breath in shock and disbelief as the flaring light illuminated his face, and revealed not the expected features of Lord Allardyce...but those of Guy Renshaw.

Sarah felt as though all the breath had been knocked from her body. She was breathing hard and shivering violently. What was Guy doing at Blanchland when he had been summoned home to Woodallan? Why had he not told her of his return? What was his purpose at the revels? And why had she ever trusted him at all, when it seemed clear that he was utterly untrustworthy?

All those thoughts raced through Sarah's mind in an instant, followed by a wave of anguish so painful she could hardly bear it. She clung to the outside wall of the grotto to steady herself, calming slightly at the physical sensation of the cold snow and rough earth beneath her fingers. She would confront Guy. Now.

The shadows shifted and he walked past her, so close that Sarah almost imagined she had felt the brush of the monk's robes against her own cloak. He was moving purposefully, unlike the others who could still be heard shrieking and tumbling in the snow. Another worse suspicion grasped Sarah. She had assumed that it was Allardyce who had discovered Olivia, but supposing that it was Guy? He had claimed that he did not agree with his father's plan to spirit Olivia away, but was that true? Perhaps he had lulled her suspicions in order to remove Olivia before Sarah could prevent it…

Half of Sarah's mind argued that this could not possibly be true, whilst the other half grappled with all her doubts and suspicions. She was tired and alone, worn out with her concerns for Olivia and the accumulated tensions of the day. She loved Guy, but her tired mind was telling her that she might have made a mistake.

There suddenly seemed to be so many reasons to mistrust him; he had lulled her suspicions with soft words and kindness, had made her fall in love with him, and yet, what did she really know of him at all? Her instincts might tell her to trust him, but those instincts could be very wrong, and Olivia's life was at stake…

Sarah slid from her hiding place and began to follow Guy between the trees. She went slowly, keeping in the shadows, careful not to make a sound. Other figures in loose-flowing robes flitted across her line of vision. Her head swam with the lingering smell of the brazier. It was like another horrible dream. At one point a hooded figure with Sir Ralph's girth loomed out of the trees in front of her, but before he could utter a word, she pushed him hard into a snowdrift and he collapsed without a sound.

They were heading for the Folly Tower. Sarah could

see its dark shape against the lighter sky, and watched as Guy slipped inside. Now was the time to follow him in and confront him, but still she hesitated. She knew that it was the only way to learn the truth, to be reassured, to let Guy explain…

The blackness of the doorway yawned before her. Tip-toeing as softly as she was able, Sarah trod up to the door and peered in. The moon was bright through the tumbledown walls; it lit up the whole of the interior, including what looked like a bundle of rags on the earthen floor.

Sarah forgot her fear. With an exclamation, she hurried forward and turned the bundle over to reveal the white, unconscious face of Olivia Meredith. Her niece was as limp as rag doll and made neither sound nor movement. There was a bruise very similar to the one administered to Tom Brookes marring the perfection of her pale forehead, and a small cut that was sticky with blood.

Abruptly the moon went behind a cloud and plunged the whole tower into darkness. Sarah heard a step on the earthen floor beside her and felt the brush of cloth against her face. Someone caught hold of her arm in a punishing grip, dragged her to her feet and thrust her hard against the tower wall.

As abruptly as it had gone in, the moon re-emerged, flooding the tower with light again. It shone on Guy's furious face as he roughly thrust the hood of Sarah's cloak aside and stared down into her face.

'You! What the hell are you doing here, Sarah?'

Sarah struggled, but he held her tightly. He shook her hard. 'Well? What are you doing out here on the night of the revels? Answer me!'

Sarah's mouth tightened into an angry line. 'What do

you think I am doing, sir, joining in? Surely the question is to you rather than me—what are *you* doing here? You are supposed to be at Woodallan, or so you let me believe! You are the one skulking around in those ridiculous robes! And what have *you* done to my niece?'

Guy let her go so suddenly that she almost stumbled. His voice was drained of all expression. 'You think that I did that?'

'Why not?' Sarah gave him a look full of flashing anger. 'You told me yourself that the plan was to remove Olivia before anyone could know of her existence! Pay her off—bundle her out of the way... What does it matter how the thing is done? The honour of the Woodallans is paramount!'

She saw the glitter of rage in Guy's own face now and was perversely determined to provoke him further.

'You lulled my suspicions, made me believe you in earnest! I thought that it was Allardyce who was the danger, but I have made a mistake, have I not?'

Guy swore. He took a step closer, and suddenly Sarah was afraid. Her own pain had made her want to lash out at him, but now, belatedly, her instincts were telling her that she had made a terrible mistake.

'Allardyce is in the grotto, tied up to prevent him from carrying off your niece,' Guy ground out. 'That is the extent of the danger he poses! As for me, I told you the truth this morning, though you obviously did not believe me! And to think you believe me capable of hitting a defenceless woman—my own flesh and blood! Your opinion of me is truly flattering, Miss Sheridan!'

The sarcasm flicked Sarah on the raw. She recoiled from the disgust she saw in his face. 'If you had told me the truth from the start—'

'We shall leave the recriminations until later, if you

please, Miss Sheridan!' Guy said coldly. 'Just now it is *your niece*—' he stressed the phrase '—who needs your help.' The tension had left him now, replaced by something that chilled Sarah more—a cold indifference. The tone of his voice, the way he addressed her as 'Miss Sheridan' rather than by her name, suggested that he was unlikely to forgive her quickly, if at all.

Suddenly Sarah was overcome by an enormous lassitude. The light-headedness induced by the brazier's fumes and the accumulated shocks of the night had left her feeling tired and faint. She slumped against the wall of the tower. Guy's voice seemed to come from a great distance.

'If this is intended to gain my sympathy, I fear it will not work...'

'I'm sorry...' Sarah's words came out as a whisper. 'The smoke...the brazier—'

She heard Guy give an exclamation of exasperation, then his angry features swam briefly into view. 'Damnation! Sarah—' He shook her hard and her head swam all the more.

Beyond his shoulder, another face appeared and then another. Sarah closed her eyes. She knew she must be dreaming now. It sounded like Justin Lebeter's voice. 'Guy? What in God's name—?'

And then, to her immense gratitude, Sarah felt herself slide from Guy's grip into a dead faint.

Sarah opened her eyes. She was in her bedroom at Blanchland, a room that was becoming almost familiar to her. The bright light that crept around the closed curtains suggested that it was daylight outside, but the bedroom was gloomy and Amelia, sitting beside the bed, was holding a magazine up to the meagre light.

'Open the curtains if it would help you to read better,' Sarah suggested.

Her cousin jumped. 'Oh! You are awake! How do you feel, Sarah?'

'I am very well.' Sarah sat up and attempted to push back the covers and swing her legs out of bed, but her head started to spin and she lay back with a groan. Amelia tutted with annoyance.

'You see! You are not well at all! Pray keep still, Sarah!'

Sarah obeyed whilst her cousin moved across to the window and pulled back the curtains. She winced as her eyes adjusted to the flood of daylight.

'Oo-oof! What time is it, Milly?'

'About midday, I think. You have slept the clock around!'

'Olivia!' Sarah said, memory suddenly flooding back. 'What has happened? Is she safe?'

Amelia put a soothing hand on her arm and sat down beside her. 'Olivia is quite safe. In fact, she awoke before you!'

'And Tom?' Sarah struggled upright again, fighting sheets and blankets that seemed to have a mind of their own. 'What happened, Milly?'

'I shall not tell you if you do not keep still,' her cousin reproached. 'Tom is much better, although his wife is insisting he rest, which goes against the grain! All of Sir Ralph's guests have left, except Lord Lebeter, who seems barely able to leave Olivia's side! Guy has packed that poisonous Lord Allardyce off—a night tied up in the grotto soon cooled his ardour and I do not think he will approach Olivia again! Oh…' she smiled '…and Sir Ralph himself is a little sickly, I fear—we found him asleep in a snowdrift and he has taken an ague!'

'Oh, dear!' Sarah pressed a hand to her mouth, assailed by guilt at the memory of the portly figure she had pushed over in the snow. 'I seem to remember... It was all so extraordinary, Milly! Robed figures running everywhere, and that dreadful smell from the brazier—'

'Yes, Guy tells me that it was some kind of opiate used by Allardyce to induce hallucinations,' Amelia said with disgust, then stifled a giggle. 'You would have thought that there had been quite enough of that sort of thing! No wonder they were all rolling around in the snow regardless of cold! The doctor believes that you suffered an adverse reaction to it, Sarah, and that, coupled with the natural anxiety of the situation, led you to swoon! It is lucky it was not worse! That is twice that you have been fortunate!'

Sarah was beginning to remember just how bad it had been. She wondered briefly whether she could claim that it was a hallucination that had affected the balance of her mind and made her level those accusations at Guy, but concluded sadly that he was unlikely to believe her. Amelia was laughing again.

'Poor Sir Ralph, I would not wish you to misjudge him! Apparently he had not intended to hold the revels, but Allardyce needed them as a cover for his own actions, so he and Marvell conspired to arrange it all. Apparently Marvell let Allardyce down by running off with Lady Ann Walter! Meanwhile Ralph came rushing out to see what was happening and caught a chill for his pains!'

Sarah tried to smile, but the thought of Guy's anger made her feel stiff and cold. Amelia had not yet noticed.

'When we first saw you with Guy in the tower, it

looked as though he was trying to strangle you, Sarah—'

'I expect he would have liked to do precisely that,' Sarah said, so bleakly that her cousin stopped laughing and frowned.

'Why, what can have happened?'

'Only that I accused him of having attacked Olivia!' Sarah's hand smoothed the bedspread nervously. 'It is a little difficult to explain, Milly, but I knew that Guy had been asked by his father to find Olivia and spirit her away before her relationship to the Woodallans became public—so I thought that he—'

'Oh, dear!' Amelia looked stricken. 'Oh, Sarah, surely you could not think that Guy would do such a thing—?'

Sarah's face crumpled and two huge tears rolled down her cheeks. 'I know it was the height of folly—no, it was worse than that, it was a lack of trust that he will never forgive! I could have cut my tongue out when I realised the truth, but by then it was too late!'

She dabbed ineffectually at her tears, eventually giving up and crying wholeheartedly into the handkerchief that Amelia pressed into her hand.

'Well, this is very bad,' Amelia said at length, with an understatement that made Sarah laugh a little bitterly, 'but perhaps Guy will understand that you were distraught. After all, you had been through an unpleasant experience the night before, and with the tensions of the day...'

'Pray do not make excuses for me,' Sarah said with desolation. 'Guy has behaved to me as a gentleman should, and I have repaid his trust with base suspicions. Oh, I wish I had never been born!'

'I will send a tray up to you,' Amelia said, getting

up. 'You will feel better once you have eaten, and when you are well enough I will let you get up! It seems we are forever ministering to one another—it is enough to induce a fit of the megrims! '

'The Earl!' Sarah said suddenly, when her cousin was almost at the door. 'I thought he was ill? What has happened—?'

'The Earl is quite well. The message summoning Guy to Woodallan was as false as the one from yourself to Olivia!'

'But—'

'Later,' Amelia said inexorably, closing the door behind her with an emphatic click.

Sarah got out of bed and wandered listlessly over to the window. The short winter day was already closing in, and Sarah shivered at the cold view. Despite Amelia's optimism, she knew that Guy would not forgive her. She should have been running to him for help, after all, not hurling accusations at him.

Sarah dressed slowly, ate a little of the food Amelia sent up, drank a glass of spring water and went down the corridor to visit Olivia. It was easy to work out which room her niece was occupying, for Justin Lebeter was sitting outside the door in the attitude of a man who is prepared to wait all day just for a glimpse of the object of his devotion. He leapt to his feet as Sarah approached.

'Miss Sheridan! Are you feeling better, ma'am?'

'Yes, I thank you, sir.' Sarah smiled at him. 'I am come to see how Olivia is going on.'

Lord Lebeter's face glowed. 'Oh, she is much recovered! I am sure she will be glad to see you! Lord Renshaw is with her, with Mrs Brookes acting as chaperon, although as he is her uncle—' He broke off. 'Indeed, it seems odd to consider Renshaw as anyone's uncle, but I suppose...'

Sarah laughed. 'I see that he has told you the whole!'

'Well, a little.' Lebeter looked diffident. 'I understand that I have you to thank also, Miss Sheridan, for your efforts to protect Miss Meredith. Indeed, she has been speaking most highly of you. I had no idea...'

Sarah felt a swift rush of guilt. 'It was my fault. When you spoke to me of Olivia's whereabouts I was anxious only to protect her from Lord Allardyce. I had no wish to mislead you, but I thought it safer to tell no one what I knew. I am sorry.'

Lebeter shook his head. 'No apology necessary, ma'am, I assure you. I understand why you acted as you did. You will know now that I am hopeful of securing Miss Meredith's affections and I swear that my intentions are honourable.' He flushed endearingly. 'The discovery of her...erm...her antecedents is of no consequence to me.'

Sarah wondered fleetingly whether the Dowager Lady Lebeter would be so sanguine about a daughter-in-law with so dubious a family history. Justin Lebeter's mother was known equally as a demanding mama and a rampant snob, but young Lord Lebeter seemed quite determined; perhaps it would only strengthen his love for Olivia if he had to overcome adversity for her sake. The thought of adversity led Sarah to wonder about the Earl of Woodallan. If his granddaughter were to become Lady Lebeter, and take her place in society, he would have to come to terms with the fact that he could not sweep Catherine's shame aside. Those were issues for Guy to discuss with his father, but she acknowledged with a sinking heart that she could not avoid her part in the debate. As Olivia's closest relation on her father's side, she would have to be consulted.

Lebeter opened the bedroom door for her and she went in. Olivia was sitting up in bed, a clean white bandage around her head. She was chatting animatedly to Guy, who was leaning forward and smiling. Mrs Brookes knitted placidly beside the window. It was a charming family scene.

Guy looked up and saw Sarah, and the smile died from his eyes. He got to his feet and gave her a formal bow.

'Miss Sheridan. You are recovered, I see. I will leave you to talk for a little with Miss Meredith.'

'Oh, do not hurry away!' Olivia spoke impulsively. 'It is quite delightful to have both my new-found relatives here together!' She turned glowing eyes on Sarah. 'Lord Renshaw has been telling me all about my mother's family! I must own that it is almost too much excitement to take in at once!'

Sarah mentally raised her eyebrows. Guy must have done an exceptionally good job to have presented the story to Olivia in a manner that caused no unhappiness or embarrassment. She only hoped that his father would be so positive. She could feel Guy's sardonic gaze resting on her, reading her mind, almost challenging her to spoil Olivia's happiness with caution.

'I am glad to find you so much better, my dear,' Sarah said, avoiding comment. 'I was so very worried about you! When I heard you were missing—'

'Oh, it was all most horrid and quite like a Gothic romance!' Olivia shivered enjoyably, secure in the knowledge that she was now safe. 'When I received your note—or rather, the note purporting to come from you—I hurried off without a second thought! Mrs Tom did counsel me to wait, but I am too impulsive, I suppose! Anyway, I remember reaching the tower and calling for you, and then I remember nothing more until I woke up here!'

'Just as well,' Guy said laconically. 'I shall trust Lebeter to keep you from danger in future!'

Olivia giggled and blushed. 'I believe he was most disappointed that you had already dealt with Lord Allardyce! He told me he wished most strongly to plant him a facer!'

'Quite understandable,' Guy observed. 'I will see you later, Miss Meredith! Do not tire yourself!'

'Oh, no, I shall chat to Sarah for a little and then sleep,' Olivia confided artlessly. 'It has been so kind of you to spare me so much time, sir!'

'If you call your aunt by her given name, I suppose you should address me by mine also,' Guy said, making Sarah feel about a hundred years old. 'That is, if you would feel comfortable doing so!'

Olivia looked as though she had been given a present. 'Oh, may I do so, Guy? That would be most agreeable!' She looked from Guy to Sarah and back again. 'And I can now congratulate you together on your happy news! I was never more delighted than when I heard!'

Sarah knew that she was looking blank.

'Miss Meredith is congratulating us on our betrothal, my love,' Guy said, with gentle sarcasm. 'Perhaps you could try to emulate her enthusiasm!'

Sarah flushed. She had assumed that the last thing Guy would wish to do was marry her after her outburst the previous night, and certainly his cold behaviour to her had borne out such an opinion. The look he gave her was caustic, once more daring her to destroy Olivia's illusions. Sarah bit her lip and held her peace. Now was not the time to attempt to explain to Olivia that the engagement was broken.

'Before you go, you must tell us how you came to be here in time to rescue me,' Olivia was saying, blissfully unaware of Sarah's discomfiture. 'You did not finish the story! You had gone to Woodallan...'

'I am sure that Miss Sheridan does not wish to hear this,' Guy said, with a smile for his niece that pointedly excluded Sarah. 'I will finish the tale later, perhaps—'

'On the contrary, sir,' Sarah said coldly, 'I am very interested. You may remember that I asked you the same question myself—last night!'

'I remember!' Guy's dark eyes narrowed with comprehensive dislike. He resumed his seat. 'Very well, the tale goes thus. I hastened back to Woodallan and was glad to find my father better than expected—surprised even, that I had received a message summoning me back home! It did not take Dr Johnson to see that someone had tricked me in order to get me out of the way!'

Olivia giggled.

'I turned around to come back to Blanchland immediately,' Guy continued, 'but my horse threw a shoe at Old Down, and whilst I waited for him to be shod, I heard an extraordinary tale. There was a closed carriage in the yard there, and two fellows passing the time drinking in the bar. It made them loquacious. Apparently they had come down from London at the behest of a noble lord...' Guy paused. 'They were joking about what a man would be doing with a closed carriage in the middle of the night in winter, but I could think of a very good reason.'

Sarah noticed that Olivia had stopped smiling and her eyes were as huge as saucers. She looked like a small child who was being told a fairy tale. 'Oh! What did you do, Guy?' she whispered.

'The landlord of the inn was most helpful in persuading the men to enjoy his hospitality a little longer,' Guy said with a grin. 'As far as I know, they are there still! I hastened back here as soon as my horse was ready. After that, it was a simple matter to don one of those ridiculous robes, wait until the...ah...service in the grotto was over, and force Lord Allardyce to tell me what he had done!'

Olivia shuddered enjoyably. 'And that horrible man, Marvell? What happened to him?'

Guy's gaze met Sarah's. 'He was...otherwise engaged, which was fortunate, since it meant that I did not need to deal with both of them at once!'

'If you had only come to tell us of your return, my lord, I am sure Lord Lebeter would have helped you,' Sarah said sweetly, unable to resist provoking him. 'There was no need to play the hero all alone!'

'I had no time,' Guy said smoothly, only his gaze betraying his antagonism to her, 'and I did not wish to alert Allardyce to my presence when he had gone to such trouble to remove me. Even you must understand that, Miss Sheridan, for do you not justify your own secrecy in this affair with the comfortable notion that you were protecting Olivia from Allardyce?'

They glared at one another. It seemed that both had forgotten Olivia, over whose sickbed they now fought. Sarah's gaze dropped to her niece's startled face and read the apprehension there. Olivia was no fool and had already realised that she had in some way caused a rift between her new-found uncle and aunt.

The look on her face gave Sarah pause. 'Pray forgive us, Olivia,' she said hastily. 'Lord Renshaw and I have matters to discuss, but not here.' She glanced towards the door and was relieved to see Justin Lebeter hovering on the threshold. 'We will leave you now, for I see that Lord Lebeter is hoping for a little time with you.'

She bent and kissed Olivia's cheek, noticing that her niece's eyes had lit up at the prospect of another visit from her beau. The squabble was already forgotten, but Sarah was ashamed of herself. She trod swiftly from the room, not waiting to see if Guy followed, and it was not until she had reached the door of her own room that she heard his quick steps behind her.

'Miss Sheridan! A moment of your time, if you please!'

Sarah swung round haughtily. 'You wish to speak to me, Lord Renshaw?'

Guy gave an ironic bow. 'You said just now that we had matters to discuss. Let us discuss them!'

'Downstairs—' Sarah began, but Guy shook his head.

'I would prefer some privacy,' he said silkily, 'and I have been in your room before, have I not?'

Sarah blushed. He hardly needed to remind her, and she was sure he had done so simply to embarrass her.

'Very well.' She turned her back as though it was of no consequence to her whether or not Guy followed her into the room, but knew with a tingling sense of awareness that he had come in and closed the door behind them. When she turned back, he was standing with his arm resting on the mantelpiece and was watching her with a cool indifference that made Sarah feel oddly at a loss.

'Well...' he made a slight gesture '...what did you wish to say to me?'

Sarah knew he was making matters deliberately difficult for her. She looked into his closed face and her composure broke.

'I am sorry! I know you are angry with me, but you must also know that I bitterly regret speaking as I did last night! But what was I to think? You had already told me of your father's plans—plans you had concealed from me when we came to Blanchland—and then to find you skulking about the grounds...and Olivia injured... I acknowledge that I reacted strongly, but—'

She knew that her appeal had failed even before Guy spoke. The look of cold withdrawal in his eyes did not fade. He looked at her with contempt.

'You simply showed what was in your heart, Miss Sheridan! We had already stumbled through a comedy of errors, had we not—the misunderstandings over your reasons for coming here, the facts I concealed from you, the secrets you refused to tell me... I suppose it is as well to know that we do not trust each other—at least that way we have no illusions!'

There was a frozen silence. Sarah felt as though her heart was breaking. She spoke hesitantly.

'Then surely it is better to forget that our foolish betrothal ever existed? Since you feel we cannot trust one another, it would be an appalling error to compound the situation by our marriage.'

They stood staring at one another for what seemed an age. Sarah was not sure what showed on her face; she almost broke down completely and pleaded for his forgiveness, begged for him to tell her that all would be well. Only the conviction that he would reject her held her silent. She remembered Guy's kindness and his gentleness, and the fierce heat of his passion for her, and looked into his cold face and felt her heart wither.

'You are mistaken, madam,' Guy said, after what seemed like centuries. His face was taut with anger and dislike. 'Not to go through with our marriage would be a greater error than that which has already occurred! I will not release you from the engagement, no matter how ill-starred it may be! When we were at Woodallan before, I made arrangements for the wedding to be held in the week after Christmas. The banns will have been read three times—and the marriage will take place!'

Sarah paled. 'You cannot mean to persist in this! It would be the most senseless act! I shall never agree!'

Guy gave her a mirthless smile. 'Unless you are prepared to stand up in church before my family and yours and refuse to marry me, you have no choice!' He took her arm and forcibly propelled her into a chair. 'Think about it, Sarah! In order to convince my father to accept Olivia, we shall need to act together. We cannot allow ourselves a show of disunity now! Worse, there is Allardyce to consider!' He paced restlessly across to the window, then turned to look down into Sarah's puzzled face.

'But Allardyce can pose no threat now!'

'No physical threat, perhaps, but think of the poisonous malice he can and will spread against both the Sheridan and Woodallan families! I know he has no proof positive of Olivia's parentage, but he has seen her—he will draw his own conclusions! And I would wager a fortune that he is already spreading scandal about you and your cousin, and your presence here at Blanchland! Remember what happened only two nights ago! Were you to break our engagement, the damage would be appalling!'

Sarah was silent. She could see the logic of his words, but equally inescapable was the misery of tying together two people who had so hurt each other that they could not be happy together. A lifetime was a very long time to be confronted by recrimination and broken dreams.

'It will not be so bad,' Guy said, and somehow his indifference was more painful for Sarah than ever his anger could have been. 'You will have regained you place in society, after all, and I am sure you will make a gracious mistress of Woodallan.'

It sounded quite chilling to Sarah. She wondered with despair how she could bear half a marriage when she still loved Guy, and knew beyond a shadow of a doubt that she had already lost him before the knot was even tied.

Chapter Eleven

They left for Woodallan the following morning. Olivia was well enough to travel and her mother was also sufficiently recovered to contemplate the short journey with equanimity. It was slow going, for the roads were icy and pitted with holes, but eventually they rolled through the gates and disembarked with gratitude.

Sarah felt both relief and discomfort in almost equal measure. Her apprehension about the imminent wedding was quite overshadowed by nervousness for Olivia, who was staring up at the house with awe and trepidation. Sarah also felt for Mrs Meredith, whose own concerns must include the worry of losing her daughter to relatives far grander than she could have anticipated.

This time there was no welcoming party, just the Countess of Woodallan awaiting them in the panelled hall and looking almost as nervous as her guests. The generosity of her welcome could not be faulted, however, and she hugged Olivia with tears in her eyes and offered a very warm greeting to Mrs Meredith. A moment later, Guy's two sisters and their families came flooding out into the hall, and in the general round of kisses and exclamations, the tension eased considerably.

No one commented that the Earl was nowhere to be seen, but Sarah saw Guy draw his mother aside for a brief word, before he disappeared down the passage to the Earl's study.

The day dragged for Sarah, who had not expected Guy to spare any time for her but was nevertheless disappointed to be neglected. She thought of their bitter words the previous day and reflected that it was probably a state to which she would, through necessity, become accustomed. The Countess had given her the rose bedroom, in deference to her new position as Guy's future bride, and Sarah felt a complete fraud as she sat in splendid isolation watching the short day fade to winter dusk. Greville Baynham rode in at nightfall, but, apart from a flurry of activity to greet his arrival, the house sat in a brooding silence, waiting for the Earl to make his decision.

Guy and his father were the only members of the party missing when everyone assembled in the drawing-room for dinner that evening. The same tension was present as had been apparent earlier, as the family chatted amongst themselves and waited, with one eye on the door. The Countess checked the clock surreptitiously, well aware that dinner was spoiling. Olivia was almost white with anxiety and Sarah's heart went out to her. Such a public meeting with her grandfather would be enough to daunt all but the strongest spirit and, if he chose to not acknowledge her, the humiliation would be crushing.

Then the butler opened the door with a flourish and the Earl came in, leaning heavily on his son's arm, a gold-topped cane grasped in his other hand.

'Good evening,' he said, the same sardonic glint in

his eye that Sarah had often seen in Guy. 'My apologies for keeping you all waiting. I wished to be seen at my best when greeting my new relative. Miss Meredith—' the fierce glare softened as it rested on Olivia's pale face '—pray come here.'

Everyone seemed to be holding their breath. Mrs Meredith gave Olivia a little push, and she stepped forward to confront her grandfather, dropping a deep curtsy and allowing him to take her hand to raise her. The Earl's dark gaze travelled over her face.

'You are the image of your mother,' he said gruffly, at length. 'You are very welcome here, my dear.'

Everybody sighed in unison and a brilliant smile lit Olivia's eyes. The Earl offered her his arm and led her through into the dining-room, and Greville went up to Guy and clapped him on the back.

'Well done, Guy! I knew you'd pull it off!'

Justin Lebeter was shaking Guy's hand and Mrs Meredith was wiping away a tear, whilst the Countess was smiling and talking to her in an undertone. Amelia came up to Sarah and put an arm around her. 'Oh, Sarah, was that not wonderful! I can scarce believe that we are all one extended family now! Is it not extraordinary!'

Sarah was conscious of Guy watching her across the room. She ignored her own heavy heart and smiled brilliantly.

'Oh, it is delightful! I am so very happy for Olivia! Things have turned out so much better than I had hoped!'

'For all of us!' Amelia said, giving Greville a ravishing smile as he came over to her to lead her into dinner. She gave Sarah a swift hug. 'I am sure Olivia will always remember what you have done for her, Sarah! She has turned out to be most fortunate in all her relations!'

There was a lump in Sarah's throat. Self-pity, she told herself sternly, was the least attractive of emotions. Besides, it would achieve nothing. Guy had made his feelings for her plain, but she had no intention of making the rest of his family privy to the shaming truth.

With a sinking heart, Sarah saw the Countess instructing Guy to take her in to dinner. Lord Lebeter was busy charming to Mrs Meredith, who looked utterly bowled over, and there was a feeling of amity amongst the guests that made Sarah feel like the spectre at the feast. Guy reached her side and sketched a careless bow.

'Miss Sheridan, my mother suggests that I lead you into dinner.'

Sarah did not know whether he was deliberately trying to annoy her with his perfunctory attitude, or whether he cared so little to please her that he could afford to be offhand. Either way, she did not intend to let her irritation show. She gave him a cool smile.

'That would be quite appropriate, since we are betrothed, my lord!' She took his arm lightly. 'Come, let us not keep everyone waiting!'

Guy paid her very little attention during the meal, confining his conversation to his sister Emma, who sat on his left. Sarah ignored this manfully, for her part maintaining an animated discussion with Justin Lebeter on her other side and with Guy's sister Clara and her husband across the table. She was aware of more than one speculative glance as both Amelia and the Countess noted Guy's neglect of her, but this just served to bring more colour to her cheeks and an angry but becoming sparkle to her eyes.

It was inevitable that, at some point, the conversation would turn to the forthcoming marriage.

'We were so excited when Guy told us of the wedding!' Clara said, smiling across the table at her future sister-in-law. 'A whirlwind romance, and to your childhood sweetheart, too! Oh, Sarah, it is entirely delightful!'

Sarah could sense that Guy had paused in his conversation with Emma and was listening. She did not even glance at him.

'Yes, is it not a charming story!' Remembering how she had once denied that they had even been childhood friends, Sarah still managed to hit exactly the right, easy note. 'As soon as we met in Bath, Guy reminded me of how close we had been as children!'

'It is a tale to tell our own grandchildren, in fact,' Guy interposed, an edge to his voice. 'Just like a fairy tale!'

Sarah smiled at him blithely. 'What an enchanting thought, my lord,' she said sweetly. 'We must make sure to do so!'

'You must have been pleased to discover that the marriage could take place so soon,' Clara said, beaming. 'What with Olivia's arrival and the twelve days of Christmas and two weddings in the family, we shall be as merry as grigs!'

'It will be utterly thrilling!' Sarah gushed.

Guy shot her a speaking glance. His dark eyebrows snapped together. Sarah felt a strange exhilaration, like taking too much wine. She might not be able to make her husband love her, but she could surely irritate him. She knew that the frown on his brow, the ceaseless drumming of his fingers on the table, indicated that she had managed to break through the barrier of indifference that he had erected about himself.

The gentlemen rejoined the ladies swiftly after the meal, but Guy again showed little interest in talking to his fiancée. Instead he chatted to Amelia and Greville, affording Sarah the opportunity to study him covertly whilst she sat talking with Clara. The soft lamplight burnished his fair hair and cast a shadow across the planes of his face, accentuating the strong lines of cheekbone and jaw. He was smiling as he talked and Sarah felt her heart twist with longing and despair. She wanted him to love her, but she knew it was too late. She had had his love for the asking—and had twisted it out of recognition. As though sensing her regard, Guy looked up and his eyes, darkly shadowed, met Sarah's. Then he looked away with apparent boredom, and such misery choked Sarah's throat that for a moment she could not breathe. Was this, then, how her life was to be in future? In the middle of the warmth and love of this family, she alone would feel cold and alone.

She excused herself to the Countess and made her way unhurriedly to the door, intending to slip away to an early bed. To her surprise, Guy stood up and came across to her just as she was leaving.

'I will escort you to your room, Sarah.'

Sarah did not demur, though she felt awkward in his company. She knew that he was only offering to accompany her in order to show his family that all was well between them. They went slowly up the stairs and along the gallery, where more haughty pictures of Woodallan ancestors looked down. It was Sarah who broke the silence.

'Thank you for everything that you have done to help Olivia, my lord. I am very grateful that you were able to persuade your father to accept her into the family.'

Guy stopped walking. In the shadowy gallery it was too dark to see his face clearly.

'I have not forgotten,' he said slowly, 'that you were

the one who was brave enough to answer Olivia's plea for help in the first place.'

The compliment was unexpected. He took her hand, his fingers, long and strong, interlocking with hers. Sarah felt a shiver go through her.

'Brave?' She knew her voice sounded shaky. 'Surely you mean obstinate—or damnably foolish!'

'Maybe.' She heard the implication of a smile in his voice and felt her hand tremble in his. She tried to withdraw it. 'It was still courageous.'

For what seemed like hours, Sarah stood staring at him, captured by the expression in his eyes. One tiny tug of the hand would have brought her into his arms, but he did not move. It was Sarah who pulled away first, and her feet tapped on the wooden floor of the gallery as she fled from him.

It was Christmas Eve. Sarah, acting the part of the future mistress of Woodallan, accompanied the Countess on visits to tenants and villagers to distribute Christmas presents and good wishes. The carriage was laden down with everything from coal to oranges, tea to plum cake. Sarah was sure that she even saw the Countess slip some tobacco into the gnarled hands of various old gentlemen and a bottle of gin to one ancient lady. It was great fun and they were greeted warmly wherever they went, Sarah especially so as the young lord's future bride.

Naturally, Guy did not accompany them. His excuse had been that his father's illness made it essential that he act as host and entertain his male guests, but as these were all either family or close friends, this rang a little hollow. It rankled especially with Sarah, who could not avoid the assumption that he did not wish to be with her. The Countess noted her goddaughter's frozen expression but wisely held her own counsel, knowing that there were some times when even friendly advice was unwelcome.

Dinner that evening was very different from the family affair of the night before. The Woodallans were hosting a dinner and informal dance for the whole neighbourhood and numerous coaches drew up at the door decorated with holly and mistletoe. The great hall of the old house had been cleared for the banquet, a huge fire blazed in the medieval hearth and torches flared on the walls. It looked dramatic and festive.

Amelia had chosen a dress in Christmas scarlet for the occasion. 'I hope it does not seem too daring for the country,' she said doubtfully, turning before the mirror in Sarah's bedroom. She gave a little giggle. 'I am indeed a scarlet woman, so it is most apt!'

'You look wonderful,' Sarah said truthfully, for the deep red was most striking against Amelia's white skin and black hair. 'I wish I could wear something as bright as that to give me confidence! And you are no scarlet woman, Milly, but a Christmas bride!'

Greville, taking advantage of the special licence, had pressed Amelia to marry him the day after Christmas, and she had been happy to agree.

Amelia smiled. 'You look charming.' She considered Sarah's green silk with its overdress of gold gauze. ' I am sure Guy will have no complaints!'

'I am sure Guy will not even notice,' his fiancée said glumly.

The evening did nothing to disprove her opinion. This time Guy did not even lead her into dinner, and he spent the entire evening away from her side. They did not exchange a single word. Sarah chatted and smiled until she thought her face would ache, and anticipated how mortified she would be when her fiancé neglected to dance with her. Dinner seemed to last forever, but eventually the tables were cleared away and the hall prepared for the carollers.

The press of people was becoming greater by the minute, and Sarah felt very vulnerable as she stood alone on the edge of the throng. She reflected wryly that it was lucky she was dressed in green. At least some people might mistake her for the Christmas decorations.

A lot of wine had been consumed during dinner and the hall seemed to be becoming very hot. Sarah fanned herself and looked around surreptitiously for Guy. She could see Amelia and Greville, amorously entwined beneath some mistletoe and gazing into each other's eyes. Olivia and Justin Lebeter were standing together, heads bent close. Sarah stifled a sigh. Only she, it seemed, was on her own…

'Miss Sheridan?'

Sarah spun around. A tall young man with dark hair and an easy smile was looking at her hopefully. He gave a slight bow.

'Daniel Ferrier, at your service, ma'am! You may remember that we were neighbours once—'

'Daniel Ferrier!' Sarah gave him her hand. 'I remember you well! How are you, sir? Why, it must be all of six years since we met—'

'Seven, I believe, ma'am.' Mr Ferrier smiled warmly. He seemed quite dazzled that she should have remembered him at all.

Further conversation was cut short by the arrival of the bell ringers and the village carollers, who gave a hearty rendition of several traditional tunes before turning with gratitude to the pork pie and elderberry wine that Lady Woodallan had laid out for refreshment. More villagers were arriving for the dance, and the throng of guests was quite overwhelming now. Sarah found herself pressed against Mr Ferrier rather more closely than propriety demanded. Mr Ferrier did not appear to object.

'Would you care to dance, ma'am?' he asked her, as the music struck up for the first set of country dances.

Sarah could not see Guy anywhere in the mêlée. With a mental shrug, she accepted Daniel Ferrier's invitation, and allowed him to swing her around to the music with as much abandon as all the other guests. Sarah found it pleasant not to be overlooked, even if she was dancing with the wrong man. Bright-eyed and breathless, they sat down as the music ended, to catch up on all the years that had passed since they had last met.

Mr Ferrier's uncle, it transpired, had purchased him a cornetcy in the 10th Foot and he had progressed to the rank of Captain before selling out six months previously. He gave Sarah a very lively account of his time serving in the Peninsula. In turn, Sarah told him of her life in Bath, and they were so engrossed that at first she did not notice that Guy had actually come across to ask her for a dance.

He greeted Ferrier with a pleasant nod of the head, but the expression in his eyes was watchful, his voice cold.

'Please excuse me for stealing my fiancée away from you, Ferrier. I fear I shall not have the opportunity to dance with her otherwise!'

Daniel Ferrier could not miss the warning implicit in the words. His gaze met Guy's for a long moment and Sarah felt the sudden tension between them. This was ridiculous, for Daniel Ferrier had never been any more than a family friend, and besides, Guy had shown no interest in asserting his claim to her hand before. The silence threatened to become embarrassing, then Ferrier gave a nod of acknowledgement even slighter than Guy's.

'You are most fortunate, Renshaw.'

'So I think,' Guy agreed smoothly.

Sarah was beginning to find this male arrogance very irritating. She got to her feet slowly, making her regret rather more evident than was strictly necessary.

'Excuse me, Mr Ferrier. No doubt we may continue our conversation at a future date.'

'I should like that, ma'am,' Daniel Ferrier said, with a ghost of a smile. He bowed and sauntered away, and Guy put a firm arm about Sarah's waist and guided her into the set. It was clear that he was furious, for his mouth was set in a straight line and his eyes glittered with suppressed anger.

'Miss Sheridan,' he said, under his breath, 'you will do me the courtesy of forbearing to flirt with my parents' neighbours!'

The injustice of the remark took Sarah's breath away and prompted her good resolutions to fly out of the window. Suddenly a wholesale argument seemed a most attractive way of clearing the air. She could see that the other couples in the dance were watching them with curiosity, and she gave Guy a ravishing smile.

'You are speaking nonsense, my lord! Mr Ferrier is simply an old friend!'

'So I believe,' Guy said tightly. 'He will not become a new one, however!'

The steps of the dance forced them to part at that moment, but both of them knew the topic was not closed. When they came back together again, Sarah said, with a melting smile, 'It shows a certain arrogance, my lord, to ignore your future wife for the best part of three days and then to take exception when another pays her a little attention!'

Guy glanced around to make sure they were not overheard. His face was set.

'I do not care for other men paying attention to my wife!'

'Pshaw! You are just a dog in a manger!' Sarah twirled merrily to the music. 'You do not care for me yourself—you have made that clear!'

'It is scarcely appropriate for you to console yourself before the knot is even tied! I saw the two of you earlier—pressed so close a sixpence could not have come between you!'

The steps separated them again, giving Sarah the chance to prepare her next salvo.

'I had not realised that it would be more appropriate for me to wait until *after* the wedding!' she said, as they were reunited. She was well aware that she was starting to behave very badly and she was enjoying it, particularly as Guy did not appear to see the amusing side.

He spoke through gritted teeth. 'It would not be. As well you know!'

'Then I am condemned to a most lonely existence, am I not?' Sarah flourished an exaggerated curtsy at the end of the dance, and clapped enthusiastically. 'You are the most dreadful puritan, my lord! Since we are to make a marriage of convenience I am simply making the best of it!'

Guy kept hold of her arm. His grip was tight. He made no move to steer them back into conversation with any of their friends, but started to lead Sarah purposefully towards the door. Sarah could see everybody watching them whilst pretending that they were not doing so. She hung back, prevaricating.

'I am in need of a drink, my lord—'

'You may have one in the drawing-room. Whilst I speak to you.'

Sarah frowned. 'I do not wish to speak with you any further. You are being quite absurd!'

She might as well have saved her breath. Guy's arm was hard about her waist and he half-carried her across the hall and through the door of the drawing-room, kicking it shut behind them.

'Why do you not lock the door?' Sarah suggested helpfully. 'It was so effective last time!'

Guy looked almost murderous. 'Listen, Sarah—'

'I think not. I have heard enough.'

Guy continued as though she had not spoken. 'If you think that ours will be a marriage of convenience, you are sorely mistaken!'

Sarah paused. She had not expected this. She frowned a little. 'But that was the agreement! Since we are obliged to marry, it should be in name only!'

Guy smiled. 'I see! Not just a marriage of convenience, but one in name only! I do not think so! Certainly, *I* never agreed to such a thing!'

'But—' Sarah's mind skittered across the conversation they had had at Blanchland when Guy had pointed out that she would have to marry him for the sake of Olivia and of her own reputation. Perhaps the phrase had not been used, but the implication had surely been the same thing. The marriage would be for form's sake only. She looked at him accusingly.

'Surely you cannot pretend to have any feelings for me! Not when you condemned me outright for believing you capable of hurting Olivia!'

Guy drove his hands into his jacket pockets. 'Very direct, Miss Sheridan! Are you sure that you are prepared for an equally direct response?'

Sarah stared at him. She was half-wondering whether she did, in fact, want to know his feelings for her, or whether some things were better left unspoken. However, it was too late. Guy strolled across to the window, looking out into the snowy dark.

'Since there is to be truth between us, Miss Sheridan, I confess that I find you very attractive. I have always done so.' He turned back to look at her. 'So there is no possibility of a marriage in name only. Even were I to promise it, I know I would break the promise at the first opportunity.'

Sarah's throat was dry. 'But that is iniquitous! Why, you do not even *like* me! How can you expect—?' She stopped as he came across to her. He picked up one amber ringlet and let it slide through his fingers. Sarah turned her face away. She was trembling and she could not bear him to see the effect he had on her.

'I know you understand me.' Guy spoke a little huskily. He let go of the ringlet reluctantly and his fingers drifted across the soft skin of her neck. 'For you feel it, too. It is the one thing that unites us.'

Sarah clenched her fists. 'But I will not give in to it!'

Guy laughed. 'Ah! That must be the difference between us!'

Sarah was afraid that she would cry with frustration and hurt. 'It is not right! How can this be, when we have hurt each other and dislike each other and can never love each other—?'

Guy's only reply was to bend his head and brush his lips against the hollow at the base of her throat.

Sarah was really struggling now, against him, against

her treacherous feelings and, most of all, against the sensual excitement that was prickling along her nerve-endings, reminding her of how it had been between them. The touch of his lips was light, brushing first one corner of her mouth then the other in a teasing caress. Sarah's eyes drifted closed as he captured her lips, tenderly, seductively...

She wrenched herself away. 'No! I will not give in to this!'

Guy stepped back in an exaggerated gesture of deference. 'Very well, Miss Sheridan. But have you thought how it will be living with me, day in, day out, yet denying the craving of your body, refusing the comfort of my arms?' His dark gaze held her still. 'We shall see who wins in the end!'

It was late afternoon on the day before the wedding when Amelia found her cousin sitting quietly in the old chapel. The winter sun was slanting through the stained glass windows, making pools of colour on the stone floor. Amelia shivered, for the air was cold. It was three days since she had married Greville in a quiet family ceremony in this very place, but now the wedding decorations had gone and the dusty chill had settled again, and it seemed it had settled on Sarah as well. She had seldom seen her cousin look so pinched and drawn. Sarah was sitting quite still, her head tilted back as she apparently contemplated the faded gold stars on the white-painted ceiling. Her cloak was wrapped tightly around her and she seemed to have shrunk within it, drawn in on herself. Amelia frowned.

'Sarah? Have you been here all afternoon?' Amelia slid into the pew beside her cousin, noting that Sarah jumped as though she had not even heard her approach.

'Oh! Amelia! I am sorry, I was woolgathering! It is very peaceful here. No, I have been here but ten minutes. We have spent the afternoon on the final fitting of my wedding gown…'

Her voice trailed away. To her cousin, she looked very unlike a young lady excited at the prospect of imminent marriage.

'Have I missed much entertainment?' Sarah asked listlessly.

'No, not really. The children have been on an owl hunt!' Amelia said, laughing. 'Do you remember that from when you were young, Sarah? As though one could possibly catch an owl with those little broomsticks! Anyway, Clara's little boy got stuck up a tree and had to be rescued by Guy! The owl flew off, of course!'

Sarah smiled a little. 'He is very kind, is he not, Amelia? I remember you saying how kind Guy was when he spoke to Jack Elliston at your ball…' Her voice trailed off again.

Amelia frowned again. 'You sound very low, Sarah. Are you suffering from last-minute nerves?'

Sarah shrugged tiredly. She drew her cloak more closely around her, as though to keep out the cold. 'Surely you must have noticed how Guy has been avoiding me over the past week?'

Amelia looked uncomfortable. 'Well, I'll allow there seems a certain distance… But he is very busy—there is much to do here.'

Sarah shot her a withering glance. 'You know full well that not a host of duties could keep a man from his fiancée's side if he wished to be with her! Consider yourself and Greville! No, Guy chooses to shun me because he is trapped in a marriage he does not desire!

Having undertaken to marry me to avoid scandal, he knows it will cause a greater one to break the engagement now!'

There was a sudden scrape of stone on stone behind them. Both girls jumped and spun around, but there was nothing to be seen amongst the cold shadows of the church. The carved faces of the Woodallan tombs stared back at them.

'A mouse...' Amelia said doubtfully, drawing her skirts away from the floor. 'You speak of a marriage of convenience, Sarah, which is strange when you remember how ardently Guy courted you! What can have changed that?'

A shade of colour tinged Sarah's cheeks. 'Matters went awry from the start, Milly. It just took a little time for the whole to unravel!' She sighed. 'We neither of us trusted the other. I fell in love with Guy so swiftly, yet I barely knew him!' Sarah shook her head. 'Before we even reached Blanchland, I had overheard a conversation between Guy and his father that suggested that he was withholding information from me. So in return I did not confide when I had found Olivia...' She gave a despairing shrug. 'So you see, we had already sowed the seeds of distrust between us.'

'I suppose it only made matters worse when you found out that he had been searching for Olivia,' Amelia prompted gently.

'Yes...' Sarah fixed her gaze on the bright lozenges of colour on the stone floor. 'Guy told me that his father had asked him to find Olivia and persuade her to vanish without any trouble. I was appalled. It sounded so callous—as though Guy would do anything to prevent his sister's reputation being harmed! Oh, Guy swore that he would not have carried it through, that it would not serve...and I believed him, but I was shocked, and once again the doubt was there.'

'So when you came upon him in the Folly Tower, when he was supposed to be here at Woodallan—'

Sarah nodded dolefully. 'I told you that I rashly accused him of attacking her! To tell the truth, I was in turmoil, Milly! I had just convinced myself that I trusted him, and then I saw him acting so suspiciously! When I found Olivia unconscious...' her shoulders slumped '...well, I was tired and distraught, but it is no excuse. I showed that I did not trust him, and he cannot forgive me, and that was the end, as far as we were concerned! Whatever love was starting to grow between us has been crushed by this!'

Neither of them spoke for a little, then Sarah shivered convulsively. 'How can I marry Guy when this is between us? I would run away if I had anywhere to go, and damn Blanchland and damn the danger to my reputation! This is breaking my heart!'

Amelia put her arm around her. 'Come away from here. You are frozen, Sarah!'

They went out of the chapel slowly, still talking in low voices. Amelia latched the heavy door behind them and their footsteps died away along the gravel path to the house. It was only when they had gone and the silence settled once more that there was a flicker of movement behind the leper squint, the soft footfall as someone descended the stone steps. The figure paused by a window, waited until the two girls had disappeared from view, then quietly let himself out of the chapel.

It was late that night when Guy received a summons to his father's study. The room was set up much as it had been on the occasion when the Earl had broken the momentous news about his secret grandchild: there was a warm fire, a good book and two glasses for brandy.

'Sit down, Guy,' the Earl said, gesturing to the chair his son had occupied on the previous occasion.

'Another brandy, sir?' Guy raised his eyebrows. He poured for himself and brought the decanter across to his father.

'Thank you.' The Earl put his book down and considered his son thoughtfully. 'In point of fact, I asked you here so that I *could* thank you—for persuading me not to be such a stiff-necked old fool as to turn away my own grandchild because of the misdemeanours of her parents! It has been a pleasure to meet her.'

Guy smiled. His gaze was on the amber liquid swirling in his glass. 'I am glad that you like Miss Meredith. She is a credit to her adoptive parents, I think.'

'They did a good job,' the Earl concurred. His thick dark eyebrows drew together. 'Young Lebeter seems to know what he's about. I dare say I may trust Olivia to him. A fine thing to find and lose one's granddaughter in the space of a few weeks!'

'It is not as bad as that, sir,' Guy pointed out. 'The engagement is likely to be a long one. There is the Dowager Lady Lebeter to bring around, after all!'

'Difficult woman!' the Earl said feelingly.

'I understand that Mama is trying to persuade Mrs Meredith to take a house on the estate here, at least until Olivia's future is settled,' Guy added. 'A sound idea. Yours, I take it?'

'You do your mother too little justice,' the Earl said gruffly. 'It was her idea, and I was happy to endorse it. I should like to see more of the child.'

'Of course. I believe that Greville and Lady Amelia have also invited the Merediths to stay with them in

Bath, though I should imagine that with their own wedding…'

'They may wish for some time alone together first,' the Earl observed. 'We must give some thought to Olivia's presentation to society in a little, when matters quieten down.'

Guy moved to build up the fire, then resumed his seat across from his father.

'We spoke before of the danger of Allardyce spreading scandal,' he said, a little hesitantly. 'Do you think—?'

The Earl made a dismissive gesture. 'There will be speculation over Olivia's birth—it is inevitable. We need not regard it, however. With powerful friends…' He let the sentence hang.

Guy knew what he meant. The Earl of Woodallan had immense influence, for all that he had lived retired for the previous few years. Allardyce's malicious stirring could do little damage, particularly with Olivia safely betrothed and Catherine Renshaw long dead. Society would always gossip, but equally a new scandal would always come along to distract attention. Guy drained his glass and stood up.

'Well, I am happy that all has turned out for the best. You must excuse me, sir, if you will. There is much to be done before tomorrow—'

'There is another matter on which I wished to speak with you.' The Earl's tone had hardened slightly. 'I have been thinking that it would be better to postpone your marriage to Miss Sheridan.'

Guy's gaze narrowed. 'I beg your pardon, sir?'

'I believe you heard me. You had better sit down again.'

His son obeyed without demur. 'What is this all about, sir?'

The Earl sighed, fixing his son with his steely dark gaze. 'We have all observed that there is an estrangement between yourself and Miss Sheridan. It is hardly the best way to approach a marriage!'

Guy looked away. He spoke a little stiffly. 'It is true that there are some difficulties—'

'All the more reason to delay, then, assuming that you are able to untangle these difficulties at all! Perhaps it would be wiser to cancel—'

'No!' Guy put his glass down so abruptly that the liquid spilled. 'That cannot be, sir. We spoke just now of scandal—if my marriage to Miss Sheridan does not take place, the rumour and gossip will rip her to shreds!'

The Earl shifted slightly. 'So this is solely an altruistic act, Guy?' His voice was dry. 'Very noble of you, my boy, but another poor reason for marriage! No wonder you resent the girl so much that you can barely bring yourself to speak to her!'

Guy flushed. 'It is not like that, sir—'

His father continued as though he had not spoken. 'No, your motives do you credit, Guy, but it will not serve.' He lowered his voice confidentially. 'To tell the truth, it quite relieves me that you do not care for the girl. You are my only son, and heir to an Earldom. Why throw yourself away on a match that brings us no material benefits? Oh, the Sheridan name was once respected in this county, but she has no fortune or connections to recommend her—'

'You mistake me, sir,' Guy said, a note of barely concealed anger in his voice. 'I still wish the marriage to take place and I am surprised to hear you speak thus of your goddaughter!'

The Earl avoided his gaze. 'Well, I say that it shall not happen. The more I think about it, the more I am convinced that it would be a mistake! And do not trouble yourself over Miss Sheridan's situation. I will help her!'

'Help her, sir?' Guy's tone was dangerous. 'In what way will you...help her?'

'Why, to find a position, of course!' The Earl gestured largely. 'It would be best for her to travel at first, until the scandal of her trip to Blanchland dies down. There must be someone—a respectable lady travelling abroad—who would appreciate a companion. I can easily persuade Miss Sheridan that it would be in her best interests—'

'I do beg you, sir, not to interfere!' Guy's tone was clipped. 'I have said that I still wish to marry Miss Sheridan—'

The Earl brought his fist down hard on the arm of his chair. 'And I say you shall not! I will find some solution, deal with the girl—'

'As you would have had me deal with Miss Meredith?' Guy's body was rigid with anger now. He stood glaring at his father. 'I know how you like to arrange such matters, sir! Miss Sheridan is to disappear conveniently—'

'Is that so?' his father said, in an entirely different tone. 'You think that I will just sweep her aside, pay her off? You have known me for twenty-nine years, Guy—in all that time, how often have you seen me act thus?'

'Never! But I—'

'But you remembered that I had threatened to do so with Miss Meredith, so when I spoke of helping Miss Sheridan, you assumed I planned to treat her in the same way. No!' The Earl held up a hand as his son attempted to speak. 'Hear me out. There is something I wish you to consider. Imagine for just a moment that you have known someone not thirty years but a week…ten days, say.' His gaze took on a sardonic light. 'Think of Miss Sheridan, for example, as you knew her ten days ago.' He paused and took a draught of the brandy.

'She was alone in a difficult situation. She had always been alone, when one considers it! Her cousin gave her support, but Lady Amelia did not know the matter that took them to Blanchland! And you and I—who should have supported her, who had *promised* our aid—' he stressed the word '—we were the worst of all, for we deceived her! I never told her my secret desire to find Olivia first, and neither did you!'

'I told her later—'

'Too late! Miss Sheridan had started to trust you. You were someone on whom she thought she could rely, but slowly she began to feel that you were not being open with her. She did not know what to do. She had known you for less than two weeks and…' the Earl's voice was dry '…an instant and mutual attraction is not necessarily a basis for trust! She kept her own counsel, waiting for you to reveal the truth. Eventually you did—you admitted to something that appalled her! I had asked you to spirit away her niece, to pay her off, to help her to disappear!'

Guy was watching his father very gravely now. He did not interrupt.

'Imagine,' the Earl said, shifting in his chair as though he were in pain, 'how lonely it must have been for Miss Sheridan! She was the one who was brave enough to originally respond to Olivia's plea for help, she was alone in the world with only Lady Amelia to help her, she thought she could trust you and then she finds she knows not what to believe. Is it so surprising that, when Miss Sheridan finds her niece unconscious and apparently in your power, she jumps to the obvious conclusion?' The Earl smiled faintly. 'You yourself have demonstrated how easily that is done but five minutes ago!'

There was dead silence. A rueful smile began to curl the corners of Guy's mouth. 'Forgive me, sir, but you have the most damnable way—' He broke off, shaking his head.

'Of making you see the truth?' the Earl said drily.

Guy sat back in his chair with a sigh. 'How did you know what had happened between Miss Sheridan and myself?'

The Earl spoke with some considerable satisfaction. 'I heard it from Miss Sheridan. Those parts I did not hear, I worked out for myself. I was right, was I not?'

'Perfectly, but…' Guy frowned '…surely Sarah did not tell you this herself?'

'No.' The Earl smiled. 'I overheard. Miss Sheridan was speaking to her cousin and unaware that I was there. She said plenty more, Guy, but that is not for me to pass on. By the way…' a smile warmed his voice '…my real opinion of Miss Sheridan has been expressed once before. She is good and brave and true—so do not lose her, I beg!' His shoulders shook with laughter. 'I thought you were about to plant me a facer when I spoke so slightingly of her earlier!'

'If it had been anyone else, sir,' Guy said feelingly, 'I would have done so!'

'Well,' the Earl said gruffly, 'it was damnably hard to deceive you, but you needed a lesson! I could see you were about to throw away all that you held dear!'

Guy drained his glass. 'I had better go and find my bride...'

'And be quick about it!' his father advised.

Guy took the stairs in double time, but he was too late. A scandalised Lady Woodallan answered the door of Sarah's room and told him in no uncertain terms that it was bad luck for a groom to see his bride on the night before the wedding. Guy was left to kick his heels and hope against hope that he had not secured his own bad luck through his foolish pride.

Chapter Twelve

The church was brilliantly lit. Hundreds of white candles threw their light down from the sconces and illuminated the passages from the scriptures that were framed in red panels on the wall. Everywhere was Christmas greenery: branches of holly and laurel, pine cones and berries, red and gold streamers… Sarah, escorted up the aisle on her godfather's arm, caught her breath at the bright beauty of it all.

In the end there had been no escape. Lady Woodallan had come to her the night before and had spoken to her gently and sincerely about the family's happiness that she was marrying Guy and the conviction his parents held that she was exactly the right bride for him. The Countess had touched delicately on the short acquaintance between them, encouraging Sarah not to be afraid, and suggesting that she already knew and understood Guy so well that they might have known each other far longer. In the end, Sarah had burst into overwrought tears and her godmother had hugged her gently and told her that all would be well. Then Sarah had slept, and now it was her wedding day…

She was very aware of Guy beside her, so handsome

in green and white to complement her gown and the colours of the season. When she stole a look at his face, she thought he seemed grave, a little withdrawn, until he gave her a smile of such sudden brilliance that her heart leapt and she allowed herself to think that now, even if only for a little, his remoteness had vanished.

The service seemed to be over in minutes, both of them making their vows in clear and resolute tones. Sarah walked up the aisle on her husband's arm, aware of smiling faces all around them.

'Sarah, you look so beautiful,' Guy whispered to ner. 'I *must* speak with you—'

He broke off as they reached the church porch and were inundated by a crowd of villagers all wanting to wish them well.

'A kiss for the bride!' someone shouted, holding up a sprig of mistletoe.

Guy bent his head and touched his lips to Sarah's. The kiss was light and cold, like the brush of a snow-flake. Sarah shivered. The sky was darkening ominously with the next fall of snow and the air was chill, but she felt as though a tide of heat had swept through her. Aware of her blush, she turned closer into Guy's arms.

'Make way there!' The crowd parted good-humouredly to allow them through to the carriage just as the first flakes of snow started to fall.

Guy helped his bride up into the coach and took the seat opposite her. He leant forward urgently.

'Sarah, I know we have not much time alone, but I *must* tell you—'

The door swung open.

'Guy! I am so sorry—' The Countess of Woodallan was in the doorway, looking apologetic as her gaze moved from her son to Sarah. 'Would you object to taking up Olivia and Lady Amelia? They walked over to the church, of course, but now that it has started to snow…'

Guy gave Sarah a rueful smile. 'Not at all, Mama! Let them come up at once! This is no weather to be standing about…'

Olivia was very excited and chattered about the wedding for all of the short journey back to the house.

'Was it not fine? You look so lovely, Sarah… And the candles and the greenery—such a beautiful alternative to flowers…'

Sarah listened, and smiled and answered, and all the time she was aware of Guy's gaze resting on her. She felt his glance like a physical touch brushing her skin and making it seem curiously sensitive. The faint smile was still on his lips; when Guy's eyes met hers, she saw a flash of heat in his that completely flustered her. She lost the thread of what she had been saying to Olivia and fell silent. Guy's smile broadened slightly.

It was extraordinary. She could not understand it. Sarah frowned as she tried to make sense of this latest mystery. The last time she had seen Guy had been across the room at dinner the previous evening. He had ignored her, as had become his wont. Then, later, he had sought her out to speak with her—too late, for his mother had turned him away and they had not met again until they were in church… And now, mysteriously, his coldness had been banished by a warmth that threatened to be her undoing. He was treating her with an ardent attention that reminded Sarah of when they had first met. It was entirely appropriate for a bridegroom, but it was also deeply disturbing.

The carriage had completed the short journey from the church to the house, and Sarah gathered up her skirts in one hand as she prepared to step down. Guy was too quick for her. He swept her up in his arms, carried her over the threshold and put her down in the hall to a round of applause from the assembled guests. He was laughing as he took the congratulations of his friends. Sarah caught Amelia's arm.

'Milly, pray step aside with me for a moment—'

Amelia turned questioning eyes on her cousin. 'Sarah? Are you quite well?'

'Yes.' Sarah's grip tightened urgently. 'Quickly, before Guy sees—'

They slipped away to the ladies' withdrawing-room.

'What has happened?' Sarah lamented, viewing her fearful face in the pier glass whilst Amelia helped her adjust her gown and pinned the silver coronet more securely on her curls. 'Yesterday he would not even speak to me, yet now—'

'The little coronet was a good idea,' Amelia murmured, tweaking a curl into place. Sarah pulled her head away.

'Are you listening to me, Milly?'

'Yes, of course,' her cousin spoke soothingly. 'I only wished to compliment Lady Woodallan on recommending the coronet instead of a wreath of flowers, for in winter—'

'Yes, yes!' Sarah said impatiently. 'But what about Guy's behaviour—?'

The door opened and Sarah turned, expecting to see her mother-in-law come to summon them to the wedding breakfast. It was her husband who stood in the doorway. Their eyes met, Sarah's apprehensive, Guy's glittering with an emotion that set her pulse awry.

'Lady Amelia,' he drawled, 'I would be obliged…'

Amelia, accurately reading the instruction implicit in

the tilt of Guy's head, smiled and started to walk towards the door. Sarah grabbed her arm, wondering if there was some sort of conspiracy going on.

'Milly, don't go!'

'Don't be foolish, Sarah!' Amelia gave Guy a conspiratorial smile and edged out, closing the door very deliberately.

Sarah, suddenly overcome with panic, turned away. She could see Guy's reflection in the mirror as he came across the room towards her.

'I imagine the others are waiting for us—'

'They can wait a little longer. Sarah—' Guy pulled her round to face him. 'I do need most urgently to speak with you…'

Sarah's eyes widened. 'On what matter, my lord?'

'Don't look like that,' Guy said raggedly. 'Damnation, this is enough to try the patience of a saint!'

He took hold of Sarah's upper arms and pulled her to him, his mouth hard on hers. Sarah's lips parted instinctively and she drew closer to him, sliding her arms around his neck. The kiss deepened, desire spinning up to engulf them.

The door opened.

'Guy,' the Countess's voice said, a little plaintively, 'your guests are hungry! There will be plenty of time for that later—'

Guy let Sarah go and she heard him swear under his breath. 'Very well, Mama. We will be with you directly.'

'Now!' the Countess said inexorably. She bustled forward to rearrange the lace dress that had once more become disarranged. Sarah knew that she looked ruffled and rosy as they rejoined the wedding guests, and knew also exactly what they were thinking. Her mind was in complete confusion. All she seemed able to concentrate on was the fact that Guy had something to say to her and that she was as devastatingly aware of him as she had been that morning at Blanchland.

The wedding feast was long and complicated. There was a warming soup to help the guests thaw out, followed by turbot in a herb sauce, dressed capon and a haunch of venison. Sarah barely noticed the dishes come and go. She picked at her food, too nervous to eat properly, and responded to the chatter of the family and friends around her, whilst watching Guy out of the corner of her eye. They had little chance to speak, but every so often Sarah would feel his gaze on her and her skin burned.

'Sarah.' Guy touched her hand lightly and she dropped her knife. She looked up to meet his gaze and blushed at the expression in his eyes. 'I wanted to tell you—'

'May I press you to a slice of Christmas pudding?' the Earl enquired genially, from Sarah's other side.

Guy made a slight gesture and turned away. Sarah could have wept with frustration.

The wassail bowl was brought in, a highly spiced mixture of wine, apple, nutmeg and ginger that smelled absolutely delicious. The Earl toasted the bride and groom and took the first drink, passing the bowl to Sarah. She drank deep, her head swimming a little. The other speeches followed, then the dancing was announced.

It was only when Sarah stood up that she realised how intoxicated she felt. The sauces had been liberally laced with wine, and the wassail bowl was particularly strong. She felt Guy's arm go around her waist and leant against him gratefully.

'Sarah?' His breath stirred her hair. 'Are you well? We may retire soon, but perhaps one dance first—'

'That would be very pl...pleasant.' Sarah tried to pull herself together. She swayed a little, and Guy looked at her closely. 'Why, I do believe that you are foxed—'

'Nonsense!' Sarah said with aplomb. 'I will dance with you, my lord!'

It was fortunate that Guy had requested a slow waltz as the first dance, rather than the more boisterous country dances that were customary. He held her gently and decorously as they circled the floor, but as the dance ended they were pulled apart and whirled off by the other guests, passed from partner to partner as the music speeded up and spun them into a progressive country dance. Finally, laughing and breathless, Sarah collapsed onto one of the benches and requested a lemonade.

After that, the dancing was fast and furious. Sarah saw Guy a few times across the room, but it was impossible to fight her way to his side. Whenever a dance ended there was someone else waiting to claim her, and Guy was similarly besieged by ladies taking advantage of the informality of the celebration to beg a dance. At one point, their eyes met and Sarah felt as though the whole noisy crowd had simply melted away. There was an intent look on Guy's face, a determination in his whole bearing that suggested it was only a matter of time before they would be quite alone.

Eventually Sarah extracted herself from the crowd and slipped unseen out of the ballroom. It was very quiet in the hall, the sound of the ball muted behind closed doors. Sarah peeped out of the window. The snow was falling fast now, swirling amongst the trees, smothering the landscape. It looked cool and tempting.

Taking a cloak from the closet, Sarah wrapped herself about and went outside.

The Woodallan gardens were like a magical white wonderland. Sarah tiptoed along the paths, her footsteps leaving indentations in the snow. She peered in at the ballroom window, feeling like a small child playing truant, then ran down the yew avenue to the spreading oak tree at the end. A wild excitement filled her, impossible to explain. The cold air stung her cheeks. She spread her arms wide and twirled around in the snow, the cloak swinging out around her.

'Sarah! What in God's name—?'

Strong arms captured her and held her still. Guy pushed the hood back from her face. There was snow in his hair and eyelashes, and he smelled of the cold air and, more faintly, of sandalwood cologne. Sarah felt her knees weaken.

'I'm sorry,' she said, raising a hand to brush the snow from his hair. 'I just needed to get away for a little.'

Guy gave her a little shake. 'Whilst you have been here carousing in the snow, I have been looking everywhere for you! You weren't in the ballroom, you weren't in your room—I thought you'd gone!'

Sarah frowned. The raw emotion in his tone cut through her wild spirits and brought her back down to earth. 'Gone? Gone where?'

'I don't know!' Guy let her go and took several paces away. 'Just gone—because you didn't want to be married to me!'

Sarah blinked. The cold air had sobered her considerably and she was quite composed enough to realise that this did not make much sense.

'Guy—'

'No, hear me out!' Guy swung round on her, full of tension. 'All day I have been trying to tell you—'

'Renshaw!' A voice roared out of the gloom. 'How d'ye do! I've come to toast the nuptials!'

'It is Sir Ralph,' Sarah whispered, trying not to laugh at the look of frustrated fury on Guy's face. 'He must have found the keys to his wine cellar!'

'Devil a bit!' the indignant baronet exclaimed, overhearing her. He came up and enveloped her in a bear hug, snow and all. 'This is spring water, my lady, and every bit as refreshing as I used to find brandy to be! I'll have you know that this water cured me of my ague—had to do, for it was all I had in the house!'

'You should not stand about in the cold when you are only just recovered!' Sarah said, slipping her hand through his arm. 'Pray come inside, Sir Ralph, and join in the celebrations!'

They retraced their steps to the house, where Sir Ralph divested himself of his cloak and gave the bride another hearty kiss.

'You will excuse us, sir,' Guy said, with barely repressed impatience, 'if we do not accompany you back into the ballroom. I have something very urgent to discuss with my wife—'

Sir Ralph winked. 'Know what you mean, my lad! Go to it! I'll find my own way to the party!'

He headed off towards the music, cannoning into the Countess of Woodallan in the doorway.

'Beg pardon, my lady!' they heard him say warmly. 'May I interest you in a glass of this delicious water, drawn from my own spring—'

Lady Woodallan excused herself, turning to Guy and Sarah with an enquiring frown as Sir Ralph wended his unsteady way across the ballroom. 'Who is that odd man? I positively do not remember inviting him and he seems quite inebriated!'

'Only on water, ma'am,' Sarah said, laughing. 'I fear that is my disreputable cousin, Sir Ralph Covell! I believe he has just discovered his potential as a merchant of fine spring waters!'

Lady Woodallan raised her eyebrows. 'Well, never mind him! You must both rejoin us—'

'No, Mama,' Guy said, very definitely. 'The entertainment is going very well without us! Besides, you will see that Sarah is in urgent need of a change of clothes, and more importantly, I wish to speak with her—uninterrupted!'

Lady Woodallan looked scandalised. 'But you cannot retire now! Everyone will know where you have gone! Besides, Sarah must be attended to her room and helped to undress—'

Guy raised an eyebrow.

His mother paused. 'Outrageous!' she murmured faintly. 'Not even your father would—'

'Pray return to the festivities, Mama,' Guy said, grinning, 'and leave me to attend to my wife!'

He took Sarah's hand and pulled her up the stairs, so fast that she was almost running by the time they reached the bridal suite.

'Oh, dear!' Sarah was laughing and out of breath at the same time. 'This is not at all the way in which the Countess would wish her new daughter-in-law to behave! I am sure she thought me quite lost to propriety!'

Guy closed the door behind them and leant against it as though he could not quite believe that they were alone at last.

'Sarah. I need to talk to you—'

'Yes, you have been telling me that all day—'

'Please!' Guy held up a hand. 'I cannot bear any more interruption!' He looked at her thoughtfully. 'However, before I start, you really must change out of your wet clothes, and so must I. I will be back directly.'

He started to walk towards the connecting door, but Sarah's voice stayed him. 'Guy...your mother was right, you know. I do need help with this dress. It buttons down the back, you see...' Her voice trailed away at the look in his eyes.

'Very well.' Guy's voice was brisk and impersonal. He took Sarah's cloak and draped it over the chair by the fire. 'Turn around...'

Sarah was desperately conscious of his deft fingers unfastening the dress. She could feel his tension communicating itself to her, making her tremble. The fastenings fell apart and she felt Guy's hand brush the transparent chemise beneath, heard him catch his breath. He cleared his throat.

'That will do, I think. You should be able to step out of it now. I will leave you to change.'

He went through to the dressing-room and closed the door with a decided snap.

Sarah raised her eyebrows. She understood just how much self-control he had been exercising and how difficult it had been for him. Whatever he had to say must be very important indeed.

She stepped out of the dress and removed her soaking satin slippers. They would never be the same again. Whatever had possessed her to run out into the snow without dressing properly? She went over to the window and looked out. It was dark and the snowflakes were still falling, and suddenly the firelit room seemed a far better place to be.

A noise from the next room recalled Sarah to the fact

that Guy would soon be rejoining her. She hurried to slip out of the chemise and into the only clothing that seemed to be available, a nightdress of fine lawn and a matching peignoir in a beautiful shade of eau-de-nil. She was standing before the mirror and brushing her hair when Guy reappeared, wearing a dressing gown in a dark shade of blue. For a moment they just looked at each other. Guy's face was shadowed and Sarah could not see his expression.

'If you would just sit down…' Guy looked around, but there was only one chair. After a moment's hesitation, he took her hand and led her across to the bed. Sarah's heart started to race, but then he sat down at the foot, as far away from her as he could get.

There was a silence.

'Guy,' Sarah said beseechingly, 'if you do not tell me what is going on, I will become very anxious…'

Guy's sombre expression lightened. 'I am sorry. It is simply that I have been wanting to have you to myself for the whole day and now that I have, I do not know where to begin!' He ran a hand through his hair. 'You know that I came to see you last night?'

Sarah nodded. 'Your mother was with me. She turned you away because it is bad luck to see your bride the night before the wedding!'

'It was bad luck for me *not* to see you!' Guy said drily. 'I had just been speaking with my father and he made me realise…' he looked up and met her eyes '—that I have treated you very badly from the start, Sarah. The way I behaved in Bath, slandering you and then practically coercing you to marry me… I was not truthful with you at Blanchland, and then I blamed everything on you and was too proud to see that I must bear some censure as well! I know I have made you very unhappy these last few days, deliberately avoiding you—'

'Oh, stop!' Sarah cried, unable to bear a rehearsal of all the things that had gone wrong over the past few weeks. 'I was equally to blame for making such a shocking mull of everything! Let us forget all about it—'

'I am happy to do so if you will forgive me,' Guy said sombrely. He shifted slightly. 'The truth is that I started to fall in love with you very quickly, before I really had the opportunity to know you. My feelings were so sudden and so violent that they took me by surprise—'

'You do not know me very well now,' Sarah said quietly. She traced a pattern on the bedcover, suddenly unable to meet his eyes.

'I think I do.' Guy's voice was insistent. 'I know enough to realise that I should have trusted my instincts all along. I know that you are brave and kind and good, and that I love you... Why are you crying?'

Sarah knew that her eyes were full of unshed tears. 'I did not know...I thought...I did not know that you love me.'

'It is true. What is the matter? Do you not love me? You have never told me that you do!'

There was a vulnerability in his face that Sarah had never seen before. She smiled brilliantly through her tears. 'Of course I love you. How can you be so foolish? I have loved you for *at least* as long as you have loved me—'

Somehow, she was not sure how, Guy was beside her and holding her very gently in his arms. She could feel the heat of his body through the silk of the dressing gown and she instinctively pressed closer to the comforting warmth. His lips moved against her hair.

'We have made a fine muddle of everything between us, but the important thing is that we care for each other and that we are married now...'

Guy's fingers were stroking the nape of her neck. Sarah found the gentle circular motion most distracting. The faint fragrance of sandalwood mixed with the scent of his skin made her want to touch him and she turned her head and pressed her lips to the hollow above his collar bone.

The effect of her tentative caress was dramatic. Guy bent his head swiftly and captured her lips with his, kissing her with all the fierce sweetness she remembered from before. All the frustrations of the day, the doubts and difficulties, were washed away as the simmering awareness between them finally flared into outright passion.

Sarah fell back against the pillows, drawing Guy with her and sliding her hands inside the robe. She realised with a sudden shock that he was wearing nothing at all beneath it; her hands slid over his bare chest and met with taut, smooth muscle. Her shocked gasp was lost as his mouth claimed hers again, drinking from its sweetness as she gave unstintingly, opening her lips to his, pliant with need.

Guy pulled back a little to shrug himself out of the robe and Sarah watched in fascination as the firelight enhanced the golden nakedness of his skin.

'This time,' he said breathlessly, 'you have the advantage over me, Sarah...'

Sarah's mind finally let go of the last shade of inhibition as she reached out to pull him tightly against her. She dug her fingers into the hard smoothness of his shoulders, smiling a little smile of satisfaction as she heard his sharp intake of breath, the groan of pleasure he could not hide.

'Sarah…'

He raised himself a little above her and undid the ribbon of the peignoir with fingers that shook slightly. The night gown beneath was of very fine lawn, almost transparent, and as Guy's hand skimmed over it, Sarah was achingly aware that it revealed as much as it concealed. Nevertheless, Guy was clearly not content to leave it where it was. Sarah felt him slide the slippery material down from her shoulders and closed her eyes as he bent to caress her breasts. Her body arched and writhed under the onslaught of such pleasure; his lips returned to hers to kiss her with a savage tenderness that was utterly sensuous and made Sarah squirm with wanting.

The nightgown soon joined the peignoir and Guy's robe in a tumbled heap on the floor. Sarah's lips felt swollen with kissing, her whole body suffused with desire, a painful longing in the pit of her stomach that demanded satisfaction.

'You said,' she whispered, 'that you would remember I owed you something…'

Guy paused. He propped himself up on one elbow and pushed the tangled hair away from her face. 'So I did…' He smiled a little. 'Are you ready to pay your debt, Sarah, because I must tell you that this time I will not stop…?'

For answer, Sarah pulled him back to her, a delicious smile curving her lips. 'You had better not,' she said.

The room was cold but Sarah was delightfully warm, the bedclothes wrapped around her and her new husband wrapped closer still, one arm lying possessively across her. She stirred and turned to look at him, her heart full of love as she considered his face, softened in sleep. Guy stirred and curled an arm about her, pulling her back down to his side.

'Sarah…'

'My love?'

Guy opened his eyes and smiled sleepily with remembered pleasure.

'I did not hurt you, did I, sweetheart?'

'I do not remember,' Sarah said honestly. She blushed. 'It was…most enjoyable…'

'Then you might be prepared to repeat the experience?'

'I do not know,' Sarah said, sounding prim. 'Is it morning yet?'

'I doubt it. It is still dark and no one is stirring. We did retire rather early.' Guy yawned and stretched, reaching over to light a candle. Sarah watched, fascinated, as the bedclothes slid from his powerful frame to reveal the taut line of shoulder and thigh, the slim waist, the muscular torso.

He caught her gaze on him, smiled and picked up one of her curls, tickling her neck. Sarah put up one hand to fend him off, realised that the sheet had slipped from her, too, and made a grab for it. Guy was too quick for her, snatching it away.

'Such modesty, after all we have done!'

The rosy colour flooded Sarah's face again. 'Oh, please…'

Guy pulled her down beneath him. 'I should like to please you, Sarah. Like this…and this…'

This time he made love to her with concentrated passion, lingering with infinite slowness over each caress until Sarah thought she would melt with pleasure.

'Did I tell you I love you?' Guy asked afterwards, cradling her to him.

'Yes...' Sarah's mind was cloudy with happiness '...but you may tell me again, as much as you wish, just as I shall tell you!'

They were awoken much later by a discreet knock at the door. Guy knotted the robe about his waist and went to answer, whilst Sarah hid behind the bed curtains and wriggled back into her nightgown and wrap. Guy reappeared, carrying a tray and put it down on the table by the bed.

'Mama thought that we might be hungry—I cannot imagine why! There are rolls and butter, ham, eggs, and this...' He gestured towards the large jug.

'What is it?' Sarah asked curiously.

'Blanchland spring water!' Guy poured it into a glass and toasted her with it. 'Mama tells me that all the guests are taking it with their breakfast and swearing that it is sovereign against the evils of too much drink!' He took a sip. 'Mmm, not bad. I do believe your cousin Ralph may at last have struck success with the *ton*!'

Sarah smiled. 'So Blanchland has at last given up the last of its secrets,' she said softly.

Guy leant over and kissed her. 'And in the process it has made everyone very happy. Olivia has been restored to her family and has found Justin Lebeter into the bargain! Amelia and Greville are united at last, and Sir Ralph has his spring water!' He kissed her again, his hands beginning to stray across the seductively smooth material of the peignoir, undoing the ribbon that Sarah had so carefully done up only minutes before.

'As for me,' Guy murmured, as his lips returned to hers, 'Blanchland gave you to me, Sarah, so I am the most fortunate of all.'

* * * * *

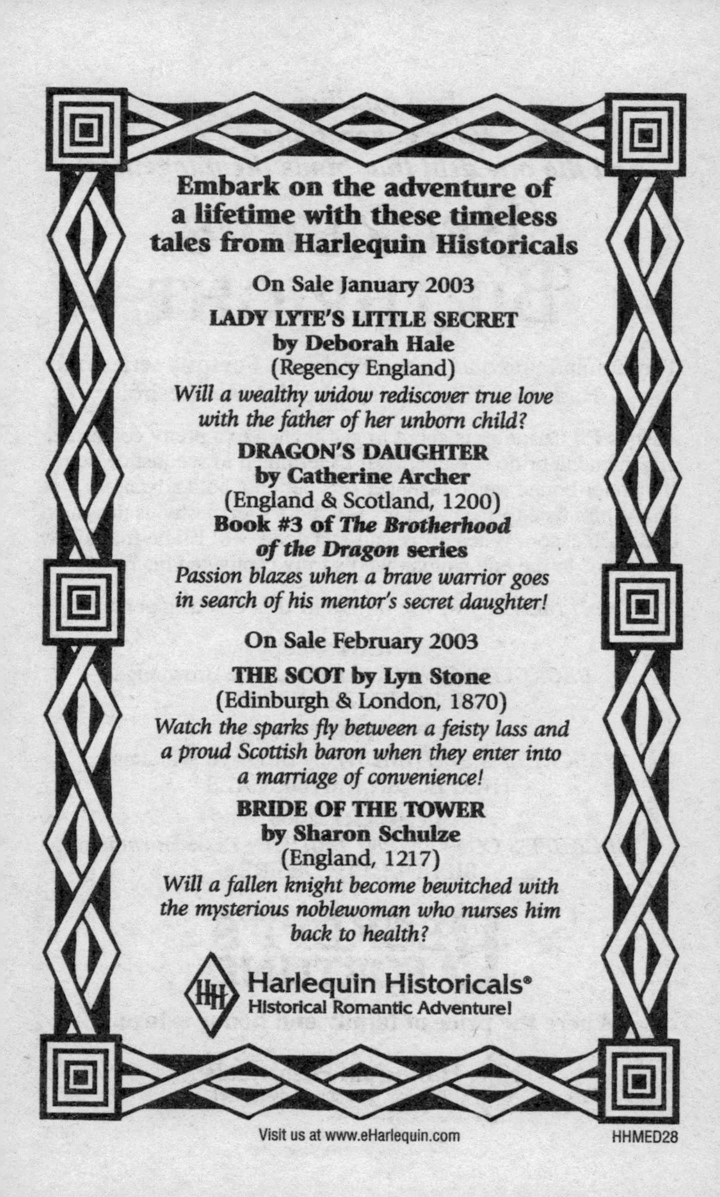

COMING NEXT MONTH FROM

HARLEQUIN HISTORICALS®

- **GIFTS OF THE SEASON**
  Mainstream historical author **Miranda Jarrett** joins Harlequin Historicals and Silhouette Intimate Moments author **Lyn Stone** and RITA® Award winner **Anne Gracie** for this Christmas anthology of three stories set in Regency England.
  HH #631 ISBN# 29231-7 $5.25 U.S./$6.25 CAN.
- **RAFFERTY'S BRIDE**
  by **Mary Burton,** author of THE PERFECT WIFE
  Ravaged by the Civil War, a military man bent on revenge goes in search of the bewitching nurse who betrayed him and his men. But he never bargained on the explosive desire that would ignite between them!
  HH #632 ISBN# 29232-5 $5.25 U.S./$6.25 CAN.
- **BECKETT'S BIRTHRIGHT**
  by **Bronwyn Williams,** second book in the *Beckett's Fortune* series
  Having lost the trail of a man who wronged him, a down-on-his-luck rancher takes a job in North Carolina. Sparks fly when he meets his boss's daughter, a fiery bluestocking, but will his need for vengeance destroy their budding love?
  HH #633 ISBN# 29233-3 $5.25 U.S./$6.25 CAN.
- **THE DUMONT BRIDE**
  by **Terri Brisbin,** Harlequin Historicals debut
  A wrongly imprisoned French count is forced into a marriage of convenience to an English heiress with a secret to hide. When he discovers his wife is pregnant with another man's child, he must choose between honor and a love finally found….
  HH #634 ISBN# 29234-1 $5.25 U.S./$6.25 CAN.

KEEP AN EYE OUT FOR ALL FOUR OF THESE TERRIFIC NEW TITLES